SMOKE JUMPERS

A NOVEL BY

Paul Freeman

BASKERVILLE
PUBLISHERS, LTD
DALLAS · NEW YORK · DUBLIN

BASKERVILLE Publishers, Ltd.
7540 LBJ/Suite 125, Dallas, TX 75251-1008

Library of Congress Catalog Card Number: 91-077073
ISBN: 0-9627509-1-3--

Manufactured in the United States of America
First Printing

To Carole, Shannon & Christopher
For putting up with my secondhand smoke
And for loving me, despite it.

CHAPTER 1

The dog strained at the leash. It took all of Malcolm's strength to keep control of the hound now that the quarry was so near. The other twenty in Malcolm's band fanned out. Billy Farquhar was the first to pick up a rock. They knew they were only minutes away from earning the badge.

The leader looked down at Malcolm. "Be certain," he whispered. He took the leash from Malcolm's hand and retreated stealthily up the hill. He knew it would be more fulfilling for them if he wasn't a witness.

The hiker in the clearing below tossed down his ten-pound pack and re-laced his boots. It was a good day to be in the woods near the Appalachian Trail. He reached inside the lining and took out the wallets and rings he had lifted from campsites during the evening. He stuffed them back in their compartment and reached inside the pack again, withdrawing his hand at a hint of movement in the brush of the mountainside. He stood and strained his ears and eyes for more than a minute. Several squirrels scampered across the rocky trail.

He laughed at his caution and grabbed the canvas pack again. His hand emerged with a package of Marlboros and an antique Zippo lighter. He flipped the wheel of the lighter and took a deep drag on the Marlboro before Billy Farquhar's rock smashed into his right temple.

The stones rained down from all sides. He dropped the burning cigarette and scampered down the trail as the joyful whoops of Asheville Cub Scout Troop 121 rang in his ears.

***

In a previous generation Billy Ray Chubb would have

been in television commercials. His face was as rugged as the countryside around him, but much better looking. Billy Ray's body belied his last name. A muscular six-foot-two, Billy Ray Chubb looked graceful, even on Rocky. Billy Ray loved everything about Rocky, except the gelding's stiff pasterns.

A good quarter horse usually has a gait that's as easy as a porch swing, but Rocky wasn't usual. Billy Ray named him Rocky not in honor of the indomitable spirit of Rocky Balboa, but because of his straight-legged, butt-busting gait. Rocky was a good cow pony, though, and he and Billy Ray had the herd moving toward the slow-moving cesspool called the Rio Grande. It was an easy walk in from here. Billy Ray's Catahoula hound would take the herd across with little or no attention from Billy Ray and Rocky. The herd, even the two unbranded and unmarked five hundred dollar steers that Billy Ray picked up, would be on the way to a Mexican sale barn before nightfall. He stopped Rocky and surveyed the countryside. Billy Ray's rough-hewn face showed something approaching contentment. God Himself would have felt serene in this lonely part of South Texas.

Billy Ray turned slightly and opened the saddlebag on the left side. He tossed away the uneaten cheese sandwich and opened the metal case that contained a half-empty package of Camels and a matchbook from Billy Ray's favorite Mexican whorehouse. Billy Ray carefully extracted one Camel and pushed his Stetson hat slightly backward. He touched the lighted match to the tip of the Camel and drafted deep on the unfiltered cigarette.

Rocky bolted left and Billy Ray Chubb ducked onto the horse's neck as the first helicopter darted from behind the little mesa. The landing skid brushed Billy Ray's Stetson, sending it spinning down then wafting up in the backwash of the copter's rotor.

The heavy mesh net spun out of the belly of the second helicopter. Its weight dragged Billy Ray out of the saddle. He rolled as far as he could, managing to stay just out of reach of Rocky's lashing hooves. He saw the squads of white-suited men leap out of the two helicopters and start trotting toward him. Billy Ray lay back on the sandy soil and pulled hard on the Camel. It glowed in volcanic contempt in the gathering dusk.

***

The pneumatic hammer made short work of the flimsy apartment door and the white-suited squad of burly men and muscular women stormed inside.

Officer Kate Campbell swept the combination living and dining room with the tiny detector. The machine beeped and a tiny arrow on its instrumentation began flashing in the general direction of a cedar chest.

"Open it," Campbell said. Officer Joseph Harper lashed his leather boot at the lid of the chest.

"It's not locked, stupid," Campbell said. Hopping from the pain in his right foot, Harper kneeled and opened the chest. He tossed a few hundred pictures onto the floor and grabbed a wrapped package. "Cocaine," he muttered, tossing it on the pile of pictures on the floor.

"Keep going," Campbell said. Her voice cracked with the tension of the moment.

Harper dug frantically, tossing his way through documents and some yellowed newspaper clippings. A bulge between two clippings caught Kate Campbell's eye. She tore the papers apart and triumphantly held up the cellophane-wrapped white package.

"We've got the little creep!" she screamed as the rest of Smoke Jumpers Unit 5 cheered.

CHAPTER 2

Things got different right after we got into the 20th Century. The beginning of the 21st Century was supposed to be a big improvement over the shank of the Twentieth, but it hasn't worked out that way for much of anybody. Especially for us. The confirmed people are now confined to three colonies. They get "confirmed" when they confess or get caught. One colony is in Nevada, another on the arid plains of west Texas and a third in eastern North Carolina. I'm one of those who tries to live free among the general population. I don't even have it all that deeply, but I've always had a tendency to get my back up when somebody is being bullied. If you get caught, you're on the way to one of the colonies — if you're all in one piece and haven't been caught by the roaming squads of quiche-stained civilian bastards who call themselves the Air Police. Air Police could have taught the Ku Klux Klan a thing or two.

Some Air Police like to torture the ones they catch. They seem to get really worked up ahead of United Way banquets, AIDS benefits or anything to do with the downtrodden. Most of the downtrodden. All except us.

The government spends millions on smoke-detecting helicopters and surveillance airplanes. The air armada spits tons of pollutants into the air every day, looking for us. Crime has never paid better down where we are. It's several quantum leaps worse than it was in the early 1990s and it was bad then. The nineties' people did the usual thing to try to find safety. They scurried to what they thought was safety in the suburbs and country. The crime wave followed as if on a leash.

I guess maybe this is the mobile society the sociologists

have been yammering about. Crime is the growth industry now. It's hell on wheels, even if it's not as bad as the figures indicate. Now the figures: the figures are another story.

The crime index went bonkers when they put us into it. It was like tossing every grandfather in the country into the database for serial rapists. But we're criminals now, by decree of our government. We smokers.

I guess it all started in the 1980s. There were so many problems around that people couldn't solve that they started looking for one they could handle. They decided that smoking was the worst thing since Jimmy Carter, which made it pretty bad, by my way of thinking. I've talked with some of the people who used to have to follow Jimmy around. He must have been something. Anyway, Jimmy came from tobacco country in Georgia and said he didn't smoke. His mother, the one they called Miss Lillian, must have smoked when she was carrying him. It's a well-established fact that mothers who smoke have a better shot at having brain-damaged kids. Miss Lillian probably was a three-pack-a-day Georgia Peach, since it's pretty obvious that you could have turned Jimmy's brain into lighter fluid and not been able to light a Lucky Strike.

But wimpy politicians like Jimmy didn't start it. Maybe the smokers did. Maybe it was the non-smokers. I had never seen anybody smoking in an elevator, but somebody must have because they turned elevators into no-smoking zones. Next came restaurants. After that, public buildings. The prisoners in the jails could smoke but the people who processed their paperwork couldn't. It was the way it was, and it got more so.

I don't know if the smokers could have done anything — except quit, as millions of them did. Quitting is not even good enough now. The smokers lost the debate over "passive" smoke. We probably should have, but passivity was in vogue. Passive is, I guess, another word for "shame." Serial rapists would look at the nearest female cop and say, "You're next, honey..." and get counseling for their maladjustment. Serial shitheads could crash their cars into a playground and they'd get treatment for their drinking problems. Serial smokers would apologize, snuff it out

5

and shuffle off to someplace where there were no non-smokers to offend. They couldn't go far enough. Some of the non-smokers were still offended.

There was a time when people owned up to their mistakes and maybe all smokers should have lived then. But we didn't and we were shuffling off behind the trees, trying to get out of the sight of non-smokers, while other people were screaming at the tops of their voices that they were victims of somebody else. Or everybody else. The women said they were victims of the men. The men who belonged to a union said they were victims of management. The managements said they were victims of the government. The blacks said they were victims of the whites. The young were victims of the old and the old yelled like hell about "age-ism."

I'm a reporter and I've run into a few thousand "isms." I've grown to hate reporters and lawyers, so I figure the most dangerous "isms" I've ever met personally have been legalism and journalism.

I guess smokers are old-timers, like me. We never defended our malady. The so-called gay people did it for theirs. Even while their disease was sweeping through society like the black plague, they intimidated everybody and everything in sight. They had people so afraid that one restaurant owner I know waffled for two days over whether he should put up a sign. It said: "All Deliveries In Rear." He decided it wasn't worth the risk. It had taken him about thirty seconds to decide to make his restaurant off-limits to smokers.

The saga of Farmersville might tell you what I mean. It's a story I picked up when I was working for a newspaper in North Carolina. There was this radio station in the heart of tobacco country. Now the people who own radio stations dearly love to identify them by call letters that hint at something. WNYC in New York City. KPBA in Pine Bluff, Arkansas. KBMN in Bozeman, Montana. Some of them go pretty far out. In the 1970s some people out West tried to get KGAY, but the Federals held the line and Radio 69 had to settle for announcers who sounded gay, although usually unhappy.

6

SMOKE JUMPERS

Then there was WVOG. It was a religion station in New Orleans. It sold time to preachers. Most of the preachers who bought their way onto WVOG were so fundamental they wouldn't screw their girlfriends (boyfriends with a couple of them) standing up. They were afraid the Lord would think they were dancing. Baptists used to be death on dancing.

WVOG was owned by a bunch of businesslike Jewish guys from the East Coast and managed by a fun-loving Irisher. He had a good perspective on his clientele. You could tell by the plaque in his office. It read: "In God We Trust — But Preachers Pay Cash." He was the one who came up with the idea for WVOG's station identification. It was a guy with a doomsday voice who would intone: "This is WVOG. The Voice Of God." The announcer sounded like God. Or maybe God would have sounded like the announcer if He had a sound studio.

Anyway, the station in North Carolina had call letters that more or less told about what had kept Farmersville afloat. They had to do with an outdated way of identifying a cigarette, but it was part of the history of Farmersville and the people who owned WFAG thought gay people would understand. They were wrong. FAG radio now goes by something that the Gay & Lesbian Coalition thinks is a little more sensitive. The guys have gone back to looking through novels from the 1930s and '40s where some character would ask for a smoke with, "Slip me a fag..." I guess the dames are checking for stories where the little Dutch boy puts his finger in the dike.

The tobacco companies couldn't help poor old WFAG and they couldn't organize smokers, even when they tried. It turned out that the smokers didn't like the tobacco companies any more than the non-smokers did.

The restaurants organized the smokers, taking their cue from the way Hitler organized the Jews. The restaurants moved smokers to farther corners and cubbier cubbyholes and the smokers took it. Some motels and hotels started banning smoking altogether, and charging higher rates. Smokers sneaked a few puffs outside, if they couldn't get a "smoking" room at one of the hostelries that still took their business.

7

The airlines snuffed cigarettes on all flights short enough that the smoking clientele might not start a riot. It's pretty hard to grab a few puffs outside an airliner, so smokers did it in the short space between the destination and the terminal, or went to the bar. Bars were the last refuge of the haze crowd. Smoking and drinking went together in more than the lyrics of country and western music. For a while. Then came Winston DeWeerd.

CHAPTER 3

Winston DeWeerd ran for the U.S. Senate when he was just forty, moving toward Washington from a one-term stint as Governor of Montana.

Winston became governor out of boredom. He had bought a ranch near Big Timber, Montana, with part of his inheritance. He liked the life but craved some excitement. Winston caught the germ of *the issue* in his bid to become governor of all of Montana. His opponent was a Republican sheep rancher from a place in the northern portion of the state, yet inexplicably called Center. Ed Jones took delight in pointing out that Winston had been born in North Carolina and didn't know a wooly Montana sheep from a North Carolina Camel.

Winston's love for afternoon tea got to be a campaign issue and Winston bridled like crazy when people would ask him, "Hey, Winston, one hump or two?"

Winston hired a political consulting company out of some place in Maryland and they said it was simple. They would just pick a flashy issue and wrap it around Winston. It was easy. Winston was what the literary types like to call an Empty Vessel. He didn't have any beliefs and didn't really know much about anything, except spending inherited money and chasing women.

Winston doesn't look like an Empty Vessel. He looks a little like the pictures I've seen of David Millar. You probably think you've never heard of David Millar and probably think Winston could look like Woody Allen, for all you know. But anybody who is older or who has been exposed to the government's anti-tobacco stuff knows David Millar. David was a Marlboro Man. They put him in ads, on his horse. Millar looked like the

9

kind of guy who could work a herd of cattle, go to bed with three or four women, drink a case of beer and whip anybody in the bar. All without drawing a long breath.

Of course he had trouble drawing even a short one. Millar died with a bulging bank account and bilging lungs. Emphysema.

Winston looks as healthy as David Millar ever did. And that was what turned the political consultants on. They figured they'd orchestrate Winston's attack on two fronts. First, Winston would stress health issues. Half the people in Montana are health nuts but they think they're sick because they're hung over so much of the time. One way to the health nuts was to lay waste to the tobacco industry. There were no tobacco crops in Montana and fewer smokers than in most places, except in the bars, which were as smokey as any in Las Vegas.

The second part of their advice was a whispering campaign. Winston's people would put out the word that his opponents indeed knew sheep. In the Biblical sense. They figured they could give Old Ed Jones an image problem on the issue. They found the ammunition at the library in Billings, Montana. The Billings Gazette had taken a series of photos of Ed for a big, boring, story on sheep-ranching. There it was. Photos that showed Old Ed on the ground, wrestling with a sheep of the female persuasion. Ed was just trying to get her wool, but Winston's folks put a different spin on it. They circulated the photos with their own caption, which read: "Ed Jones loves it when they play hard to get."

Between Ed's ewe turn-ons and the tobacco companies, well, it worked. Old Ed Jones started getting the smart-mouth questions when he campaigned in bars. Everybody in Montana campaigns in bars. That's where the folks are. Winston's political consultants staked out some watchers and they reported Ed was getting asked "One hump, or ewe?" three-and-point-four times for every time some smartass asked Winston about "one hump or two?"

There was even a cottage industry that grew up around old Ed's supposed predisposition to the southern regions of north-pointing animals. There were cartoons galore. The one Winston liked best captured the essence of the whispering campaign and his strong attacks on the tobacco companies. That one featured Old Ed and a satiated female sheep in bed. Both of them puffing on cigarettes. Winston used several intervening people to put up a five-thousand-dollar scholarship for the young woman who did that one.

He might have done the same over a video put out by some broadcasting students at the University of Montana. It keyed on the theme that "Old Ed Jones would walk a mile to hump a camel." He didn't do anything for them, of course, because the video had been produced by his own political consultants, who paid the students to front it. It was a cult hit as far away as San Diego, which is where the consultants had to take their Ed Jones look-alike to get him on camera, appearing to be ready to have his will with an ugly camel, if that's not redundant. Winston joked that his people had to ignore physical accuracy to make the Camel video. Winston explained that he had visited the Middle East and was one of those rare people who knows that the sexual business end of a male camel points toward Mexico when the camel's nose points toward Canada. Winston told his people to be certain they never accused Old Ed of being *built* like a camel. "The women would all vote for him. They'd think he'd be tons of fun to dance with," Winston cackled.

So Winston moved from his big high-tech mansion on the ranch to the little down-in-the-mouth mansion on Patterson Street in Helena. He credited victory to his loyal supporters, especially the tough women of MASK (Mothers Against Smoking & Kancer). MASKers got network television time by staging a topless demonstration against a smoke shop on Helena's scenic main street, known from the gold-mining boom days as Last Chance Gulch.

They called it "Baring Our Lungs for Health" but the networks liked it simply for pluck and art. Pluck because the shivering women did their demonstration in an early snowstorm. Art for their beautiful blue breasts, their nipples black from the cold and the entire scene highlighted by a shimmer of white snow. It was beautiful.

11

Of course Winston gave some credit to his campaign staff, but mainly, he said, his victory was due to his courageous stand against the Merchants of Death — the tobacco companies. That was bull, of course. The stories that Ed Jones was as one with his flock was the mover for Winston DeWeerd. Montana people are a prideful lot and they blamed Ed Jones for their being the butt of jokes from every wiseass on every network television show. All of them had his version of the line that Montana was the land "Where Men Are Men and Sheep are Nervous." The voters haven't figured out to this day that it was Winston who caused it. And, being proud people with little except scenery to be proud of, they take pride in Winston's celebrity.

Winston DeWeerd knew he couldn't ride the sheep deal any farther than the North Dakota line. But he had figured the way to get out of Montana and on the road to Washington. He told me he saw the path to big power as a one-way street, cushioned with tobacco and cloaked in a lovely haze of smoke. Winston said he was tired of Montana and he knew the quickest way to Washington curved through the Carolinas, Kentucky, Georgia and Virginia. Tobacco country.

I ought to know quite a bit about Winston. He's my half-brother. The guy who ran the Merchants Of Death right out of town. And he's still pissed about it.

CHAPTER 4

Joe French stood over the machine that turned them out. They rolled out by the thousands. Little pieces of death that bumped happily down the line. They looked innocuous. Joe wished they hadn't looked so innocuous when he was tending bar at the Holiday Inn in Buffalo. Joe knew nobody had ever served his or her time and gotten out of The Line in Packaging.

A couple of people had gotten out of Administration. The brass said they had "resumed smoke-free and productive lives in the never-ending struggle against the Tobacco Demon." They didn't identify them but French had recognized one of them. People in the bars had bet on, and against him. He had been a pretty fair tennis player at one time. Milano Nagurski was his name.

Joe French didn't know anything about the one they called Two Shoes. He had heard that Two Shoes was a two pack-a-day guy and some kind of computer freak. Everybody who knew Two Shoes had been transferred to Power and never heard from again. No one ever mentioned Two Shoes. That couldn't have been his real name, unless he was an Indian and Indians didn't get busted and sent here.

The brass said there was a separate Colony for Indians but that was probably bullshit. Joe Looks Behind said it was. Joe was one of the slime guards. He was a Blackfeet Indian. He admitted he had killed an FBI agent but Joe Looks Behind thought it had been a bad rap. Joe explained that he had been drunk at the time. Joe Looks Behind was always sober here and he said nobody got busted on the Indian Reservations for smoking.

It didn't seem fair. The history books said Indians started

all this crap in the first place.

Joe French remembered the story he had read about the Great Spirit of the Indians. The story said the Great Spirit sent an angel, or something like an angel, to save the poor humans on earth. It had been a big job. She had to touch the land to get it going again. What she touched with her right hand turned into potato plants. What she touched with her left hand turned out to be stalks of corn. She finally sat down to rest and when she got up, a new plant sprouted from where she was sitting. It was tobacco.

It seemed somewhat balanced to Joe French, like that bullshit phrase a lot of people used. The one that went: "What goes around comes around." It came down from an Indian angel's butt and now Joe French was getting it in the ass. It was finally coming around.

Like the damned trucks and trains. They came in all the time, bringing more and more of the stuff. It had to be dried and quick-cured. The whole process took a ton of electricity.

Joe's job in Packaging sucked but it beat working in Power.

Electricity killed people worse than smoking. The people in Power went fast. Their lungs went. Their livers went. Their bones turned to mush and they more or less disintegrated. People said they didn't need night lights in the cells for the Power people. They said they all glowed in the dark. They probably didn't glow. They probably just lay in their bunks and smoked themselves to sleep, like most everybody else in the damned place.

You could tell from the security that Packaging beat the hell out of Power. The second-meanest people in the world were guards in Power. It took a mean bastard just to put up with wearing the lead-lined suits all day at work. They said Dean Stanley, one of the con guards in Power, had come there from the federal slammer at Marion, Illinois. He had been serving time for murdering a guy, then eating his heart. That was the only heart the bastard ever had, by all accounts.

The first-meanest bastards in the world were the ones assigned to guard the guards in Power, who were the second-meanest bastards in the world. Actually, there wasn't that much difference between the real guards in Packaging and the real guards in Power, but the ones in Power had more opportunity to show how tough they were. People in Power were dying to get out.

Joe French thought the security was overdone. He thought smokers in the Colony were just like smokers had been on the outside. Most of them were passive and easy to push around. It was a behavior pattern intrinsic in being told they were walking mass murderers who destroyed the lives of thousands of other people while committing slow-motion suicide.

Overdone or not, everybody said there wasn't a week that the real guards didn't kill somebody in Power.

All the real guards were lean and tough. The brass put the real guards' training on the closed-circuit television every day, just so the inmates could plumb the futility of trying to fight their way out, or of making a run for it.

There was little chance a lung-impaired inmate was going to fight his or her way out, even if it was hand-to-hand, which it wouldn't be. The reason the real guards mainly guarded the slime guards was to keep their weapons out of reach of any inmate.

The weapons were better than the Army had. The closed-circuit television showed real guards popping targets at a half-mile. One of the perennial reruns on the closed-circuit entertainment was Joe Bob Rains, a three-pack-a-day inmate from Hot Coffee, Mississippi. The camera caught Joe Bob's death throes when he ran into a five-foot rattlesnake about a mile from the perimeter. The announcer said Joe Bob might have lived long enough to have been killed by the guards if his heart hadn't been weakened by the habit.

If you got a chance to go out during the evening you could always hear the rattling death out on the desolate countryside, even over the persistent rumble of the generators down below in Power.

The real guards had clothing that looked to be snake-proof. Even without the special leggings and boots the guards wore, there was no chance that any lung-impaired inmate was going to outrun the real guards. They drove that point home, time and time again on the evening telecasts. You didn't have to be brainwashed or drugged to believe it.

The announcer on the ten-mile run part of the guard-workout telecast liked to point out that the guards were a lot like the Apache warriors of old. The Apache couldn't catch his sprinting runaway horse, but his steady, loping gait could run the horse to ground. The announcer always said: "The Apache didn't kill the horse, once he caught him. Inmates should remember that they are not horses."

Joe Bob Rains was only one of several inmates who had made a run for it. The bodies of the others had been frozen and displayed in the common area for days. Their captures, and their deaths, were televised, over and over, on the closed-circuit television. It motivated a body to stay put, light up a cigarette and hope that things will change. But Joe French didn't believe there was much chance of change.

French was a hard-twisted one-hundred and eighty pounder who had boxed some before he dropped out of college. The skills he learned in boxing had served him well in the hassles that develop as a normal part of the bar business. And his years on the business side of drinking had honed his instinctive sense of who was tough and who was bluff. Joe French figured the real guards here were more tough than bluff. They were uniformly pissed but even the women guards carried themselves with the easy assurance of people who knew how to rip out your Adam's Apple with their hands.

Joe respected the real guards. He had heard that they, like the convicts and the slime guards, knew they were never getting out of this place. You couldn't tell for certain if that kind of talk was true, or if it was just some bullcrap the administration put out to make the cons think the guards didn't have any reason to be afraid of anything.

The real guards were impossible to read except for body language. You never got to see their eyes, except on the television videos. When they were working they always wore the full-head helmets with the mirrored visors were part of the air-filter setup. It made the real guards look like aliens from some science-fiction movie.

The slime guards never got to see their faces either, but Joe French had heard the slime talking about the real guards. They said the real guards were people who ought to be on the inside, with us. When you get caught smoking cigarettes in the Smoke Jumpers, you get a one-way ticket here. That's what the slime said. You couldn't believe anything the slime said, but Joe thought maybe it had the ring of truth. Sort of a smoke ring.

The people the real guards watched were a bunch of sludge that would give sewer scum a bad name. But the slime got the job done. The job being simple: keep the cons working. They loved to do that and there was more work all the time. The story was that Power was expanding. People had seen bulldozers and shovels working on about fifty acres next to the Colony.

More work and more smokers to do it. A woman who worked in Administration said the smokers were getting younger. Some of them looked like college kids, for crissakes.

An English teacher in the crowd said the guards worked them "with a vengeance." Joe thought it was a stupid phrase but he had heard it for years before he got busted that night in Buffalo. He thought it didn't mean anything. Until he got here. Now he was Packaging Death with the S-mark on his forehead. The S would be pretty subdued when he woke in the morning but there was so much nicotine and tar in the air of the work area that the S blazed by the time he hit the sack. It was funny how they could treat your skin so the mark would come up the way it did. He wondered if you could still see the S on the tennis player. The Nagurski guy. Or the one they called Two Shoes. The slime guards took their measure of you by how bright your S-mark shined. That was one reason Joe French worked to stay at least a three-pack-a-day man.

The guards were getting meaner and the slime was getting slimier. It had always seemed strange to Joe that the slime guards who were murderers were a couple of cuts above the robbers. Murderers weren't bad people, by and large. They were the only ones Joe would like to talk with if he ever got back to his bartending job in Buffalo. But he knew he would never do that.

17

They had gotten a bunch of rapists to staff the slime line. The rapists weren't all that hard to deal with, for the men. Rapists were afraid to take a man to the discipline room without help. And they knew better than to ask one of the fellow non-rapist slime to come help them beat the hell out of you. Joe French figured the pecking order among the slime was about the same as it had been in the prisons they had come here from. Rapists only outranked child molesters in the outside jails. It was the same here. One of the rapist slime guards had shoved Joe French into the Discipline Room one afternoon a year ago. Joe took his baton, then beat him bloody with his fists.

A second guard, a cop-killer from California, came into the room and handcuffed Joe after the first guard was a bloody wreck. "I was tryin' to give you time to kill the sonofabitch," the guard said, "but I guess your friggin' lungs quit on you."

Joe French was so out of breath that he could only nod.

The guard Joe whipped was never seen again and his fellow rapists on the crew took the lesson to heart when it came to dealing with Joe French.

The rapists were still burning hell on the women, though, even with the Sex Drive Suppressant.

Everybody got the Sex Drive Suppressant, except for the real guards. The Sex Drive Suppressant was supposed to be one of the big benefits that came out of the Smoker Colonies. A pack-a-day woman nurse who worked in Pharmacology said the Sex Drive Suppressant was supposed to kill your libido forever. Joe didn't doubt it. He hadn't had an erection in years. He could figure how it worked on a man but he wondered how they did it with women. The nurse said it was the same drug and worked both ways. She said she hadn't had a tingle between her thighs since she got the drug. Joe would bet the drug wouldn't have taken the edge off his ex-wife.

The Sex Drive Suppressant had taken care of the problem of rapists sexually molesting the women but the rules apparently allowed beating the hell out of them and anybody else who doesn't perform up to quota. Joe French didn't know what the rules really said, of course, because he had never seen them. He

18

had every confidence he never would.

Some of the women inmates had tried, at first, to assert their rights to be treated like the men. That worked with everybody but the rapists in the guard corps. A woman who got picked out for discipline by a rapist was in for a whaling. Being meek didn't help. At least the Colony had proved, forever, that rape and sex had nothing to do with one another.

There was no one around who had been in the place since the beginning. People didn't last that long. That seemed to be the plan, right down to the air. The place was so completely insulated that the air never was clean. The cigarette smoke from the production lines was a constant cumulus cloud over the workers and the slime guards. Any emissions from the machinery and paper bits from the wrappers hung in the air. You never got away from it.

A Smoker who got to leave the building would gulp the outside air as if it were an unfiltered Camel.

One reason you got to leave now and then was to do a videotape for the people you left behind, if there was anybody. It was easy time. They took you to the drug center for at least a day while they fine-tuned the dose. Joe had tried to fool them, but their equipment was too good. It was like trying to fool a good bartender into believing you needed that last hit just before closing time. The medical people would ask you questions, then read the data they got from the electrodes on your penis, earlobes and toes.

They'd zing you, adjust the dose then zing you again. They called it Total Behavior Modification. At the end of getting his behavior totally modified a man could go on camera, swear he was a lesbian Doberman Pincer and still score a 90 on the Truthfulness Indicator. Funny thing about that first Total Behavior Modification was that it took away your need for the weed.

Now the hardest adjustments the lab people had to make were to restore the need for the nicotine fix. That was necessary because you had to smoke when you did the video.

Joe was one of the first cons to get the cure, then the uncure. It happened the first time he went in to do a video. The drugs

19

worked, all right, but he didn't want to smoke any more.

The little doctor with the funny accent had been hyper when Joe refused a phony Camel. He had jumped up and down, screaming, "It's over! I've done it!"

"Done what?" Joe had asked.

"A cure. It looks like a cure."

The little doctor had put Joe in Hospital Isolation for a week. They even gave him a carton of cigarettes and a lighter. There was a refrigerator full of Labatt Beer. They must have known that Labatt and a smoke had been a heavenly combo. The Labatt was pretty good, but the lighter should have been a treasure. Joe had wished he could cop the lighter and smuggle it to the outside. It would bring five-hundred bucks on the black market. But he didn't use it to light cigarettes. The funny little doctor's stuff had kicked his habit.

They had given him a telephone. He couldn't call anybody on the outside, but people inside rang him occasionally to chat. Joe knew his file showed that he, like most smokers, had started patting for his weeds when the telephone rang. The phone could ring and Joe just answered it. The compulsion was gone. He looked in the mirror one morning and he couldn't even make out the outline of the S on his forehead.

At the end of the week a new doctor showed up and put Joe through a new drug series. The Demon was back. He was smoking five packs a day when they finally yanked him out of Hospital Isolation and sent him back to Packaging.

The little doctor with the funny accent was gone. Joe was too savvy to ask about him. Curiosity got you sent to Power.

The new drug people were getting better all the time. Joe French figured the drugs were being refined as they got more experience with Totally Behaviorially Modifying people. It was getting close to perfect. When he first came a home video would take a bunch of takes. Joe French once joked that there was so much redo that it must be like making "Gone Is My Wind." He thought that had been pretty funny, but none of the drug people laughed.

They didn't have a sense of humor but their stuff was

doing its job. Once they had a smoker fine-tuned, he or she would go through the routine like a trained sheepdog. Maybe even a politician. You did what they said, said whatever they wrote, even cried when the script called for it. That was the one that still mystified Joe French. The crying.

The background checks must have been pretty damned thorough. They had known that the manager of a Wal-Mart store in Buffalo had caught Joe French stealing baseball cards when he was ten years old. He didn't tell them that, so they probably got it from his mother.

They had known that Veronica was burning hell in the sack and he didn't remember their asking him that. Hell, after six years they could probably ask anybody who ever got it up in Erie County, New York. Veronica could do without a lot of things, but not that. If they'd asked him about Veronica's sex drive, he could have gone on for hours.

The drugs were so good that you'd tell them anything they asked but they couldn't know everything because they couldn't ask everything. For instance, nobody would ask a man if he cried.

Everybody in 21st Century America cried. The last two Presidents had cried while running for office. Winston DeWeerd sometimes cried when he talked about the victims of smoking. The coach of the Chicago Ground Cover cried when they canned his porky butt because the Ground Cover couldn't cover any ground. Crying was sensitive. Everybody cried. Everybody but Joe French.

Joe French loved it when the script called for him to cry. His ex-wife knew damned well he never cried. Veronica said it had been his biggest failing. She couldn't believe it when their daughter died of leukemia and he had just stood there with a sad face. The tears just didn't come. Joe thought about it a lot. There had been a lot of sad stuff in his life, but he didn't remember crying. Ever. Until he got here.

The brass must have hired a writer from a down-and-out soap opera to do the to-home videos. The last three scripts had called for Joe to cry; to denounce his crime, then sob while he said he knew he could never be cured. The tears came. Every time. Joe sobbed like a television evangelist caught with his pecker in half the congregation and both hands in the till. It was amazing.

Veronica must think he had changed completely in his five years inside, if she still gave a damn. He could tell that she sent him a video now and then, because some parts of the script were obviously intended to answer questions. You couldn't tell whether anybody on the outside gave a damn about the people in the Smoker Colonies. They probably didn't.

The jailers ran videos all the time that told the inmates that people on the outside were happy they were in custody; that nobody gave a damn if they ever got out. Winston DeWeerd said it all the time: "Every smoker is a slow-motion mass murderer, killing his or her loved ones and the innocents who come into contact with the evil taint of the Demon Weed."

Could be that everybody outside here believed that. You couldn't put much stock in what they told you in this damned place, but that much just might be true.

There was a lot of fact in the video scripts, but not much truth. Or Joe hoped there wasn't. The last script had called for Joe to tell his wife he had been diagnosed with lung cancer. Hell, he hadn't been inside the hospital for two years but his lungs felt fine. Joe French figured the line meant he was due for a transfer to Power. They said six months was about it when you worked in Power, especially if you were a lifetime smoker and couldn't fight off whatever it was that came at you.

Veronica wouldn't get any money when he died. The story was that OTA had a team of people in Washington who visited the former spouses of smokers to tell them that tobacco had finally taken its toll. Nobody was married in a Colony. Regular convicts just lost their civil rights. Smokers got a government-paid divorce the minute they were convicted.

Winston DeWeerd had said it was fair to the poor smokers and to their wives and husbands and to whatever it was the gay people called theirs. They played a lot of DeWeerd on the television around here. Joe French always thought of Veronica when they put on the tape in which DeWeerd said: "Smokers are doomed and their husbands and wives should not bear the stigma of tobacco-ruined relationships. It is a caring and loving government which ends that relationship before the further ravage of the Demon Weed is complete."

Joe French took the ballpoint pen from its hiding spot in the heel of his shoe. The slime guard was wandering down the line and wouldn't be back for a couple of minutes. Joe wrote three notes and slipped each one inside a package on its way to the loading dock.

It probably wouldn't help. Whoever got them probably wouldn't give a damn. Nobody had yet, as far as he could tell. He had been sending the notes for four years. There was no chance he would get another pen, so the notes had gotten shorter and shorter and the ink was getting dimmer and dimmer.

He really didn't have any idea where the damned things went. It could be that they were going in a shipment to Katmandu, or someplace in Africa, or Asia. Joe had been on a work detail in the administration building one day when a bunch of well-dressed Asians hustled around the corner. Most of them were wearing the masks like the guards wore. All but the old guy, the one who appeared to be the Big Dude in the crowd. A young woman was carrying his mask. She looked like an American. The Oriental guy was smoking a cigarette. Joe thought he must be a heavyweight dude, to smoke in this place.

The thought of the scene spurred Joe French's nicotine habit anew. He went to the electric lighter and fired up another phony Camel Filter.

CHAPTER 5

*SPOKANE, Washington — Smoke Jumper troop-
ers arrested twenty people at a rock music concert on Saturday. The officer in charge of the unit
said there would have been more arrests except
the marijuana smoke from the crowd was so
dense that the tobacco detectors were not fully
effective.*

***

I have always wondered whether the Air Monitor's
background checks are incompetent and management doesn't
know that I'm compromised in the job because I'm Winston
DeWeerd's half-brother. Maybe it's more likely that they knew
all along and that was the very reason they hired me.

The guy on the telephone knew about me and Winston
and that bothered me a little. He said he is a Paris-based investigator for Amnesty International and wanted to talk to me. He
wanted to come by the newspaper but I put him off. It sounded
like Mr. Pierre Letouf of Amnesty International hasn't read the
Air Monitor editorials about Amnesty International.

Amnesty International has raised hell for years about the
Smoker Colonies. My newspaper says Amnesty International
represents the tobacco-hazed thinking of a discredited class of
European smokers who fail to grasp the wisdom in protecting the
smoker and his or her "victims" by isolation.

Amnesty International suspects we may be protecting the
smokers the same way Hitler protected the Jews.

I was curious as to how Amnesty International came upon
my Winston DeWeerd connection. And I wanted to know what

Mr. Pierre Letouf might know about the Smoker Colonies. I guess that would be just idle curiosity, since nothing bad about the Colonies would wend its way onto the pristine pages of the Air Monitor.

I recognized Pierre Letouf the moment I walked into the bar. It was a pretty good trick, considering the slender Frenchman looked like another slender Washington denizen. His smoker grapple gave him away. He was glancing around the room and reaching for his non-existent cigarettes. Pierre Letouf was obviously a French puffer who couldn't wait to get back to his embassy where he could have a smoke. Embassies are the only places in Washington off-limits to our Smoke Jumper goons.

Letouf saw me and recognized me immediately and waved for me to join him at his table. "Mr. Reynolds, very good of you to meet me," he said.

"Call me Rob, please," I said.

"Whatever is your preference," he said, smiling with that peculiarly irritating condescension that Europeans often display at the informality of their unwashed American cousins.

"You look like a man who needs a cigarette," I said, smiling with my own brand of condescension, which is probably not arrogant enough to get me a good table at an empty restaurant in Paris.

Letouf laughed. "Ah, the habit. The Demon Weed of your brother."

The bar was packed and I didn't want my slimy genetic link with Winston DeWeerd to get on the grapevine by way of a sharp-eared gossip. I leaned over the table and spoke in a low voice. "I am not particularly proud to be associated in any way with the Senior Senator from Montana. Very few people know he's my half-brother. One of the reasons I came here is to find out how you know."

Letouf's Gaelic arrogance was slightly dampened by my directness. "Please accept my apology," he said. "It was in the computer files of InterPol. It was thoughtless of me to mention that you and the Senator had the same mother."

The bar was becoming even more crowded. Two young

men at the bar appeared to recognize me. "Friends?" Letouf asked. "More than likely they saw my face on one of the Air Monitor billboards," I said.

One of the men walked to the table. "You're Robert Reynolds," he said. "I just wanted to tell you how much I enjoyed that historical story you did on the flight of the Merchants of Death."

I thanked him. Pierre Letouf got the check and suggested we go to his temporary office to complete our conversation. It was all right with me. Besides, I could tell from his involuntary pocket-grabbing that he was lusting for a date with a Demon Weed.

We caught a cab and settled in for the short trip to the French Embassy. "Ah, you're an expert on the flight of the tobacconists," Letouf said. "In Europe we were somewhat...somewhat...amazed."

The United States economy still is having aftershocks from the amazing departure of the Merchants of Death. The tobacco companies. It had been one of the most effective moves in the history of mankind. I guess Moses crossing the Red Sea was more dramatic, but Moses didn't have to comply with just enough Securities and Exchange Commission regulations to make the move stand up. Christianity probably would have ended at the shore of the Red Sea if Moses and his band had to do their thing today. There is no way in hell our environmentalists, lawyers and politicians would have let Moses, or God, get away with parting the Red Sea. Not without an Environmental Impact Statement, a tedious debate over the whether some fish was an endangered species, two years of public hearings and a bunch of politicians reading statements for C-Span and the cameras of the Egyptian News Network. Not to mention the lawsuits, which have been going on for years. If I have any grandchildren, I hope they find out how all the lawsuits came out.

"Senator DeWeerd says the departure of the tobacco companies was the beginning of the greatest American economic renaissance since Henry Ford," I said.

"We Europeans have our economic problems and our

own versions of your Senator but we have tried to work them out without the terrible trauma that you Americans have brought to the endeavor," Letouf said.

He asked for my opinion on the sudden departure of the tobacco companies. His voice rose when he said, "the ones you Americans call the Merchants of Death."

"An increasing social unacceptability of smoking, I guess, and the fact that every lawyer in the United States either had filed a lawsuit against the tobacco companies or was trying to find someone who would allow him to file one."

"You Americans and your lawyers..." Letouf said, flipping his hand in a gesture of disgust.

I had to agree. Our lawyers would have tried to make Moses come back and face a special prosecutor.

If they ever got the Merchants of Death back in court there wouldn't be a showroom yacht in America without a "SOLD" sign on it. The government's own Special Prosecutor in the case of the Merchants of Death spent more than half a billion dollars before Winston DeWeerd and his buddies put the Special Prosecutor's budget in with the Central Intelligence Agency's. Winston observed that public scrutiny in this case was not necessary because it dealt with "significant ongoing matters of National Security." Special Prosecutor Walsh Larry did manage to convict a bank officer in McComb, Mississippi, for transferring five thousand dollars to the account of a relative of one of the departed Merchants of Death. And he promises this is just the beginning.

Walsh Larry would have gone after the money trail on Moses, just like he did with the poor jerk in Mississippi. Moses could have beaten the rap only if he had money, airplanes, facsimile machines, computers, greed and electronic-funds transfer. The Merchants had all those and they knew how to use them. When Black Monday dawned in Tobacco Country they were long gone. Every tobacco company headquartered in the good old USA had done a Moses and an Elvis at the same time. The Moses part involved parting the airspace of the Atlantic, the Pacific and the Gulf of Mexico. Lear Jets stuffed with corporate brass and billions of dollars in cash and notes screamed into the air, heading for safe haven. The Elvis part was more minor. Our politicians kept looking for the Merchants of Death in strange places. They wanted to keep on taxing the hell out of them and their products. About a fifth of the population had been hooked on cigarettes. The political system was hooked on the tax money from them.

"As you know," Letouf said, "the rest of the world has had a great economic bonanza from the taxes your tobacco companies are now paying."

I laughed at his understatement. "American politicians went crazy when they woke up and found the tobacco companies had fled. It was a little like Dracula waking up and finding out that the fat paraplegic in his basement had taken the noon carriage out of Transylvania."

Letouf smiled. "The people at Amnesty have frequent contact with the tobacco people. It is the concern that some of them have voiced that has brought me here," he said. "They seem to be very capable and sane people. Not the wild and undisciplined gaggle that your Senator DeWeerd says them to be."

I had to agree. The tobacco companies had to be well-organized and disciplined to flee the United States with hardly a murmur of advance notice.

The preparations had been impressively quiet. There was one exception. A stringer for The Associated Press in Tokyo had reported seeing the chairman of RJ Reynolds' tobacco division, walking with about twenty aides and a short ton of Japanese real estate people. The stringer said the tobacco baron and his smiling hosts were looking at one of the few vacant large office buildings in the town.

The AP's Tokyo people figured their stringer might be onto something and sent a message to the stateside bureau in Raleigh, North Carolina. The Raleigh Bureau called the tobacco giant's public-relations people and was told the Big Guy was playing golf at Pinehurst, North Carolina.

The AP Carolinas staffer explained later that the RJR public-relations people had never lied to her before. On reflection, she admitted she probably could have been a little more suspicious. She never told her bosses that she distinctly heard a voice in the background asking: "Do those file cabinets make the trip to Tokyo?"

"Have you personally interviewed any of the tobacco people about the smoking issue?" I asked.

"Not any of your people. My work takes me mostly to the backwaters of the world and the giant corporations chose not to relocate to them," he said.

It figured. Few of the backwaters of the world had good golf courses and no American bigwig was going to give up his citizenship and his golf handicap at the same time.

Once conglomerated in their former tobacco-growing empires, the Merchants of Death spread across the world, avoiding only United States territories and protectorates.

Some joined RJR Tobacco in Asia. The Americans who had to go to Japan were uniformly upset by the prices of recreation in Tokyo. Foreign newspapers said the once-American tobacco companies sponsored company-owned golf and tennis spas on South Seas Islands to try to take the sting out of relocation for their American executives.

Some companies sought safe haven in the Cayman Islands, where nicotine-stained billions melded into banks bulging with drug-stigmatized zillions. The locals in the Caymans hardly raised an eyebrow. They knew that tobacco killed more people than heroin and cocaine combined, but business was business and money was money. The death was someplace else. The money was working in the Caymans.

"I tried to make entry to the North Carolina Smoker Colony," Letouf said.

"I'm certain I know what happened," I said.

"I'd imagine you do. The gendarmes you call Smoke Jumpers ushered me into a little town called Goldsboro and warned me that I should not return," Letouf said.

"Grim place, Goldsboro," he said with a shudder.

I agreed. Goldsboro, North Carolina had been a gem of a small city in the heyday of tobacco but had gone into a decline

29

with the rest of the former American Tobacco Belt when the Merchants did their Moses routine. Unemployment in the old tobacco capitals has been at least double the national average since the Merchants of Death left.

The people from RJR/Nabisco in the United States were left with no smoke, no salaries and benefits and tons of cookies and food products. In cities across America people adopted the tactics of the 1990s. They had, after all, worked for the gays, the minorities and even the women.

They took to the streets with guns, fire and violence. It was a typical nineties kind of thing. The RJR tobacco employees and Winston-Salem business people provided their own smoke, burning everything in town that bore the trademark of RJR or Nabisco. The police were of little help. Every cop in Winston-Salem had a spouse, brother, sister or close friend among the rioters.

The cabby had to let us out a block from the Embassy. I saw a Smoke Jumper van, parked in the shadows in the next block. The Jumpers make quite a few smoking busts after Washington parties, especially after those in embassies where liquor flows freely and the Demon Weed can be smoked with a moment's impunity.

"There's a reception for some politician who is the chairman of one of your government's appropriations committees," Letouf sniffed. I chuckled inwardly at his characterization of Eddie Guidry as "some politician."

"Eddie Guidry," I said, "you mean some jerk politician." Letouf laughed without reservation, for a change. I told him that I have interviewed Eddie Guidry several times. "If I knew I had one minute to live, I'd want to spend it with Eddie. That way it would seem like a year," I said. He laughed again. I got the impression that he had read Eddie Guidry's file.

Eddie was at the head of the political stampede when the tobacco companies left the country. A Democrat from Louisiana, Guidry introduced a bill to require the companies either to return to the United States or just send money. Guidry said the government's needs were small. He just wanted the annual tax

30

bill that the companies and their customers paid to every level of government. Every politician who had ever had a chance at taxing cigarettes had boosted the take at every opportunity. Governments at all levels collected more than sixteen billion dollars in tobacco-related tax revenues as long ago as 1986 and the take had grown to more than twenty-five billion when the Merchants of Death did their disappearing act.

Cigarette smokers had provided a friendly target for the politicians for years. Their addiction to nicotine had cut their options on tax evasion.

Guidry acknowledged that the golden nicotinic goose was dead as a source of new revenue. He said he simply wanted the companies to keep paying their "fair share" of current taxes and to adjust future tax bills to reflect the percentage of increase in the national cost of living index.

Guidry said the payments should continue to state governments for no more than 25 years. He proposed to end the payments to the federal government after 50. Guidry explained his proposal on television time and again. He told me he was willing to consider a compromise at 20 years for the states and 40 years for the feds. I thought it laughable but the Air Monitor editorial page didn't. It praised Guidry for his "statesmanlike and reasonable proposals" and mentioned his "coolness under fire" during the panic associated with the tobacco companies' joint departure. That was meaningfully ironic, since Eddie Guidry had run to Canada to avoid serving in the U.S. military during the Vietnam war.

We walked inside the Embassy against the onslaught of several hundred well-dressed Washingtonians.

The cracking Cajun voice made me want to hide behind a philodendron.

"Rob Reynolds. Good to see you made it heah foh mah reception, even if it's almost ovuh." I took Eddie Guidry's proffered paw and shook it. "You'all be shoah to quote me as sayin' that Franco-American cooperation is jest as fine as a sunrise in Nahlens, 'ceptin' foh the problems we still got on the tobacco folks," Guidry said.

31

"One of our society reporters is covering the reception, Senator, but I'll pass the word along," I said.

Letouf and I stopped to get a drink at one of the four bars set up in the wide hallway. "What's Nahlens?" Letouf asked, sipping tentatively on a glass of California chablis.

"It's the way a Cajun politician like Eddie Guidry pronounces New Orleans," I said.

"The Senator is almost as much of a barbarian as your...as Senator DeWeerd," Letouf sniffed.

He had a point. Chicken Eddie Guidry of the Vietnam era turned into Tiger Guidry when the Merchants of Death took their tax bonanza and left town. Eddie proposed using the Armed Forces to make the Merchants of Death keep supporting their abandoned government. Eddie's press secretary, a decorated war hero, kept telling everybody who would listen that the Senator was both tough and reasonable. He did it with a straight face. It was remarkable.

They didn't laugh at Eddie in the Senate. Most of its members had about the same history of physical bravery as did Fast Eddie Guidry. The fleet-footed Democrat of the Vietnam era got twenty co-sponsors on the bill that required the Armed Forces to conduct maneuvers in Thailand and the Caymans, with the object of the maneuvers being the seizure of the former USA tobacco barons and their assets. Eddie helped fight back an amendment to add the Japanese to the list. Guidry explained that the Japanese had suffered enough.

Skeptics like me thought it could be possible that Guidry wasn't so senile to remember that the Japanese owned about twenty percent of his state's privately held assets and paid a couple of million a year to Fast Eddie's law firm in Baton Rouge.

The Washington Post wanted to avoid being tarred with a pro-tobacco position. The Post, however, tried to point out rather wimpily that Guidry was calling for "...a unilateral declaration of war on non-belligerent nations," even with Japan excluded. Guidry was unimpressed.

Newspapers in tobacco country found reasons to support Guidry. The Charlotte Observer pompously opined that the legislation was unconstitutional, but could be rewritten to conform to the law. The Observer editorial writers crowed that they had found the smoking loophole that everyone else, even Eddie Guidry, had missed. The Observer said the tobacco companies had failed to file an Economic Impact Statement before fleeing the country.

Eddie Guidry said the Observer editorial was balanced, fair and well-reasoned. Which meant, of course, that it was full of crap.

We made our way through the crowd and ducked into a tiny office.

"My government allows me use of these grand quarters only temporarily," Letouf said.

He lit a cigarette and drew smoke deep into his lungs as I watched. I wanted to ask him for a smoke but I still didn't know what to make of the man.

Letouf must have been a good investigator. Like good reporters, good investigators can sense something of what other people are thinking.

"Cigarette?" he said.

"I really shouldn't."

"I understand completely," he said.

"I'd appreciate it if we could come to the point," I said.

Letouf's calm face became stony. "I understand your American directness," he said. "The point is your Smoker Colonies. I believe you could be of great assistance to the cause of freedom if you would use your position to gain entry to one of the Colonies. I believe you will be appalled at what you will find."

"I don't know that you are wrong. What I cannot understand is why you are saying this to me. You know I am the half-brother of the man who built the Colonies. You know that I work for the Air Monitor. My newspaper's management can identify the sweet strains of Mozart in the sound of one of Winston's farts."

"Those are only two of the reasons I want to make a presentation to you," Letouf said. "You are a nonconformist. And you are, I think, an honest man. You are uniquely situated to gain

33

entry to one of the Smoker Colonies. If our reports are groundless, then I will find other work to do. In the business of oppression there is always other work."

"What do you think I might find in the Colonies?"

He waved the new cigarette in a circular motion. The smoke looked inviting.

"I must admit our information is little. You might look at this." He took a package of filtered cigarettes from a plastic bag.

I smiled. "I might find a cigarette? The Colonies are the only places in America where smoking is legal."

He handed me the package. "These cigarettes came to us from a person in Tokyo. Look at the piece of cigarette paper inside the package.

I found the cigarette paper. There was writing on it. The message said: "They're killing people in the Colonies."

"We have had similar messages found by people in Canada and South America," Letouf said. "Most are written by the same person and convey the same message."

Letouf's telephone rang. He asked me to wait, saying the call involved a Brazilian case in which thousands of children were reportedly being held hostage by their government. I looked over his sheaf of clippings on the three American Smoker Colonies. I couldn't listen in on his end of the conversation because he was conversing in French.

I decided to make no commitment to do anything. I wouldn't go so far as to indicate I might check into the Colony rumors. I had covered crime before coming to work at the Air Monitor and I had a police reporter's suspicion of anything written by any kind of convict, even the bland variety that populates the three smoker Colonies.

Winston DeWeerd was able to get the Colonies into operation because of the flood of arrested smokers. Winston pointed out that it wasn't fair to America's rapists and murderers to have to breathe the foul pollution that accompanied those with *the habit.*

There was some skepticism about the Colonies but the crime wave in the streets took care of that. People wouldn't put up with secondhand smoke and first-person crime.

Some newspapers decried the Colonies as un-American. Others saw them as a necessary answer to a problem that smokers had created.

It was America at its most illogical. Things tended to get a little more balanced in cities closer to Canada. Canada had managed to cut back on smoking without the cataclysmic experience of its bumptious southern neighbor. Canada had taxed cigarettes at a rate roughly adjusted to the actuarial cost indicated by the health figures associated with Canada's National Health Insurance. The average tax on a pack of cigarettes in Canada was $3.30. It was only 49 cents in the U.S. before they became illegal.

Canada's idea of separating smokers from their habit at the pocketbook had showed results and promised more. Canadian cigarette sales dropped 30 percent in the 1980s and had continued to skid in the 1990s. The galloping departure of the Merchants of Death had thrown even the Canadian government into a tizzy. Most Canadian cigarettes came from the United States. The taxing authorities had no trouble toting up the billions on cigarettes through the proper channels. But the disruption in the normal supply caused a budgetary crisis that brought down Premier Pierre Laurent's government. The Canadian taxes remained in place but the bureaucratic chain had been broken.

The New York Times foresaw a budget crisis of its own. The Times, which had lost money for decades on its New York City operations, owned five newspapers in the Carolinas. Its top executives saw the corporation's financial life flashing in front of their corporate eyes. Normally attuned to dispassionate plumbing of depravity or disaster in Turkey or Tupelo, Mississippi, The Times could see there was a financial Armageddon in the making in Tobacco Country.

The Good Grey Times pontificated that the President should, at minimum, send a couple of carriers toward the Caymans and the Far East and use every diplomatic avenue available to ensure the return of the Merchants of Death and their tax billions. The Times editorialist didn't mention the possible return of the hundreds of millions it sucked off every year from its

35

Carolinas properties. The Times editorial page has always stayed above the grubby concerns of the marketplace. The take from the Carolinas had helped it keep it that way.

Letouf ended his call over the Brazilian case. His eyes misted, but only for a moment. "Have you been in contact recently with the rehabilitated smoker, Mr. Milano Nagurski?" he asked.

"Not recently. I've done some stories on Milano's return from the Smoker Colony but I haven't heard from him in quite a while."

Letouf adopted his conspiratorial look, which didn't take much adopting. I assume constructive paranoia is part of your job description when you go into his line of work.

"Possibly you might find something interesting. The Smoker who got the message, unhappily, destroyed the paper. But she said she distinctly remembered that the message stated `Nagurski knows the truth about the Colonies.' "

I gave him my halfhearted assurance that I might get in touch with Milano Nagurski. It was halfhearted because my past contacts with Milano yielded nothing more than his parroting the joys of freedom from the thrall of the Demon Weed and his pledges of allegiance to the Office of Tobacco Abatement. The OTA had, after all, helped him to become productive and smoke-free.

I left Letouf as he was returning a call from Brussels. I stopped at the bar for another drink. Senator Eddie Guidry was roaring drunk and was fondling the wife of a South American diplomat. "Cher," he said, "you ain't never had it 'til you've had it from a registered Coonass," he said. I could tell from the woman's expression that she knew that a Coonass and a horse's ass were the same. At least in the case of Eddie Guidry.

I felt two wonderful pressures at my back and looked over my shoulder.

"Hello, Cecilia," I said. The woman whose world-class chest was gracing my back was Cecilia Word, Winston DeWeerd's press secretary and mistress.

The voice could have melted titanium. "Hello, Rob, it's

nice to see you," Cecilia said.

"Where's your boss?" I asked.

"Working on a new anti-tobacco bill at the office. He asked me to come by. He and Senator Guidry are quite close."

I figured that Cecilia, who is probably the most beautiful woman in Washington, had gotten close to me to avoid close contact with Eddie Guidry.

"Let's have lunch sometime," she said.

"Sure. Call me at the office," I said.

"I'll do it," Cecilia said. "Pardon me, Rob, but there is someone here I really must talk to."

I joined every other man in the room in watching her walk down the hallway. We watched until she reached the hallway. I wondered if Pierre Letouf's French instincts would warn him that he should hang up on Brussels and open the door for an eyeful of Cecilia Word as she walked past.

Probably not. Letouf is a pretty serious fellow.

CHAPTER 6

WASHINGTON — A special three-judge panel of the U.S. Circuit Court of Appeals on Tuesday dismissed a lawsuit brought by relatives of a man who contended arresting Smoke Jumpers used a "throw-down" package of cigarettes as a reason for his arrest.

***

Barranca Lopez pulled at the hem of her dress. She had decided she hated Washington and everybody in it. She wanted them to buy her a leather miniskirt and they made her wear this stupid dress with flowers on it. They were all so phony and they all smelled like a perfume factory.

Barranca was the daughter of a janitor from Gallup, New Mexico, and not yet accustomed to attention, much less adulation. She knew she could get accustomed to it. She felt a little like a rock star. People turned and looked at her on the street. Everyone knew who she was. The OTA said more people had seen the Barranca Lopez videotape than had watched the San Diego Smoke-Frees whip the New York Hills in the last Super Bowl.

She had seen the videotape a hundred times. The bitch from the Office of Tobacco Youth Division had told Barranca she had done the right thing. Everyone had told her she had done the right thing. After watching it and watching it, Barranca was still not certain she had done the right thing. She had been afraid somebody would catch on, but nobody had yet.

Now Barranca was going to have to watch the videotape again and all those Anglos, and the Hispanic senior senator from

New Mexico, would set their faces in phony sorrow, rub their chins when the tape ran, then look sorrowfully her way. They always did that. They had never caught on before. They wouldn't this time, either. Barranca, a slender fifteen-year-old with only bumps for breasts, was self-conscious about her appearance. Especially without the miniskirt. She had tons of pretty hair and nice legs. She would have looked great in the miniskirt.

One thing she was certain of. None of the bastards really felt any emotion about her, or her mother. It was all a show. All she had gotten out of it was a trip to this stinking Washington and a new dress with stupid flowers on it.

Her stupid father had sold the videotape for two thousand lousy bucks. Tommy Jimenez told Barranca the guy who bought it had already made a half million out of it. Tommy said the guy was going to make that much again just off a movie deal.

Barranca secretly wished that it had been her father outside the door. Her mother might have had enough brains to wait a couple of days before she sold the tape. Probably that was true for certain because her mother didn't drink nearly as much as her father did. The two thousand was already gone and Pedro Lopez had lost his janitor job. Barranca definitely wished it had been her father on the videotape, but she wasn't going to say that. Ever.

Tommy Jimenez said Barranca could make a bunch of money herself, if she was smart. Tommy said Barranca should wait until she was 18 and then she could go into the movies and on the speaking things and all of that crap, unless her face changed so much that people wouldn't recognize her anymore.

Tommy was pretty smart. Barranca figured Tommy believed her face wouldn't change. Tommy had thrown over Yolanda Cordero right after the tape came out. And Yolanda was sixteen and had a body like she was twenty-one. But Yolanda was no more. Tommy was Barranca's steady boyfriend now and he took her to bed two or three times a week, more often when her father drank himself to sleep right after school. If the pig had enough brains to keep the tape for a day or so he could have enough booze to drink himself silly every day. She and Tommy could have done it all the time if her dad wasn't such a fool.

Barranca thought the big, gray-haired creep with the phony smile had a pretty good name, if you pronounced it Winston The Weird. She wouldn't have been here if it hadn't been for The Weird one. He was the one who was always in the videos they watched at school, talking about the Demon Weed. Now her cousin, Alejandro, he knew about Demon Weed. Alejandro smoked peyote. Alejandro's brain probably looked like the inside of a peyote plant. Nothing but water and mush. Barranca figured her father probably had smoked a lot of peyote before he turned onto booze. Alejandro was almost as nuts as her old man.

Winston The Weird was coming to her side. He smelled like the whores her father rubbed up against when he had a couple of bucks he didn't spend on booze. She wanted to turn up her nose but everybody was looking at her and The Weird. There had to be five hundred people in the auditorium. Some place, this Office of Tobacco Abatement. Tommy Jimenez called them the Master Abaters. She always laughed like hell when Tommy said that. Just like Tommy did, but Barranca never got what was so funny.

Winston The Weird patted her on the shoulder and looked at her. She could see that the old creep looked at her little tits. That pissed her off, but she wasn't going to do anything stupid. She had to suck up to this Weird shithead. He was talking about her being a symbol. He didn't talk as good in person as he did in those videos of him they had seen in school.

She had heard his crap about The Tragedy of Barranca a hundred times before. He'd never know it wasn't a tragedy. He probably didn't give a damn. She was just tired of the goddamned smoke. She knew she'd never get a guy interested in her if her hair smelled like goddamned smoke all the time. That had been the whole deal but if Winston The Weird wanted to pretend she was some kind of heroine, that was all right with Barranca. Barranca fixed her eyes on Winston The Weird like maybe the old creep looked like Tommy. The drama teacher at school had told her that kind of thing would relax her. It was the only thing the Anglo bitch had ever said that was right.

Barranca Lopez had practiced the expression before. She knew how to time it. She had worked it out with Tommy. When the tape started rolling she was supposed to look at it with wide eyes. Like she was seeing Freddy Krueger on the foot of her bed. Then she was supposed to look like somebody kicked her in the gut. Then she was supposed to stiffen up. Tommy said she should sit there like she was a sleepwalker who was having a bad dream. It always worked. She wanted to laugh.

***

Winston DeWeerd looked at the blue-ribbon crowd of educators, psychologists, psychiatrists, child-behavior experts and anti-tobacco activists. Their presence in the OTA Auditorium proved that even his closest staff members could be abysmally stupid when it came to an issue.

Even Cecilia Word had advised against making a cause celebre of it. Cecilia was seldom wrong, but she was this time. Winston knew the Barranca Lopez tape would be a major tool when he first got wind of it.

It was a fluke, but flukes could be better than the half-million-dollar staging that the OTA put on. An ambitious young lawyer in the Office of Tobacco Abatement Youth Crimes Division managed to get through to Senator DeWeerd. He insisted on telling only Winston DeWeerd the story of a young woman in New Mexico who had videotaped the tobacco-related death of her mother.

The lawyer told the story of a young girl who acted out of love for her mother, a two-pack-a-day smoker. The girl, spurred by the federal anti-smoking program in general and Winston DeWeerd in particular, wanted to show her mother the ugliness of her cigarette habit. The child set up the video camera and threw her mother's cigarettes outside, into a raging snowstorm. The mother, her nicotine addiction taking over her mind, had plunged outside. She refused to relinquish her cigarettes, despite her daughter's pleas.

The lawyer had seen the tape, thanks to a sharpie in Gallup, New Mexico. And the OTA lawyer told DeWeerd that he had invoked the Senator's name and reputation to convince the idiot local District Attorney that no charges should be filed in the case.

Winston DeWeerd ordered a military jet to pick up the tape and rush it to Washington. After only one screening, he called in the OTA technical creeps to add some snow to several scenes and to enhance the image of the package of rebel cigarettes. The audio people made one change in the dialogue. No one would ever know. It was amazing. The audiophiles could remove just one consonant and make the entire film more compelling and meaningful.

There had been only one mistake on adding the snow. The idiots added it blowing in, but didn't leave a dusting of it on the floor. Even if anyone happened to notice it, it would be explainable. The supposedly sharp-eyed media jerks had never caught it and never would. Only Cecilia Word had noticed and Cecilia would never tell anyone. There were thousands of copies of the tape. It even ran in Japan, where the idiots still smoked like crazy.

Winston smiled as he addressed the crowd. He dropped his hand caringly on Barranca Lopez's shoulder before he started to speak.

"The tragedy of Barranca brings us here today that we may celebrate the caring and tenderness of this brave young woman, who was driven to an act of love to try to save her mother from her deadly addiction to tobacco," DeWeerd said.

"Most of us here today have seen the tape that chronicles the Tragedy of Barranca. Most of us celebrate the wonderful impact the Barranca story has had on other people. Children and other family members of tobacco addicts take heart from Barranca's story. They know they can fight back against the demon weed that is destroying their life, and the lungs, heart and brain of a loved one."

"The tragedy of Barranca Lopez is not simply her mother's evil addiction...a violation of Barranca that was polluting her little lungs with the equivalent of six cigarettes a day. Deplorable and criminal as it was, that was not the major tragedy," DeWeerd said, thumping the podium. Scattered applause broke out.

Barranca stiffened noticeably at his words. DeWeerd

adopted his best smile of understanding. The reference to the pollution that her mother had sent into her lungs had frightened the child. "It's all right," DeWeerd said, stroking Barranca's shoulder again. Barranca relaxed. DeWeerd couldn't know that Barranca wanted to give him the finger over the words "little lungs."

DeWeerd continued. "No, the tragedy of Barranca Lopez is the tragedy of an Act of Love spurned...spurned in the quest for the addictive and demon weed!" DeWeerd's voice rose to a thunder on the last two words and the auditorium shook as the crowd moved as one body into a standing ovation. DeWeerd smiled as the roar subsided.

"And now," he said, "the story of Barranca Lopez."

***

The OTA video specialists had added clarity and color to the video made by the cheap Sony camera. The audience was as motionless as a glacier. The tape leader shows the date and time. Alicia Lopez is in her kitchen. She picks up the pack of cigarettes from the table. Barranca Lopez grabs the pack from her mother's hand, runs to the door and tosses it outside.

The OTA computer specialists had added a few thousand snowflakes to the paltry dusting that had appeared during Winston DeWeerd's initial screening the videotape. In OTA's version, Barranca Lopez appeared beset by a blizzard before she slammed the door shut.

The portly Alicia Lopez launches a roundhouse slap at Barranca, snarls something unintelligible, opens the door to another blizzard of OTA-provided snowflakes, then walks unsteadily outside. The camera captures Alicia Lopez, fumbling in the snow for the package of cigarettes. All but the top of her head disappears as Barranca is seen, slamming, then locking, the door.

Alicia Lopez's face is a mask of anger at the window in the door, a cigarette clenched between her lips. The smoke curls almost evilly against the glass.

Barranca screams. "Throw away the cigarettes, Mother!"

Alicia Lopez responds by hurling her body repeatedly against the door. The cigarette never leaves her mouth. Barranca's reed-like body is against the door, shuddering from her mother's rushes against it.

Barranca's voice is shrill. "No more smoke, Mother."

Alicia's face is against the window. Her face is absolutely demonic through the dew on the inside. She uses the cigarette as a pointer as she screams at Barranca. "Screw your air!"

There is ten minutes with almost no action. Barranca Lopez paces to and from the door. Her mother occasionally disappears from sight, then comes back, smoking a cigarette. (In the OTA version shown on television, the hiatus is taken out, and explained by an off-screen announcer, who intones: "The stand-off continues for ten minutes.")

Alicia Lopez screams for her daughter to open the door. Barranca is resolute. She pleads again, "Throw away the cigarettes, Mother." Alicia's face is becoming pinched in the sub-zero cold. Her hands appear to be made of ice as she fights the wind to light yet another cigarette. She defiantly takes a deep draft on the high-tar weed as her jaw appears to lock. The heart attack freezes the frightful visage, then the entire body. The squatty and snow-covered body falls like a poisoned oak in a blizzard. The red tip of the burning cigarette is a laser trace against the snow. Alicia Lopez is dead.

The daughter's hands go to her head. She fondles the black mane of hair absently, almost tenderly. Suddenly hyper with panic Barranca Lopez runs off camera. The audio picks up the three strokes of the 911 telephone call. Barranca's voice is quavering, but clear. "My mother is dead. Cigarettes killed her."

***

It was as if I had been sitting in a petrified forest. I needed to get up and leave but I sat still. Almost everyone sat still. The frantic movements of the photographers broke the spell. I'm a pretty good reporter but I would have made a lousy photographer. Some photographers are artists, but not many. The best news photographers are a blend of pig, coyote, gorilla and eagle. The elite of the crowd are the ones who will jump up on a casket as the pallbearers are carrying it out of a funeral, so they can get one last closeup of the body. We knew we had total equality at the Air

Monitor when fifty percent of the shooters were men, fifty percent were women, and ninety percent were pigs.

I knew one of our photographers would make the first move. Right on cue, the lovely Jewell Cross rose from the front row and started snapping pictures of Winston DeWeerd. Tears were pouring down his cheeks. I figure the creep carries an onion in each pocket. Winston could turn the Sahara Desert into an oasis. I'll bet he could even cry when he's humping Cecilia. It's an obscure talent, but Winston makes the best of what he's got.

Jewell got the last Winston teardrop, then hovered over Barranca Lopez like a condor with a Rotax camera for an eye. Jewell hates the Rotax but they're all the Air Monitor will buy. They're the only camera company that smoke-tests all employees and signs the goddamned pledge that's required of anybody who does more than a hundred dollars worth of business with the Air Monitor. We cut it off at a hundred bucks. We're reasonable people. Besides, we've got to pay people to do the paperwork.

Jewell Cross is doing her fashion-photographer routine with Barranca. The kid is eating it up. She is touching her hair, just as she did in the film. It's strange. It's exactly the same. Both hands are up and moving in circles. The kid is in love. I'm sure one of these psychiatrists would call it follicle fantasy. Psychiatrists never say "banana" when they can work in "elongated yellow fruit."

I had happened to take a seat beside Hormel Schlegel. Hormel is an interesting guy. He is a North Dakota farmer who sued American Brands and got one of the mammoth judgments that kept spewing out of the courts when the legalistic logjam broke in favor of anybody who sued anybody who made a smoking something. Hormel's lungs were fine but he contended that smoking had destroyed his hearing. We never found out exactly how much Hormel got, but he admitted to me that it was more than two million bucks.

Hormel nudged me. "Great public service, that film," he said.

"Great drama, for sure," I said. Hormel's ice-blue eyes were on my lips. He had been the first deaf person I had ever interviewed and I never had to repeat one word.

"The old bitch deserved to die," Hormel said. I couldn't go along with that, but there was nothing to gain by arguing with anti-smoking activists. Especially when you work for the Air Monitor.

Hormel appeared not to notice my lack of agreement and continued in his sing-song voice. "I've seen that film a hundred times and there's one thing I don't get about it."

He paused and I made certain I didn't turn my head away from his field of vision. "I've never understood why the woman didn't pretend to toss her weeds, then come inside and kick the living shit out of her daughter," I said.

Hormel Schlegel chuckled. "That sounds like you, Robert. You're always going for action, but you're a nice guy. You clean up things people say before you put it in the paper."

I appreciate being called a nice guy, but one thing I do not do is clean up quotes. That had gotten to be unacceptable before I got in the business. There was a day when not every event was tape-recorded and videotaped by somebody, or a dozen somebodies.

The censorship we have today is much more malignant than that of the old days. We're under pressure all the time to be "sensitive" and the pressure isn't genteel.

A reporter could be genteel in the old days. I remember reading a story that General Douglas MacArthur and his staff officers finally pushed the Chinese Communists back across the Yalu River in Korea. The story said MacArthur and his officers "strode to the bank of the Yalu and spat into it." The symbolism was right, but Douglas and his lads went to the bank, undid their flies and took a leak. If Douglas and his officers triumphed today they'd be hanging it out on television and would instantly galvanize the environmental people into opposing whatever war they were fighting.

No one at the Yalu wrote a letter to the editor correcting the spitting story and I didn't argue with Hormel. He thought he was paying me a compliment, but I quote people on what they said. Period. I started getting careful with words when I was a mere kid and was writing about a golf match involving women from competing country clubs in Fort Worth, Texas. My one stupid reference to an "inter-course rivalry" brought me enough grief to dam the Yalu.

"I don't recall sanitizing anything in my stories about you," I said.

"Nothing there," Hormel said, "it's been in your articles about the Barranca Lopez tape. You always write that Mrs. Lopez screamed `screw your *air*.' " Hormel stopped, as if he were talking to a child.

"That's what she said," I responded.

Schlegel's eyes never left my lips. "Bullshit," he said. "She said, screw your *hair*, but it's nice of you to put it in the way she really meant it."

I looked at the stage. Barranca Lopez was moving her head in animated conversation with an anti-smoking activist from New Hampshire. Barranca's coiffure was a black halo. I had never looked at the child's eyes before. They were as black as the hair and as cold as the New Mexico blizzard that had sapped the damaged heart of Alicia Lopez. I couldn't mask the involuntary shudder that came over me. It only lasted a second, but Hormel Schlegel saw it.

"You must be coming down with something," he said.

"Maybe it's a virus," I said.

"Probably ought to get a doctor to give you something for it, just so people won't think the wrong thing," Schlegel said.

The slight threat in his words was quite clear to anyone who lived in 21st Century America. Clearer still to someone who worked for the Air Monitor. We had exorcised the Demon Weed. With the exorcism, the health-related blight of tobacco had been exiled. Smokers got sick. Non-smokers stayed well.

There was no more palsy. My body was rigid with anger as Barranca Lopez turned and locked eyes with me. Barranca didn't give a damn about her pristine little lungs. She let Alicia Lopez freeze to death because she didn't want the scent of her mother's cigarette smoke in her hair. She smiled at me and turned away. She was still fluffing her hair.

CHAPTER 7

*JACKSON, Mississippi — Police put down what
one officer described as a mini-riot Wednesday
evening. A theater spokesman said the disorder
began when militant anti-smoking advocates
objected to footage which showed a Lark Cigarettes billboard in the background of the movie's
final scene.*

***

The billions of dollars the corporate tobacco barons could
command kept a lid on non-smoking initiatives for decade after
decade. They even turned back initiatives in California in the
early days. People have always called California a bellwether
state. I agree, but I think of it in terms of the natural relationship
between a bellwether and a Judas goat. A bellwether was the
castrated sheep whose bell told the other sheep where to go. Not
that different from a Judas goat, who led the other goats through
the slaughterhouse.

California has thousands of people who die every year
from crime. California has more drive-by shootings than Wyoming has drive-by drive-bys. California would beat itself every
year if the Book of Records did drive-bys. And there's AIDS.
Californians can be proud that California performed the same
service in incubating the AIDS virus as did North Carolina for the
lung-cancer industry.

California is the most anti-smoking state in the union
today. That stature is why I get to go to a hotel convention room
to listen to the speech of California State Senator Dianne Sharp.
Dianne Sharp is an innovator. She came up with the idea that

people convicted under state or federal anti-tobacco laws should lose it all. The house, the car, the boat, the Reeboks, the jewelry. Everything. Even Winston DeWeerd hadn't thought of that. Dianne Sharp, whose mother had died of lung cancer, also sponsored a bill to allow the state to use smokers for air-pollution testing. The California Supreme Court ruled the Sharp bill unconstitutional because it was too narrowly focused. She gleefully wrote a new version, which also allowed use of repeat-offender smokers for "any legitimate medical and/or health-related testing."

Dianne Sharp was at the podium, turning her head gracefully to match the angle of her favorite television camera of the moment. Funny, but her hard little eyes remind me of Barranca Lopez's and that gives me a knot in my stomach.

Dianne Sharp recounted the history of anti-smoking initiatives in California. She noted that Californians had a chance to be the first place to pass anti-smoking initiatives.

"But the Merchants of Death unleashed their billions of dollars and set their hired political minions to their evil work and the first initiatives failed," she said. There was a tone of sorrow in her voice that must have made her drama coach swell with pride.

"But Californians are a proud and sensitive people who would not long suffer the fiction of the Merchants of Death that smoking was a victimless crime," Ms. Sharp thundered. Half the room stood in spontaneous ovation. I was lucky that reporters, even reporters for sheets as suspect as the Air Monitor, are bound by the fiction of objectivity not to take part in such demonstrations. Despite that, one of the reporters at the press table stood and joined in the applause.

Ms. Sharp waited for the crowd to calm down, then noted, sadly, that Californians kept puffing their cigarettes for years. "But the people have spoken and the Demon Weed will never again befoul the lungs and lives of our citizens, thanks to an enlightened public and the God-guided work of people such as Senator Winston DeWeerd," she said. Her eyes were shooting sparks and her shoulders were shaking in anger.

Half the crowd rose again in what appeared to be spontaneous applause, then the other half joined in the standing ovation when Dianne Sharp ended her speech by shooting both arms straight out and shouting: "To clean air!" Six uniformed Smoke Jumpers in the back of the room stood at attention as they mirrored her arm movements and echoed her words. One of the Jumpers dropped his hand to his nine-millimeter pistol. His emotions were so overwhelming that he was lusting to gut-shoot a smoker in the name of clean lungs.

We've come a distance from the old days, when California voters could be convinced that cops had better things to do than bust smokers. I don't think the trip has been worth it.

As I left the convention hall, I recalled that Miami had a shot at immortality in the Office of Tobacco Abatement archives, but they blew it, too. Miami has one of the largest Smoke Jumper units in the country to try to catch the billions of dollars worth of cigarettes that are smuggled in from Cuba and the drug nations that made Miami Vice a hit television program back in the last century. I think it was 1980 when there was an election initiative in Dade County, Florida. One industry ad showed a couple of crooks loaded with loot walking past a bowling alley. There is an empty police car parked outside. "Geez, the cops!," says one crook. "Relax, Louie," says the other. 'Dem Cops is inside enforcin' da' no-smoking law."

I heard the chatter of the Smoke Jumper helicopter and watched a Smoke Jumper van, speeding down the street in pursuit of a little electric car.

***

The sight of the Jumper van made me happy that I had gone from a confirmed smoker to a protesting puffer. I had it once. The habit, I mean. I had it bad.

The telephone was the worst offender, at least at home. It would ring and I would fumble in the nearest hiding place, trying to find a cigarette. My friends got a little tired of my asking them to hold on for a second while I opened the window and turned on the fan.

They must be pretty good friends. They've never turned

me in. Several of them were smokers, too. Manley Tatum died at age thirty-five of a massive heart attack. The doctor said nicotine had clogged his heart and circulatory system beyond even modern medicine's ability to help. His lungs were already gone. I didn't remember him as being that heavy a smoker. I've never figured out how he grew up in this society and managed to grab enough smokes to kill himself.

Smoking is a challenge, almost anywhere in the United States. Smoking enough to kill yourself takes a lot of commitment. You could compare it to a guy who masturbates himself to death when his hands are tied for fifty-eight minutes out of every hour. Some people think the apparent increase in the lethal nature of the cigarette comes from the new weeds. The hundred-buck-a-pack cigarettes people smoke come from South America, mostly. Maybe the new tobacco barons have crossed the Demon Weed with something mean. Jalapeno peppers, maybe.

Horace Jistel got crossed with something mean, thanks to his habit. Horace died of smoking the old-fashioned way. He was shot in the bedroom of the woman whose husband was holding the smoking nine millimeter pistol. There was no doubt that Horny Horace was a victim of his smoking. The husband of Horace's Monday afternoon delight was a militant non-smoker. He was going to do a quick in and out at the house to pick up his Ruger for target practice after work. If it hadn't been for the odor of Horace's cigarette the guy might not have suspected someone had been doing an extended in and out on his wife. The guy kept sniffing and sniffing and sniffing.

He opened his wife's closet door and Horny Horace and his half-smoked Merit 100 both were on the way to that Big Ashtray In The Sky. The shooter was a real charmer. He told the cops he started to shoot his wife, but didn't because she wasn't smoking.

Winston hasn't yet proposed a federal reward for husbands who put a tight nine millimeter pattern in the chests of their wives' lovers, but don't rule it out. Not if the lover is a smoker.

I smoked quite a bit in college. While I was there I read about the potheads of the last century and found that a lot of them smoked marijuana just because it was verboten. It's the same thing now with cigarettes. An amazingly high percentage of professors smoke the Demon Weed and almost all the students smoke one now and then, at least if my college was an indication. It was a forgettable little school in upstate New York, but smoking cigarettes was a "statement" of some dumb kind. It was even a bigger rush to smuggle cigarettes from Canada.

A couple of the hockey players were damned near millionaires when they got out of college, thanks to the all the games they played in Canada. Now Canadians don't take second place to anyone when it comes to hating smoking, but they manage to be anti-tobacco without going nuts. They just tax the hell out of cigarettes, take care of their lungers through their national health plan and go their merry, Canadian, way. They drink a lot, too, which explains to me why they won't follow us and outlaw smoking.

I'll quit for good some day, when Winston DeWeerd and his clowns are gone, but I doubt I'll ever take a sip of beer or mixed drink without fumbling toward my shirt pocket. I wish that weren't true but I've got reason to believe it is.

There are some things that will help the urge to quit, or at least cut down. Like boxing. I was in a boxing club in college and I found that my physical well-being, or maybe my somewhat pleasant but stoic face, dictated I keep my smoking to a minimum.

I like boxing because it's so out of fashion. Insensitive, you know. And I learned I was sensitive to lung conditioning as a short-armed heavyweight. A guy who's five-eleven and wears a thirty-two-inch sleeve gets hit when he's moving in on those six-foot-plus guys with arms so long they could reach around a television anchorman's ego. Now you might think I'm being sexist, referring only to anchor-man, but I'm not. I never fought anybody with arms long enough to reach around an anchorwoman's ego.

Anyway, I smoked some in college and then more when I graduated and got my first job. That was at the daily newspaper in Raleigh, North Carolina, just ahead of the tobacco cataclysm. I knew I ought to quit even though I wasn't boxing. The only pounding I ever got on a regular basis was from the horny woman who ran the "Vistas" section of the newspaper.

A pounding from Charlotte Gay was a breathtaking experience. You didn't tell Charlotte you were out of breath, because that would make Charlotte reach down and get that something "extra" that all great athletes have. In Charlotte's case, she would put you on your back and work and work until your lungs had recovered enough from the carbon monoxide to catch up with your sex-crazed brain.

I figured a hundred bucks was a cheap price to pay to get my lungs tuned up to a general level of interest with my brain, so I flopped out a credit card to pay for a session with a hypnotist. I explained the generalities of my problem. He said he could make it easy to quit the weeds, but that he figured it would take about ten-thousand bucks more to cure me of the woman I had described. I quit for all of five days. Quit smoking, I mean. Only a fool would have quit pounding Charlotte.

I even did the nicotine mainlining that was supposed to be foolproof. It wasn't really mainlining, but this gizmo zapped a weed's worth of nicotine into your body every ten minutes or so. I was still pawing my shirt pocket like a bear cub playing with himself.

I even tried one of the cures of the Twentieth Century, nicotine gum, just before it got outlawed. It was supposed to make it easy to quit. You could keep it in your shirt pocket, which gave you something to paw for with your right hand. Then you chewed it. Then you wanted to throw up.

It made me so sick that I couldn't smoke, or eat, and upset my stomach so badly that I lost ten pounds, from a combination of the system problems and running back and forth to the rest room. If my idiot boxing coach had given me nicotine gum I could have fought as a light-heavyweight and done my roadwork in the room.

Worst of all, the nicotine gum made me vulnerable to J.R. Tyson, who has a really bizarre sense of humor. J.R. and I were sharing an apartment and working about the same hours at the newspaper. J.R. knew all too well that I was having some stomach discomfort from mainlining nicotine down the gums and into the stomach.

J.R. brought three pairs of shoes to the office one day. J.R. could glance over at the City Desk from his position in the Business News Department and calculate from the tempo of my fidgeting when I was about to make a run for the commode.

He would grab his bagful of shoes and run into the men's room, placing one pair in each of its three stalls. I'd skid into the room and see the damned thing was standing-room-only. I'd clear my throat loudly, squirm for a second, then dash up two flights of stairs to the men's room on the fifth floor.

After a couple of days of fidgeting, skidding and sprinting up the stairs I got downright familiar with those shoes. And it finally came to me that J.R. was the only SOB I knew who had a pair of beat-up, old, gray Justin Roper boots. I relieved my bladder in J.R.'s Justins. I know I should have done the other one in J.R.'s footgear, but the imagery was close enough. And it stopped his torture routine.

I didn't benefit that much, since it was only a couple of days later that I gave up the nicotine gum and went back to smoking.

I finally got my motivation revved up when I ran out of breath just before the final bell in a twelve-round championship match with Charlotte Gay's sex drive. Charlotte said she won on a NKO (that's a nicotine knockout). I viewed it as a wonderfully split decision.

Anyway, I quit the weeds cold turkey and stayed quit until J.R. and I both went to work for the Air Monitor. J.R. had never smoked until we arrived at the Air Monitor. Like me, he views a little carbon monoxide in the lungs as an acceptable price to pay to differentiate yourself from Winston DeWeerd and these brainless bastards who follow him.

Winston was enough to keep me puffing a couple a day for as long as there was the idea of rejecting him and his people. J.R. and I had no idea that we weren't too far removed from a day when we would have to think about something more substantive. I hadn't yet smoked my way into meeting Barbara Savage, the

woman who would change my silly little rebellion into something larger.

CHAPTER 8

ATLANTIC CITY, New Jersey — Two men died of gunshot wounds at a sports bar Saturday night after an argument over the propriety of an antique boxing poster on the wall of the bar. Clement Ford said no one in the history of the Boxing Bar had ever before objected to the poster of "Smokin" Joe Frazier, a heavyweight champion of the Twentieth Century.

***

J.R. Tyson and I had tickets to the football game, thanks to the Air Monitor. The Office of Tobacco Abatement had put out the word that there might be a significant amount of Smoke Jumper action at the game and J.R. and I volunteered to go. Two Air Monitor photographers were roaming and a third was standing by, poised to rush out and record the action.

Pierre Latouf had called in the morning, wanting to know if I had thought more about checking into the Colonies. I was noncommittal on that, but asked him to be my guest at the football game. He seemed to be the sort of serious fellow who would show genuine puzzlement over professional football. Latouf didn't really care about the game, but decided to join us when I told him J.R. and I were going on the chance there was going to be a big Jumper bust.

He got to see a good game, but didn't enjoy it. A long time ago he would have seen a big bust or twenty on the cheerleaders but big-chested cheerleaders are now widely regarded as exploitative. The Jumpers watched the game with us. The whole thing was a bum tip.

SMOKE JUMPERS

Latouf at a football game reminds me of a blind Baptist at an Episcopal funeral. He doesn't know when to stand, or sit, or kneel. I confused him by cheering for Dallas.

"Why are you yelling for the Dallas team?" Latouf asked.

"Because I like Texas better than the District of Columbia," I said.

Pierre Latouf didn't cheer loudly at first, but did get caught up in the Dallas fever as the game went on. There were only a few of us cheering for Dallas. I guess Dallas playing Washington in Washington just naturally brings out the empathy of a representative of Amnesty International.

It was a cold day and there were plenty of empty seats.

"I had expected more people," Latouf said.

I explained that there were always plenty of seats for a Washington football game these days. The old days of every game being sold out were the good old days for the National Football League.

Today there is an occasional full house, but not often. There are probably many reasons why the pro football games don't sell out any more. For one, professional football is a violent sport in a violent society that tries to pretend it is enlightened. People prefer to pretend that they reject violence. It's probably even simpler than that. They see enough violence on the streets and in their neighborhoods. When you've watched a drug-crazed teenager rake an entire playground with one of those old AK-47s, what thrill is it to see a couple of three-hundred-pound behemoths run at one another?

And there's the leisure-time thing. It's so "in" to be health-conscious that people say they spend their Sundays exercising instead of going to watch three-hundred-pound mastodons get their workout.

Latouf said he had seen some sumo wrestlers in Japan who rivaled the linemen in size. "I think your football players are larger and faster than the sumos," he said.

I agreed that might be true. Since Latouf appeared interested, I decided to share my theories of professional football's decline in the District of Columbia.

"The games were more exciting when they were played in Robert F. Kennedy Stadium. They couldn't keep from being boring when they named the place Jimmy Carter Stadium," I said.

Latouf confessed that he knew very little about either Robert Kennedy or Jimmy Carter.

"It was RFK Stadium but the Planned Parenthood people got caught up with the victories the various Total Sensitivity groups were scoring. Planned Parenthood wanted to get RFK's name off the stadium because Robert Kennedy and his wife had eight or ten or twelve or some whole potful of kids," I said.

Pierre's French leer asserted itself. "Aha. The French would never take an honor from a man of such outstanding sexuality," he said.

J.R. and I both laughed. "Good point," J.R. said, "From what I've read it's likely that Mr. Kennedy had eight or eighteen more children from other women, too."

"Ah, I understand," Latouf said, "the Planned Parenthood intelligentsia viewed his lifestyle as wild and undisciplined."

"No," I said, "I don't think they gave a damn about the outside kids. Fooling around doesn't count as planned or unplanned."

I've never been all that a big a Kennedy fan, either, so we can write off sour grapes as a rationale for my thinking.

The Planned Parenthood leadership chose Jimmy Carter because Jimmy and his wife had managed to produce only one homely little child.

Pierre Latouf knew more American history than do most modern Americans. "Your man, Truman, I recall that he had only the one daughter. Just like Carter. Why not Truman?"

"President Truman was a smoker," I said.

Jimmy Carter's name was the obvious one because he was a dedicated non-smoker.

"How does that explain why people don't come to the games?" Latouf said.

"Theory Number One might be that the stadium has taken on the personality of its namesake's sex drive, and it's running on empty," I said. Latouf and J.R. both laughed.

I admit that Theory Number One is pretty far out. Nobody paid much attention to Jimbob when he was alive, so it's stretching credulity to believe he would have any effect now that he appears to be gone.

So, that leaves us with Theory Number Two, which is probably the correct one. Theory Number Two holds that people lost interest in pro football when the Total Sensitivity Movement took over. Total Sensitivity had its humble beginnings back in the 1990s when American Indians found they could get on network television by protesting games played by the Atlanta Braves. It's an interesting organization. There is a national Total Sensitivity headquarters where a Board of Directors licenses subgroups after a sensitive look into their particular agenda for sensitivities. Senator Winston DeWeerd is on the parent organization's Board of Directors.

"I believe that the Total Sensitivity people started the decline of American sports when they screwed up the names of all the teams," I said.

Latouf chuckled.

"Your Sensitivists. They are intellectual terrorists of a particularly foolish stripe."

"You're absolutely correct," I said.

RFK Stadium hadn't yet become Jimmy Carter Stadium when the Total Sensitivity people started raising hell about the team that filled the place. The Washington Redskins. In the first place, the Indians were the progenitors of smoking in the world, but the Total Sensitivity people didn't make too much of an issue of that. It's insensitive to criticize Indians.

The Total Sensitivity Movement pretended mammoth outrage over the racial slur they saw intended in the word Redskins.

As often happens with dumb ideas, it became a national craze. The Total Sensitivity Movement caught on in Dallas, where there were daily demonstrations against the Dallas Cowboys. TSM-Dallas said the Cowboy was a symbol of disenfranchisement of women, minorities and people of other-than-standard sexual orientation. A Dallas talk-show host was shot by a man who claimed to be the president of TSM-Gay Dallas, a splinter group.

The golden-throat had joked on the air that possibly the team mascot should be a slender guy, carrying a quirt and wearing spike heels. He said the football team could be The Dallas Gay Caballeros. The shooter was sentenced to five years probation. The jury bought most of his attorney's argument that his client, a slender young Hispanic interior decorator, had been driven temporarily insane by the jest since it slandered his sexuality and misappropriated the Spanish word for "cowboy."

The Dallas trial took some of the heat off New York City, where there had been daily demonstrations over the insensitivity of the New York Giants. Totally Sensitive Short People took to the streets to raise hell about what they saw as a backhanded insult to little people. The knee-biters were joined by Totally Sensitive Hispanics of Heritage, who were enraged by the New York Yankees. Totally Sensitive Hispanics of Heritage railed that the gateway for American immigration should not be home to a sports team whose name invoked Latino memories of the hated phrase, "Yanqui, Go Home." The Yankees are now the New York Ozone, which at least has a nice sexual tint to it for those few of us who are doomed to wander America with a sense of humor.

There was an injury on the field. Latouf said he could not understand how there was a play without an injury. He said the violent sport contrasted rather mindlessly with the inane names that teams bore.

I had to agree.

The old New York Giants now are the New York Hills. The New Yorkers wanted to be Mountains but Totally Sensitive Short People said the New York Mountains would amount to a re-endorsement of the old Giant image. The Hills came out better than the former Cleveland football team.

I figured the Cleveland Browns were going to survive with their stupid name intact. Browns, I mean. But Totally Sensitive Hispanics of Ohio joined with Totally Sensitive Native Americans of the Midwest to prove me wrong. The environmental people were moving in and I was thinking maybe the Cleveland people could wind up as the Brown Snow, because I've never seen white snow on the ground in Cleveland. I knew it would never happen. Constructive irony is a misdemeanor today.

The Cleveland Mist hasn't been all that impressive. Maybe that was preordained when the name tells you the team stands for a bunch of little drips.

Chapters of Totally Sensitive People to Stop Exploitation of The Animal Kingdom sprang up across the country. Among the more militant of a strident lot were the members of the Miami Chapter, who defaced thousands of signs bearing the emblem of the Miami Dolphins. The Miami defacement experience was replicated in Philadelphia, home of the Eagles. Demonstrators in the City of Brotherly Love staged a "fly-out," in which they stormed the zoo and pet stores, freeing birds to fly into Philadelphia's smoggy skies.

Most of the birds died. Freeing a bird into Philadelphia's skies is a little like liberating a bunny into a wolf pen. But symbolism, not reality, was the issue and the bird people took to the streets. They were joined by other rioters, who freed thousands of television sets from stores and liberated hundreds of automobiles.

The San Francisco 49ers calculated, erroneously, that they were immune from the silliness. The error of such logic was demonstrated when Totally Sensitive Gay Bay Residents began bashing the 49er image. The 49ers, they said, were a band of horny fag-bashing spoilers, who drank, smoked and debased women when they weren't busy raping the land. The Chicago Bulls came under fire from the animal-rights people and from Totally Sensitive Lesbians of Illinois.

The list ran on and on until the owners of America's sports teams got together. In a previous age I would have said they "cried Uncle" but that would invoke male chauvinism and saying they "cried Uncle or Aunt" sounds brainless. But they gave up and did the Sensitive Thing. They formed a National InterSport Committee on Sensitivity in Nomenclature to come up with recommendations for sensitizing the names of sports teams. The committee recommended a nationwide referendum, of sorts, conducted on interactive cable television, where Americans could submit substitute names.

There were some deviations, but the national environmental groups generally dominated the submission process and the national voting that followed.

The first name change brought us the Green Bay Greens. The bad guys who once played football in Oakland or Los Angeles as the Raiders became the Oakland Trees. The guys in Dallas — the ones who had pretended to be America's Team — became the Dallas Naturals. The Naturals had to pay a half-million bucks to the former Chicago Bears, who also liked the Natural name. The Bears should have hung in. They're now the Chicago Ground Cover.

There were some surprises. The Los Angeles Lakers came out best of all. The National Basketball Association powerhouse only lost one letter. They're the Lakes, which makes them fun to pick in one of the national sports betting pools. The New Jersey Nets figured to be in good shape, but the Jersey owners hadn't counted on emergence of Totally Sensitive Friends of Fish and Other Marine Animals.

The Nets fought too long and most of the pure environmental names had already gone. They're now the New Jersey Soil, which is highly scatological when you consider that most of their games are played at night. I've considered taking a job with one of the New Jersey newspapers for one week so I could write a headline: "Night Soil Flushed With Victory."

The biggest trouble came in San Francisco, where owner Giovanni Restino dug in her spike heels at the Number One choice for the new name of the 49ers. Ms. Restino stressed that she was as sensitive as the next person, but couldn't enjoy owning the San Francisco Neutrals.

After painful negotiations toward a compromise, Ms. Restino accepted the Voice of the People and now presides over the hard-hitting San Francisco Compassionates, which played the most-dramatic Super Bowl game of the new-names era against the unpredictable Denver Wind.

Ms. Restino's refusal to accept Neutrals had spawned a

budding boycott of the team, so she knew she had to do something to boost her sensitivity rating. She did that by proposing a National Football League rule to change the name normally used to refer to the largest pass receiver on a team.

It swept the nation, down to the kiddy leagues. Today our football teams take to the field with a large lineman known as the Close Catcher. The ploy satisfied the Gay Bay Athletic Sensitivity Conference, which had long screamed that calling a position "Tight End" amounted to a subliminal slur of the Gay Lifestyle.

Latouf had caught the Dallas fever and was cheering the Naturals at the top of his voice. The game ended with the Naturals driving, but the Washington Legumes picked off a last-minute pass and wound up with a 24-21 victory.

After the game, we were walking to the car. We happened to be behind a squad of Smoke Jumpers. One of the Jumpers was desultorily sweeping the lot with his tobacco detector. It flashed while pointed at an electric-powered recreational vehicle and Pierre Latouf got to watch the ten Smoke Jumpers storm the vehicle.

A Smoke Jumper captain emerged with an elderly couple in tow and an evidence bag containing a counterfeit carton of Marlboros.

"It is a unique use of law-enforcement that you Americans do," Latouf scoffed.

I had to admit that we have come a long way from the old Texas Rangers, whose reputation was reflected in worldwide knowledge of the slogan, "One riot, one Ranger."

"Full employment," I said. "One pack, one Fascist."

***

Latouf negotiated the purchase of one of the arrest photographs. He signed the Air Monitor photographer's form, in which he pledged that the photo would not be used to promote sale or use of tobacco or tobacco products.

J.R. and I dropped him off at his embassy. He trotted up the steps. "I'd guess the man smokes a couple of packs a day when he's not protected from his habit by our marvelous pro-health legislation," J.R. Tyson said.

PAUL FREEMAN

"You forgot to mention his opportunity to be under the nurturing care of two-hundred pound goons carrying automatic weapons," I said.

***

Tyson laughingly suggested we recruit Latouf for the Air Monitor staff party.

"Just what we need," I said. "Katricia Coyne would have us in for Random Tobacco Testing every day for the next decade."

"Maybe she won't come to the party," J.R. said.

The boy does a terrific amount of wishful thinking, especially for a war hero.

Katricia is one of our editors. She wants to get me into bed. I gather she would enjoy the sex, but what Katricia really wants is to assert her dominance over me. Once she has a couple of drinks, Katricia goes on the prowl for a bed partner.

I've never turned her favorite insult against her. She always says I am "totally penis-oriented," whatever that means. I think she means I'm a prick.

We arrived at Lars Jensen's apartment and found the party was going full bore. Katricia Coyne was wobbling and screeching with laughter. It was a bad sign. Katricia would make her move on somebody, soon.

Katricia could have cured Teddy Kennedy from lusting after women. Given a personality-ectomy, Katricia would improve to highly unattractive, moving up from absolutely hideous. She's about five-foot-five and has the body of fifteen-year-old male marathon runner. When provoked, which is both easy and usual, her skinny neck extends about a half foot and she shakes her head from side to side, which roils the cowpie-shaped crown of reddish-brown hair. Her thick glasses reflect darting beams of light. It looks like a scene from one of those science-fiction movies where everybody is firing away with lasers.

She lurched our way. I said hello and quickly moved away. J.R. did the same.

I was talking with one of the sports guys when Katricia slithered around the bar and cornered me. She stuffed her hands down my pants and gripped me, cooing, "I want it. I want it."

64

SMOKE JUMPERS

J.R. Tyson still has nightmares about his sexual encounter with Katricia. I hated to do anything evil to a friend, but I invoked his name to cool her off. "I don't think it would be fair to J.R.," I said, gently but firmly pulling her hands out of my pants. I love fairness, but Tyson says I'd best not set Katricia on him again. Not unless I want to go to that big Newsroom In The Sky. J.R.'s martial-arts talents don't frighten me. My hands are as fast as his. It's the nagging memory of the story about Marine sniper J.R. Tyson, killing two men who were a mile away.

I know J.R. wouldn't shoot me, but I still hated to do it. Hated it right until the time I could tell it was working. The reminder of the quickie in the apartment set Katricia after him. It was a pretty even match.

Katricia's aggressiveness against J.R.'s evasion. J.R.'s footwork is impressive and his general fleetness made him a good opponent for Katricia. I made a mental note to congratulate him, especially on the great move he made when Katricia had him backed into a corner and was throwing combinations at his fly with all ten fingers.

J.R. wiggled and wiggled, then downed about four ounces of bourbon in one gulp and collapsed in a heap at Katricia's feet. I know how the Devil felt in the Garden of Eden when he saw Eve, or maybe Adam, get the First Headache. My admiration for J.R. Tyson ended quickly. Katricia came after me again. I'm not nearly as nimble as J.R. The dirty bastard was smiling, pretending to be passed-out drunk on the floor.

I kept back-pedalling and carrying my hands low. I thought Katricia had thrown in the towel after she fell for a fly-feint, closed her eyes blissfully and grabbed with both hands. I made a great move and she wound up with both hands on Lars Jensen's private parts.

She knew before she opened her eyes that she had landed limp and languid Lars. She decided it was time to go to the bathroom and regroup.

I thought it best to stick close to Lars Jensen and the bar. Lars saved me a couple of seconds ago and bourbon and I have been friends for half my life.

Lars and I get along very well, even though Lars views me as hopelessly insensitive. Lars and I disagreed, for instance, when Totally Sensitive Women Against Male Domination moved in on his alma mater. My position was simple. I thought a college that had been in business since 1693 deserved to keep its name. But I'm hopelessly out of touch and Lars now gets an invitation every year to send money to Mary and William College in Williamsburg, Virginia. Lars also thought it reprehensible that I found uproarious humor in the victory speech by the president of Totally Sensitive Women Against Male Domination. Not the whole thing, just the part when she shook her fist and said, "William has been on top of Mary for far too long."

So Lars and I were talking boxing when Katricia appeared again. Bobbing and weaving, she elbowed Lars out of the way, then moved in close and sucker-humped my left leg. I've never been very good at hurting people, except with my fists. I hate psychological rejection when it comes my way and I guess I'm a patsy on the flip side of it. It's one of my more endearing weaknesses.

Lars Jensen is gay, so he had immunity. He smirked and walked away. I'll have to remember to invite Lars to go a couple of rounds some time. I'll have to remember not to kill him. I might forget.

Katricia's eyes bulged and I remembered that J.R. had described her as "a lean, mean, orgasm machine." She shuddered a little, then started working religiously on my thirty-two-inch thigh again. I say religiously because she was already on her way to the Second Coming.

"Let's get out of here," she said, just as her portable phone buzzed. It was the only time I've been saved by the bell when I had a woman riding my leg and grasping for my penis.

Her head never moved and her voice only broke once as she talked to the office. It was quite a piece of body control because her lower body was grinding away on my thigh. I could tell from her end of the conversation that she was going to have to leave the party. The paper had been a'buzz for a couple of days with reports that a big Smoke Jumper bust was imminent and this obviously was it. So I slid my hand under her skirt. She wasn't wearing underclothing but it still took a good effort to get my fingers inside her since her vesper lips had a palpitating death grip on my leg.

"Street value of half a billion dollars!" she shrieked. I pumped her mercilessly with the finger and she howled like a drunk coyote.

The poor deskperson on the other end of the line must have thought she was having a seizure. I guess he or she asked if Katricia would be available to coordinate coverage of the Smoke Jumper bust.

"Of course I'm coming," she panted. I gave her a couple more thrusts with my index finger and she squealed again as she hit the button to end the telephone hookup.

She kissed me hard on the cheek. "We'll finish this later," she said, spinning on her heels and walking toward the door.

"Yeh," I muttered. "Right about the time Winston DeWeerd does his first testimonial for Marlboros."

Lars Jensen took in the entire event. "I've told you there are vast benefits to the gay lifestyle," he smiled.

"You were always wrong. Until now," I said.

CHAPTER 9

DETROIT — Juvenile authorities said no charges have been filed against a 14-year-old boy who locked the door to a closet his father used to try to hide his smoking habit. Investigators said clothing inside the closet was ignited and the youth refused to unlock the door. The youth reportedly said his action was spawned by the celebrated anti-smoking tape known as "The Tragedy of Barranca Lopez." Officers said the family video camera had been set up in the bedroom and was consumed by the fire.

***

I got to the office and saw I had quite a few calls to answer. I took the easy ones first, then I got down to one from somebody named Veronica French in Buffalo, New York. I clicked the computer signal to dial the call but there was no answer. I hit the "Returned Your Call" option on her Message Center. The office computer list of "Sources and Contacts" pops up helpfully when you get a telephone call and Veronica French was listed as "Unknown."

I couldn't place the name, but I try to return the call of anybody who calls me. I get to talk to a lot of nuts. Once I got a loon in Wisconsin who said Martians were holding him hostage and making him smoke green Pall Malls. Occasionally the call turns out to be from somebody who has a story to tell. You can't know until you talk. So I talk.

I had cleared the decks so I could call Milano Nagurski. Pierre Letouf's suggestion intrigued me. I've always wanted to know the real story about Nagurski. I wanted to refresh my memory on what we had published, so I told the Air Monitor's on-line library to cough up its information on Milano before I called.

It was there, a bit of the reality of his life obscured inside one of our interminable feature stories on the Smoke-Free Youth Movement.

I had tried to angle the story on Milano Nagurski himself, but the Air Monitor desk gutted the interesting part about his life. Nagurski had been a championship-level tennis player despite his cigarette habit (the desk editor said that sounded pro-tobacco and anti-health) and had once been married to a female smoker who was a famous playwright ("Too glamorizing of the habit," he said). They had three beautiful and talented children (that went. The OTA has embellished the unwholesome facts about children of smokers. OTA's position is that forty-eight percent are somewhat mentally impaired, forty-six percent have severe physical and behavioral problems and the rest somehow manage to escape displaying harmful effects of parental criminal behavior).

All the copy from my original story was displayed in a separate color scheme. There were little codes to identify which editor at which editing stop had changed a word or phrase. It was typical of the Air Monitor glorification of its computers. The computers can keep the information, so the Air Monitor keeps it.

They left in the fact that Milano was one of the few people who had ever come out of the Texas Smoker Colony. I've gone through every legitimate avenue I can think of to find out how many people have come out of any of the Colonies. OTA will only say that "many" people have been "cured of the Demon Tobacco" and are back, fighting to "resume smoke-free and productive lives." If the subject were anything but the OTA, I might be able to go through the Freedom of Information Act and find out. I believe it was Winston DeWeerd's third anti-tobacco bill that took the OTA completely out of the coverage of the Freedom of Information Act. Winston said it was necessary to "protect the smoker and his or her victims from further harm."

Anyway, OTA says Milano Nagurski is one of the "many"

people who have come back among us. As far as I know, he's the Lazurus of the tobacco set: The only one who has come back to life.

My Milano Nagurski story had gone to the copy-desk computer without a quote from Winston DeWeerd. Some helpful soul — probably at Katricia Coyne's screeched instruction — called the Senator's office and got one. The computer jottings indicate it was a "statement." Anybody knows that means his lovely and talented Press Secretary, Cecilia Word, wrote it for him.

Winston's statement said Nagurski proved that "even a smoker whose life has been ruined by a one-pack-a-day habit can rehabilitate himself and rejoin moral and productive Americans." Back in the good old days politicians had to get somebody to write that crap for them on a three-by-five card. Our computerized society let's them send it to us at light speed on a computer modem. I sort of miss the three-by-five cards. They probably got lost now and then.

Winston DeWeerd and the Office of Tobacco Abatement had pronounced Nagurski rehabilitated, but the punishment didn't end when he left the Colony. The Baltimore job was a comedown for a championship tennis player who headed a college chemistry department before he was caught with a carton of bootleg weeds. OTA said its testing showed his smoking impairment amounted to a twenty percent loss in brain function. So Milano's new job involved trying to teach the Chart of the Nuclides to a bunch of heavily armed yo-yos in one of Baltimore's toughest high schools.

This was the kind of place where the kids perked up when he mentioned a Bunsen Burner, then went back to sleep when they found out it wasn't a new kind of machine gun.

***

I finished my cursory reading of the file and hit the icon that would call Milano Nagurski's work telephone. He came on the line after just one ring. He balked at first at my suggestion of an interview. He said he had to check with his boss. He called back within five minutes, a completely receptive interview subject.

He said the leadership at his school had produced some "exciting new developments in youth anti-smoking information." That usually means a two-hundred-pound freshman thug has written a rap song condemning tobacco and the principal thinks it may give the school some ink in the Air Monitor.

It wasn't a story I wanted to write, but it was the angle for me to talk with Milano Nagurski. I sent an electronic message to the desk, telling them I was going out on an interview. I called for a photographer when I got into my car and started the drive to Baltimore.

I was wrong about the story involving a two-hundred-pound freshman thug. Nagurski and his boss introduced me to a two-hundred-twenty-pound sophomore thug. He had written a rap song condemning tobacco. They were nice enough to make me a copy. One of the high points was:

> *Smokers Suck*
> *Big Time*
> *Smokers they bes nuttin'*
> *But they bes slime*

The principal asked me what I thought about the lyrics. I said I thought the kid could be a new Smokey No. Smokey's biggest rap hit so far has been "Butt Kickers." They were proud of their lad. I couldn't help but notice the young anti-smoking crusader had a bulge under his sweater. I'm pretty certain it wasn't his homework, unless he's studying pistol shooting.

I asked Nagurski and the principal to join me for a drink. I didn't really want to see Milano's boss ever again, but he would have been pissed at Nagurski if I had excluded him. Luck was with me. The boss said he couldn't make it. Milano said he couldn't either. He said he had some paperwork to do before he went to his second job. I asked him what the second job was and he said he was a researcher in drug therapy.

His day boss told him he probably needed to relax. That meant the boss thought Milano ought to go with the Air Monitor

71

reporter for a drink if the reporter asked him. It might bring some coverage for the school. Maybe even a new OTA grant of some sort.

So, Milano Nagurski and I had a few drinks at a bar far from the school. Only a fool would go into one of the bars that abuts the school.

I wanted to write something to make the trip worthwhile, so I asked Nagurski about some of his successes in bending young minds away from the evil weed.

He's one of those people who looks five-foot-nine and nervous at work, but turns out to be six-foot and interesting when he relaxes and has a couple of drinks. We were talking about boxing, music, guns and women and he was animated and fun. I mentioned his life in the Colony and his voice became metallic. He sounded like one of those poor bastards who lost his voice box to smoking.

He said, "I am fortunate to have been adjudged free of the nicotine habit and able to make a significant contribution to the anti-tobacco movement by rejoining the smoke-free society."

An inexact comparison might hark back to my encounters with Charlotte Gay. Let's hypothesize that Charlotte was building to one of her ten-megaton climaxes. For the sake of our exercise, let's agree that Charlotte had said, "In the name of the Deity to whose teachings you subscribe, grant me the preponderance of the body member posthaste."

My point being rather simple. It would have been extremely out of character, since Charlotte could be expected to moan: "Oh, God! Give it to me! Give it all to me!"

I persevered. I had asked Milano about his life in the Texas Colony before and he had handed me an eight-page document that purported to describe his years there. It was a bunch of anti-smoking boiler plate.

"Really, I've always wanted to know what it's like on the inside...day by day. I'd think it would be a pretty tough situation," I said.

I had wondered how much worse it was than his Baltimore teaching job while I was looking at the computer files. The tenuous nature of life in Milano Nagurski's job had come rushing back to me when I re-read the deleted paragraph that described how everybody in the auditorium for our Smoke-Free Youth Movement gathering had to hit the floor. Two youth gangs were trading automatic weapons fire across the auditorium. (It didn't make it into the Air Monitor. The desk said that violence had no place in a story about the Youth Movement and should be handled in a separate story. I wrote one and they killed it.)

Nagurski grabbed a paper napkin and scribbled furiously. As he handed it to me, he said, "The Colony was a healing experience for those of us unfortunate to be addicted to the Demon Weed," I looked at the note, which read: "It's worse than you can imagine." I didn't yet understand, but I didn't say anything. I looked at Nagurski and tore up the note. He nodded his head vigorously to tell me I was doing the right thing.

I'm a cynical person and I thought it possible that Nagurski was exaggerating the way ninety percent of people do when they figure you've got no way of checking into what they said. Like the old guy at the paper who said he was in the Vietnam War. To hear him tell it he crawled on his belly for six years, got shot up like a sieve, killed North Dakota worth of Commies and gave up about 18 gallons of blood to leeches, which he remembered as being about the size of an elephant's dick. Another guy at the paper recalled our Hero as an announcer for Armed Forces Radio, who might have taken a direct hit or two from the whores in Saigon.

Milano Nagurski's eyes told me his fear was real, at least to him.

I mouthed the word. "Why?"

He tugged his left shirtsleeve halfway up his forearm, exposing a substantial platinum-colored watch. He turned his arm slowly in front of my eyes, pointing with his right index finger at the watchband. It was an unbroken piece of metal. A mugger who wanted Milano's watch would have had to take his arm with it, which would be a definite possibility in 21st Century Washington. I understood completely, now.

"What time is it getting to be?" I asked.

"Four-thirty-three," Milano said, his eyes darting down to the watch and back to my face.

"Nice watch," I said.

"Wonderful piece of machinery," Milano said. There was a slight tremble in his voice that told me I shouldn't mention the watch again. He yanked the sleeve back over the timepiece. "It even works under water," he said, glancing nervously around the room.

I've read about the quantum advances that technology has made possible in monitoring. For a couple of hundred bucks you can order your car with a radio transmitter which is put into the car as an ordinary metal screw. The robots that make all the cars put them in at random. The car thieves can't disable them without tossing every screw in the car and that's more of a screw job than the amateurs are willing to take on. Consequently the car thieves of our Century have fought back in the American Way. They threw big money and high technology at the problem.

In the old days, your car might be stolen by some jerk with a piece of metal that opened the door. Then he would break the steering lock and drive away.

That doesn't happen now. Your car is stolen by a bunch of jerks who cruise in lead-lined trucks, pick what they want and then hoist their heisted vehicles into the truck. The truck speeds to a lead-lined building, where the bad guys can then use their computerized signal-finders to locate and remove the transmitter. The downside of the whole thing is that the bad guys have to steal more cars so they can justify their investment in the lead-lined vans and computers.

As I said, it's totally American. You still get a screw job, but now it's high technology and based in what the business consultants call "productivity enhancement."

Milano Nagurski was a bugged BMW who could never get rid of his tattletale screw. Some Smoke Jumper recorder, and a Jumper computer, knew where he was. They knew what he was saying, and what he was hearing. Helluva way to live.

I decided to give Milano's Jumper listener a warm feeling. "I just want you to know that we at the Air Monitor admire the work you are doing to protect the lungs of our youth," I said.

Milano smiled his thanks. "It's the only thing I live for," he said, rubbing the watchband.

CHAPTER 10

*DALLAS — The City Council met in special
session on Friday to approve new names for the
so-called "cigarette streets" of the Dallas suburb
of Oak Cliff. A guerrilla anti-smoking group has
pledged to burn down one home a night on Viceroy,
Marlboro or Pall Mall streets until less-offensive
names appear on street signs. Nine houses have
been torched so far, police said.*

***

I was depressed and angry when I left Milano Nagurski.
I ran into one of our patented traffic jams and took a coward's turn
into a covered parking lot. My mood was so lousy that the mile
walk to the office would do me good. My route would take me
through Victims' Square, which is a good place to stop and
fulminate about the Office of Tobacco Abatement and the dam-
nable Smoke Jumpers.

I count myself as reasonably brave but there had been a
time when I wouldn't have walked through Victims' Square
without an armed guard and my own automatic weapon. It wasn't
called Victim's Square in the dangerous days but there was a lot
of victimization that went on.

The police sector that includes Victims' Square was so
bad a couple of years ago that the District's Chief of Police
actually bragged about a slight reduction in its crime rate. He
crowed that good police work had slowed the pace of violent
death in the area dramatically. He said the improvement had been
so spectacular that people were dying in the sector at a rate below
that for American soldiers in the 1991 war with Iraq.

SMOKE JUMPERS

The monument, and the armed Smoke Jumper guards who patrol the area, changed all that. The monument was commissioned by the Federal Commission on Anti-Tobacco Arts. It began as a low-budget idea. Only one and one-half million dollars. The idea picked up steam so quickly it was frightening. What started out as a low-level Treasury rip-off for some of Winston DeWeerd's fellow travelers wound up as a bona fide national monument. A budget that started out at a piddling one hundred million dollars has increased tenfold. It's still climbing.

Victims' Square is the first such monument built in the country. Washington is proud of that. The Greater District of Columbia Chambers of Commerce trumpet that Washington is the center of anti-tobacco sentiment for the world. The Tobacco Victims Monument helped us get that honor.

There were several dozen people in Victims' Square, not including the six Smoke Jumper guards I could see. Most of the crowd is prototype Washington. Young, well-groomed, expensively dressed and heavily in debt. They were called Yuppies in the 20th Century.

I felt a tug on my elbow. A foreign tourist asked me if I would take a picture of him and his wife.

"I am from India. The state of Andhra Pradesh. We have much to be ashamed of." He said seventy-five thousand farmers in Andhra Pradesh grew tobacco.

I took the picture and the Indian couple walked toward the OTA display. A Smoke Jumper moved to my side. "Mind if I ask what those people are doing?"

"They're tourists," I said. "I get the impression they're on an anti-tobacco pilgrimage of some sort."

"Can't be too careful," he said. He said there had been rumors that foreign tobacco interests planned to bomb Victims' Square.

I looked up rather reverently, I guess, at John Wayne. The Duke looked down rather serenely at the mostly middle-class crowd around me. I got the feeling he might have been a little more at ease if he had been looking down on druggies and dealers. At least some of them knew how to shoot.

77

I never go through Victims' Square without stopping at the big boots of the cowboy who got famous after being born as Marion Morrison. John Wayne now extends fifty feet into the Washington sky. On Wayne's left is Jack Benny. Of course almost everybody in the world was to the left of The Duke. To Jack Benny's left is Buster Keaton, which makes political sense. The farther left you go the more clowns you run into. Then comes Humphrey Bogart and Betty Grable. Completing the circle to The Duke is Nat "King" Cole, the silken-voiced crooner who puffed on an unfiltered weed on his television show. I've seen some of the old King Cole stuff in the film presentations that the Office of Tobacco Abatement Clean Lung Entertainment Division puts on.

I always get a small surge of pride when I look at Nat Cole. He was one of the minor journalistic accomplishments of my first year at the Air Monitor. Actually he was one of the major accomplishments but I have come to the grudging conclusion that any journalistic accomplishment is minor. But I like to think it did some good.

As with many journalistic accomplishments, it began with a tip from somebody who was pissed off. In this case it was a young black woman at the Office of Tobacco Abatement. She was the world's ranking Nat King Cole fan.

She was shocked to hear that OTA's Entertainment Division was going to put Nat's music under sanction. OTA can't ban music, but the Entertainment Division hands out eight hundred million dollars a year in Enlightenment Grants. Most of it goes to broadcast stations.

It's yet another legacy of Winston DeWeerd, doled out on a sliding scale. A greater percentage of a given grant goes to media outlets which produce and air entertainment programs that are clearly anti-tobacco. Winston says it's only the beginning of a balance. Winston put it this way in a Sunday interview show: "The tobacconists at Philip Morris paid three-hundred and fifty thousand dollars to pollute the lungs of the James Bond character in the movie License to Kill. For this pittance of investment, young people saw the James Bond character smoking Lark Cigarettes. Hundreds of thousands, maybe even millions, were addicted to the Demon Weed."

Winston says the "modest" grants actually make money for all of us since they promote a tobacco-free lifestyle. Any television station, entertainment channel or video store that has anything to do with License to Kill is going to lose its shot at the Entertainment Division bonanza.

The grants get a pretty good ride. There was a movie called Lethal Weapon 2 that was a pre-Winston action classic on the television stations. Had a macho guy named Mel Gibson as the lead. Gibson smoked up a storm. The Entertainment Division was lethal to Lethal Weapon 2. I have a copy of it, hidden beneath the floor in the utility room of my condo. It's a place of honor, since I've also got a copy of Humphrey Bogart, puffing away in Casablanca. Humphrey was a piker compared with Nat Cole, who was so smokey he made Bogart look like the air over Glacier Park. Entertainment Division put its best sound technicians on Nat Cole's records, trying to find a tobacco-induced quaver in the voice. There was none, even though his lung cancer had to be booming like a Cole album on the Billboard charts.

Entertainment Division could have accepted Cole's music if there were evidence of deterioration. But there wasn't, so Entertainment Division decided to ban the man's living legacy, his music, and keep the dead man as a symbol. My story was an average tearjerker but it got the job done. I found some older black nonsmokers who said Cole's death made them throw down their Old Golds. I quoted some psychologists who said Cole's music, and his place as a victim of tobacco, could be a significant motivation to keep young people from smoking.

I felt guilty about using psychologists, who are probably the biggest bunch of frauds and misfits I know, outside of The Congress and The Bureaucracy. But I figured saving Nat's *East of the Sun and West of the Moon* was worth a little whoring around. The shrinks helped, but the clincher was, of course, the same one that worked in the 1980s and 90s. Zulu Tamara Zambora, who runs a record company that gets tons of Entertainment Division money, told me that the whole thing was "racism" and I put that quote high in the story. I neglected to mention that Zulu Zambora owned the rights to most of Nat Cole's work and made a couple of million a year out of it. Maybe I forgot.

Whatever you think, I figure I kept some of the King where everybody can enjoy it. I've seen some tapes of Cole on television. He was a fine and graceful man. And even with the smoke wafting out of his nose and mouth, the voice was baritone angelic.

OTA is shrill and soprano when it comes to smoking, even to a nice black man whose voice, even on the scratchy sound technology of the 1950s and 60s, was so incredibly smooth that it probably won't ever be matched. But the official OTA line is that the puffing by John Wayne and his monument pals is simple. They were victims. They were smoking before people knew that a big cigarette habit was a one-way ticket to the cemetery. Some journalists tried to get Edward R. Murrow into the smoker circle. Murrow was the CBS reporter who almost made television news credible before the three-pack-a-day habit stilled his booming voice and agile mind. OTA wouldn't buy Murrow. Some of his news shows had been sponsored by cigarette companies.

The Washington statues started a frenzy of imitation. There's one in Central Park in New York City that bears the names of all of the New Yorkers who supposedly died of secondhand smoke.

The monument in Hollywood was done with ten million dollars of OTA money. It's John Wayne all the way. In the Hollywood OTA monument Wayne has hogtied a creepy looking little guy and appears to be stuffing packages of cigarettes down his throat. An automated audio setup runs on command. It tells the viewer that the little creep eating his own weed is James "Buck" Duke, the father of the cigarette industry in America.

The once-famous university in Durham, North Carolina, named after Buck Duke took a new name after the Duke University riots right after the turn of the century. A splinter anti-smoking group in nearby Raleigh had invited all militant non-smoking people to converge on Duke University. The nationwide invitation, which zipped over the government's Anti-tobacco Computer Network, called for smoker victims everywhere to "tear the lungs out of this Citadel to the Evil Weed." The rioters burned some of the graceful old homes in Durham that once belonged to America's tobacco barons.

Duke University cried uncle after two weeks of riots. Its sports teams are still called the Blue Devils but they play for the University of the Carolinas. OTA rewarded the University with a fifty million dollar facility aimed at planning the economic bonanza to come from the Clean Air Dividend.

Standing at the foot of Nat Cole normally improves my mood. Tonight it made it even worse. There is something seriously wrong with a society that can think about censoring an artist because of what he sucked into his lungs. There is something even sicker about a poor slob like Milano Nagurski, tethered to an electronic bug simply because he once made the mistake of smoking cigarettes.

I had become hostile to the point of stupidity. Two punks came out of the shadows only two blocks from the office. One of them eyed my two-hundred-dollar shoes and said, "Hey, rich boy, what size them shoes I gonna' wear?"

I put my notes on the ground. "Nine-and-a-half, jerk. What size coffin you gonna wear 'em in?" They were circling me when a guy in a jogging suit zipped between us. The toughs ran when the five Smoke Jumpers came into the light. One of the Jumpers stopped to ask me which way the smoker went. I motioned down the street, then said: "I don't know what you're after him for but two young guys ran down the alley when they saw you. They tried to sell me a carton of Marlboros."

"To clean air!" the Jumper yelped. He summoned his pals and they stampeded down the alley.

I got to the office and wrote a story about Milano Nagurski's anti-tobacco program. I tried to return a telephone call from the persistent Veronica French in Buffalo, New York. She had at least given me a little more to go on with this call. She had followed the electronic "prompts" that the telephone service provides and I hit the "Reason For Call" button to see if I could finally get a preliminary idea as to why we might need to talk.

It's not that my time is so damned valuable that I have to

get the machine to screen my calls, but the machine screening is one of the only good things we've got going. If "Reason For Call" tells you the purpose is to "Discuss Aluminum Siding," you can select "Block Future Calls" and Mr., Miss or Ms. Aluminum Siding gets a computer-generated "not interested" message and has to take the pitch to another sucker on another telephone.

It's a "don't call my computer; my computer will call yours" kind of thing. J.R. and I were drinking one night and got a call from one of those companies that gets the suckers to contribute to the Smoker Jumper Auxiliaries. I tried to reprogram the "Alternate Message" to tell them, "Screw You and the Horse You Rode In On." It wouldn't take it. It's a very moral Message Center.

The reason for this call was "Assistance," and I checked the "Background" screen. Background told me Veronica French told the Message Center she was the ex-wife of Joe French. I didn't make the connection for certain until I chose "Extended Background." That searched my personal database and flashed up a picture of Joe French.

I would never forget the jut of that jaw and the strength in those eyes. My jaw and somewhat overlarge nose would never forget Joe French's right hand. They had become close when I fought Joe French in college.

The people who saw it said it was one hell of a fight. I only saw it out of one eye after the second round, but I figure the crowd had it right.

Joe French and I were both marginal heavyweights. I outweighed him by about ten pounds. Joe was slender and had long arms and I was then, as now, bulky, short of arm and long of body strength. I remembered taking shot after shot until I got inside during the third round and started working him over.

Joe French was the toughest guy I ever fought. The doctor told me after the fight that I had fractured two of his ribs, apparently in the fourth. Joe went the whole eight rounds without more than flinching. The doc said an ordinary man would have collapsed during the fight. But not Joe French. He collapsed when I hugged him after they announced I had won on a split decision.

Joe French walked on the crazy edge of tough.

I typed in the menu option that would tell me more about Joe French. The computer zipped through the outside data base and came back with the message: "No Current Data." That was strange. The computer can tell you when Joe Shitz the Ragman died or when Winston DeWeerd is supposed to give his next speech.

Thoroughly intrigued by now, I hit the "Return Call" option on the screen. As usual, Veronica French was not in. I left still another message.

A friend in Austin, Texas, called me to give me a tip that she had seen a whole battalion of Smoke Jumpers staging for a raid near the University of Texas campus. I volunteered to catch an airplane and check it out but Katricia Coyne nixed the idea as too expensive. I called our Dallas Bureau and talked with its only staff member — a woman who said she hadn't heard anything out of Austin but would check it out.

CHAPTER 11

DALLAS — A rebel anti-smoking group claimed credit Monday for burning three houses on what once was Viceroy Street. A letter from the group noted that one street sign had retained the name Viceroy. "Oversights are costly," the letter warned, noting that "Viceroy is only a couple of blocks from Profit Street."

***

All Doctor Collier Smythe ever wanted in life was to be president of the University of Texas at Austin. Cigarettes had helped him achieve his goal. Collier Smythe had given up a two-pack-a-day cigarette habit when he was a graduate student in Philosophy, but that wasn't it. Collier was an academic politician and had risen to the Presidency of East Texas State University. Cigarettes helped him even there. His lackluster record as a teacher or a scholar certainly didn't.

Collier Smythe had missed his cigarettes occasionally. He remembered his hand starting to move toward his shirt pocket when the plagiarism investigation was going on. His disarmingly charming demeanor had gotten him through that, which dealt with the blatant theft of the dissertation that had gained him his Ph.D.

Collier Smythe had demonstrated an almost-complete disinterest in reading writing on a page, but had the eye of an eagle when it came to handwriting on a wall. And the wall Smythe had seen was emblazoned with the international no-smoking symbol.

Banning smoking on campus buildings was not all that innovative. But Collier Smythe took it one step farther. He banned smoking by faculty, students and college workers at East Texas State and had instituted the first scholarship program for children of smoke-free parents. It was an innovation. No one had ever tied a scholarship to a parental couple who would pledge they had been tobacco-free during the child's entire life. Collier Smythe patiently explained that such students were more likely to be high academic achievers and less likely to fall victim to disease.

It was one hell of an idea. True to form, Collier had stolen it. Collier's victim was the president of a two-year college in northeastern Arkansas. The Arkansas educator made the mistake of mentioning his idea to Collier in the bar of the Holiday Inn in North Little Rock.

Collier praised the innovation of it and pressed for details. Doctor Knox Williams provided them. Williams knew that no college president would be so low to try to plagiarize an idea on an item of administration. Honor aside, there was a paper trail. Most important was the trust that one Ph.D could have in the honor and integrity of another.

Williams recalled later that Collier wasn't taking notes, but pressed for every innovative detail of the scholarship plan.

Then Collier sprang the trap. He told Williams that the impact would be greater if East Texas State piggy-backed the announcement. Smythe said he would gather the Texas media, issue a "me-too" press statement, praise his Arkansas cohort as a visionary in the fight for better young minds and cleaner young lungs, then back off and let the national spotlight gleam on Harrison, Arkansas. They agreed on a date for the announcement of the smoke-free parental scholarship fund. Collier took copies of Williams' contracts and press releases, pumped his hand, whaled him on the back, praised him for his vision and social consciousness and walked out without paying his share of the tab.

Collier Smythe was out of Arkansas within 30 minutes, guest on a private jet of a Texas oilman whose son had been suspended from East Texas State after being charged with rape. Collier rectified the suspension before the plane touched down. The news conference began after he and his top staff members

85

had an hour together.

It was a slow news day and the Collier Smythe announcement was well-attended. Collier did mention that the idea had an
Arkansas genesis. But that came when he said the brainstorm
came to him at a conference in Little Rock. He added that he had
been so excited about his innovation that he discussed it with
some fellow whose name he couldn't quite recall. He said the
fellow pledged to emulate the plan in Harrison if it worked at East
Texas State.

Knox Williams watched the Collier Smythe show on
television in his room at the Holiday Inn. He knew he was a bit
player in the story of the perfect intellectual crime. Collier
Smythe had closed all the doors that might expose his chicanery.
Williams summoned his wife, Mary, to watch. "Honey," he said,
"we're going to have to get me AIDS-tested next week. That
sonofabitch screwed me for two hours and then made me pay for
the drinks."

Hundreds of colleges and universities across the country
followed the East Texas State plan. One college in California
even offered a no-strings-attached scholarship plan for students
whose parents and grandparents had been smoke-free, but withdrew it after two hundred Mormons qualified for a free education.

The headlines had gone away but Collier Smythe blossomed anew as a national media star when he invoked a little-
noticed clause in one of the one-hundred and twenty-five no-
smoking contracts in force at the school. The target contract
involved a young education student from Dawson, Texas. Collier
Smythe was sad of face when he told the sordid nicotine-stained
story of Rowan Paulson.

Smythe said he became suspicious when Paulson was
hospitalized twice for lung disorders. Smythe didn't need a court
order to do a complete investigation of Paulson's parents. They
had given him that right when then signed the contract. Smythe's
investigator followed a smoking trail of the father's MasterCard
to the purchase of carton after carton of Marlboros.

The purchases had been made when Rowan Paulson was
a child but Collier Smythe revoked the scholarship and used the

86

scholarship contract to seize the Paulson's modest home in payment of the funds illegally obtained for young Rowan's scholarship. Rowan Paulson tried to explain that his first hospitalization was for acute bronchitis and probably had been brought on when he and his girlfriend got roaring drunk and went skinny-dipping in 30-degree weather.

Paulson contended the second trip to the hospital was for a virus that had swept the campus. He pointed out that three-hundred of his fellow students had been absent because of illness during the same week he was ill. Collier Smythe dismissed Paulson's lame explanations with a wave of his elegantly gleaming fingers.

Smythe had a distinct geographical advantage over Rowan Paulson, who was telling his side of the story over a telephone at the Diamond Shamrock store where he worked. Smythe's announcement was made in front of the national media in Washington.

"It is for the good of all. The nation, and our young people, must realize that cigarettes are a plague on parent and child," Smythe told a special meeting of the House Education Committee.

The wave of publicity made Collier Smythe a leading candidate for the presidency of the University of Texas at Austin. Collier Smythe viewed himself as a shoo-in. He knew that incumbent UT President Barker Mandrell was leaving soon to begin treatment for lung cancer. Smythe had overheard Mandrell discuss his illness with Margaret Moorehouse, the UT academic dean. Dr. Mandrell had been grooming Doctor Moorehouse to take his job.

Collier Smythe's quiet campaign for the UT presidency had included whispers from some of his supporters that Dr. Moorehouse, who suffered lung impairment from a childhood disease, was actually a heavy smoker and was undergoing treatment for emphysema.

The entire University of Texas had gone smokeless at its facilities in the last century and Collier Smythe had built on that tradition. Collier Smythe ordered the sale of the four hundred and fifty thousand Texaco shares owned by the University Pension Fund. He explained he took the action when he saw a television special in which a Texaco Vice President was filmed while sitting at a table with a fugitive executive of the Philip Morris Company.

The disgraced Texaco woman tried to explain that she had been a panelist at a foreign-trade seminar in Geneva and had no idea who else was on the panel. But the damage had been done. Texaco stock skidded ten points under pressure from the huge UT sale, then lost that again and more as college pension funds across the nation followed the lead of the UT fund.

Collier Smythe had taken severe heat from the oil-soaked alumni association over the Texaco stock debacle. Texaco had, after all, been born in Texas but the grousing was mostly ideological. Collier had personally contacted almost a hundred top contributors to warn them of the impending Texaco dump from the UT pension fund. That was then and today was today. And Collier Smythe had tobacco trouble today.

Students at Cilia Hall had formed a Smoking Ring and it had to be stopped before word of it could hit the national media. Smythe listened carefully as his Dean of Continuing Behavioral Improvement outlined the reports from the paid anti-tobacco informants. One of every twenty University of Texas students was on a anti-tobacco scholarship funded by the Office of Tobacco Abatement. No less an anti-smoking advocate than Senator Winston DeWeerd had told Collier Smythe that the Austin intelligence network was the finest in the history of academic anti-tobacco efforts. The completeness of the anti-smoking infrastructure made the reports of smoking within storied Cilia Hall even more abominable.

"Do whatever it takes to stop the little addicted pricks," Smythe said, adding: "Make certain the story is contained."
***
The Air Monitor had ten reporters and five photographers assigned to the convention. I was one of them. News releases by the organizers called it history's "most important single meeting of clean-air proponents and advocates of sensitive social change." Two thousand delegates from various anti-smoking groups,

joined by more Total Sensitivity people than you could shake a fixation at.

I flexed my minimal corporate muscle and turned down Katricia Coyne's initial assignment, which would have stuck me at the press table. I would have been there for a series of kooks and crazies, a few true believers and would have got to catch the big finish. The big finish at all of these events is a speech by Senator Winston DeWeerd of Montana; the ranking icon of Total Sensitivity.

The assignment I got allows me to wander around. In the past century it would have been called "color," but no one admits to writing "color" at today's newspapers. Not because we don't do it. Everyone remembers the riot that broke out in Detroit when a poor fool from a Midwestern newspaper signed up for press credentials at the meeting of Totally Sensitive African-Americans Against Violence and Oppression.

Royal Houston pecked his assignment into the convention computer, never bothering to think hyper-sensitively. He said he intended to write color. Several delegates saw the notation on the screen. One of them yelled, "Honky says he's going to write COLOR!" Then they started beating him.

J.R. Tyson had drawn the black bean from the Air Monitor and was there. The highlight of his day came when he broke the jaw of a rapper from New York who goes by the name of Mammy Jammer. J.R. is a country and music buff, but he doesn't automatically try to break the jaws of those people who do rap. But he did think it insensitive of Mammy Jammer to slash at him with a straightedged razor. It turned out to be one of J.R.'s more socially responsible acts. Mammy Jammer's career has flagged since Detroit. The busted jaw has made it difficult for him to pronounce hyphenated forms of the word "mother."

So, my assignment is known in the Air Monitor as "humanistic sensitivity." J.R. and I know the assignment is writing color: Looking for the offbeat and interesting angles to the gathering. It's one of the easier jobs. Something unusual in this group is a man without earrings or a woman with a wedding ring from a male husband.

One of the big draws on the convention floor is the Smoke Jumper demonstration area. Several muscular Jumper men and women give demonstrations in the martial arts every thirty minutes.

A Jumper public-relations specialist does a narration. She says Smoke Jumpers try to make arrests with minimum physical contact with smokers because of the health risks associated with close contact with tobacconists.

There are videos of some of the larger Smoke Jumper busts and footage featuring some of the confessions of convicted smokers now confined in the Colonies.

One video display that never gets a rest is The Tragedy of Barranca. Barranca Lopez always gets spontaneous applause when she shrills: "No more smoke, Mother." Alicia Lopez never fails to draw boos and catcalls when she is heard to say, "Screw your air!"

The convention speaker of the moment is Betsy Freebourn-Saunders, who is railing about the subject of "linguistic sensitivity." Her speech is actually a sales pitch for the New America Sensitively Abridged Dictionary, which defines "gay" only in terms of sexual orientation and gives the first definition of "sensitive" as "Politically Enlightened."

I decided it would be a good time to wander outside to get some fresh air.

There was an animal growl coming from the convention crowd at the doors and I pushed my way through the crowd to find the center of the hostility. It turned out to be a frightened woman who might have weighed a hundred pounds. She had walked close to the convention entrance and triggered a tobacco alarm. Several delegates had grabbed her purse and were brandishing a package of Cayman Island cigarettes.

"Smoker bitch!" screamed a delegate whose badge identified him as an animal-rights advocate.

Several women delegates grabbed the woman and began tearing at her hair and clothing. I was moving to intervene when a District cop took the woman away.

I went back inside for the big event. The keynote address

of Senator Winston DeWeerd.

Winston told the cheering throng that he had spent a few days recently with international anti-tobacco activists. "Our government is the only government in the world to move strongly against the Tobacco Demon. Many of our intellectual soulmates in the international movements are so disgusted that they now understand that guerrilla action is their only resort," DeWeerd said. The applause was explosive.

The American experience did amount to a success of sorts against tobacco. Sicily once tried to stop smoking by announcing that the Turks had poisoned all tobacco, but Sicilians didn't stop. The emperor of China once decreed that importers of tobacco be beheaded and the Chinese remain among the world's premier puffers. The Russian czar in 1634 prohibited tobacco completely. He said first offenders — buyers or sellers — were to have their noses slit and persistent violators were to be put to death. The countries that make up the former Soviet Union are hotbeds of smoking and some have made moves toward luring the former American Merchants of Death to do business inside their borders.

Winston gave the locations of people who would accept donations for the international smoke-fighting force.

CHAPTER 12

ALBANY, New York — Police said a friend or family member of a convicted smoker is suspected in the fire-bombing of a downtown dry-cleaning shop. Andrew Pigatti, proprietor of Andy's Cleaners, pledged to continue working closely with Smoke Jumpers, despite the arson attack that did $100,000 damage to his business. "I check the clothes of everybody what sends them in and if there's tobacco or ashes, I call in the Jumpers," Mr. Pigatti said. He said his policy is "the least an ordinary Joe can do in the fight against the Demon Weed." Pigatti said reward money paid under the government's Smoker Watch program has never been a factor in his cooperation with the Smoke Jumpers.

***

The auditorium in the Texas Colony was a haze. Nothing unusual about that. The unusual part of the inmate meeting today was the guards. There were no slime guards walking the corridors and barring the entrances. Today the crowd was under the watchful visors of the helmeted and stiff-backed Smoke Jumpers. Their eyes were masked by the smoked visors and their faces hidden by the air-filtration equipment. Their body language told Joe French that they were tense.

The warden came onto the stage, holding his nose against the smoke. He stepped into the Clean Air Cubicle that gave him refuge from the inmates' secondhand smoke.

The Warden's voice boomed over the public-address

system.

"We are expanding operations in Power," he said. "We need volunteers to work in Power. Those inmates in or nearing the final stages of emphysema will be excluded from the expanded Power Division operations and shall remain in their jobs for so long as they remain at least marginally functional."

Joe French knew the Warden's order would launch a flood of inmates complaining about the ravages of emphysema. Emphysema didn't kill you as quickly as working in Power. Everybody knew that.

"We will accept volunteers from the general inmate population," the Warden said, adding: "Those people with significantly advanced lung cancer will automatically be added to the new Power staff rolls, as well as those people whose conduct in the past has indicated behavioral maladjustment to life in the Texas Colony." The words hit Joe French hard in the gut. The last body blow that stung like that came from that musclebound guy, Reynolds, when they fought in Syracuse. Joe French looked absently at the shoe that hid the contraband ballpoint pen. He pledged to himself that he would use up all the ink for messages to the outside before they got to his name on the list for Power.

***

J.R. Tyson and I figure we would rather work in one of those old smoke-filled newsrooms we've read about than go through a Katricia Coyne staff meeting. This being the 21st Century in America, we get no choice. There aren't any smoke-filled newsrooms any more and J.R. and I get to join our fellow reporters once a week to listen to Katricia Coyne screech about the latest plans for Air Monitor projects. It's difficult to keep focused on Katricia's rantings. I try to let my mind wander while keeping one ear tuned for mention of my name.

"The Office of Tobacco Abatement will have a major announcement this afternoon for Health Beat people," Katricia said. "OTA has exciting new figures on the quantum decreases in mortality from smoking."

I made a couple of scratches on my notepad. Katricia sometimes stays off my case if she thinks I'm paying attention.

I wondered if J.R. and I could go to the Office of Tobacco Abatement and find some figures on the number of those our ink- and tobacco-stained former colleagues who died from smoking. OTA keeps the figures on all smoking-related deaths. The ones they don't keep, they just make up. Computers are great for making up figures that probably don't exist. OTA spent a couple of hundred million on programs that prove that every third person who ever died did so of smoking or because someone else smoked. They call it Retrospective Mortality Projection. I called it bullshit, even before I heard about the OTA statistician who tried to prove that Abraham Lincoln would have lived through John Wilkes Booth's head shot if Lincoln had not been hope- lessly addicted to tobacco. The OTA squashed that one. Lincoln is on the official list of OTA non-smokers, since he freed the slaves and is generally believed to have been a pretty good fellow, for a lawyer.

J.R. Tyson's theory is that Lincoln was a smoker whose long periods of depression came because Mary had hidden his cigarettes somewhere in the White House and he didn't have a Department of Nicotine Unabatement to run them down for him.

Nicole O'Toole is one of our ambitious Entertainment Writers. She has jumped onto Katricia's bandwagon and is telling us, breathlessly, that she is working on a long feature that will tell Americans everywhere that Prominent Figures no longer are smoking.

"The latest figures from my sources at OTA tell me that the mandatory nicotine testing of doctors indicates that under one-half of one percent of physicians have smoked in the past five years," Nicole said.

She said OTA's only glitch in information about Promi- nent Figures comes from musicians who have made tours in Europe and Asia, where smoking is legal and widespread. "I believe I will be able to report that OTA and Senator Winston DeWeerd have plans to announce their long-awaited International Smoke Jumpers organization to try to aid Americans abroad from succumbing to Euro-Asian addictions to the Demon," Nicole O'Toole said. Katricia Coyne beamed. Katricia beaming is an uglier sight that Katricia snarling. I'm always reminded of Dracula's smile when Katricia loses her customary full-face grimace, but Nicole's tip on the new OTA study of Prominent Figures and Smoking were clearly orgasm material for Katricia.

Everyone in the room has seen videos of OTA's labors on previous studies of Prominent Figures and Smoking. OTA says Marilyn Monroe killed herself in a nicotine-induced psychosis. One OTA video even apologized for Jimmy Carter's general lack of brain activity on the basis that Jimbob probably inhaled secondhand smoke when he was a Navy submariner. I've got to check the OTA material sometime to see if Elvis Presley was a smoker. If he wasn't that might explain why people still see him wandering around. OTA says non-smokers live forever.

"We all smoked in Iraq," J.R. Tyson whispered. "Even the generals."

It was a good point. OTA has never gotten around to explaining just how an American Army of smokers kicked ass on the Germans and Japanese in World War II. If they ever get around to it OTA will tell us that American non-smokers did all the fighting, the smokers were deserters, and that the Japanese and Germans were burdened by nicotine. They'll have to ignore the history books. Especially the part where General John J. Pershing, head of the Army in Europe during World War II, said: "You ask me what we need to win this war. I answer tobacco as much as bullets."

***

We dispersed to our various offices and desks. I'm a star reporter, so I have an office. It's not all that large. J.R. is not a star reporter, so he has a cubbyhole. It's smaller than Katricia Coyne's sense of humanity. I tell J.R. that he'd best never get an erection at work or he may topple the free-standing "privacy wall" between him and Nicole O'Toole. J.R. says he can just stand up and look at Katricia Coyne whenever the wall is in danger.

The Air Monitor newsroom is crowded. I guess the Air Monitor balance sheet is getting pretty crowded, too. We sell some of the Air Monitor the old-fashioned way, in a lump that's made from wood pulp to newsprint. We sell most of it the new way, which zips it to the world on computers.

Our circulation and advertising people say the Air Monitor is the fastest-growing newspaper in history. It started out small as one of those "niche" publications, supposedly the brainchild of a couple of sharpies who figured there was a market out there from people who hated smoking and smokers.

Our newspaper sprang up just before Winston DeWeerd blew into town on a cloud of socially unacceptable secondhand smoke. The early editions were nothing more than press releases from the Office of Tobacco Abatement and Winston DeWeerd and his fellow travelers. The early Air Monitor was pretty puny but today's pulp version runs a minimum four sections — chock full of ads for smoke detectors sandwiched between the stories and big ads for the nationwide chains of clinics where they promise to certify that you and your family are smoke-free.

That's pretty important. You can't get a driver's license if you're not certified smoke-free.

The Air Monitor was making money until a weird little duck named Benson Goodykoontz came on the scene. Ben is our publisher and owner. We don't just make money any more. We more or less print it. Benson Goodykoontz is a secretive fellow. Every business writer or reporter in the world has tried to get the background story on Goodykoontz. No one has. He arrived rich and is richer. He took the Air Monitor from a hole-in-the-wall office to a gleaming office complex. His gigantic office and a penthouse apartment share the top floor.

Everyone says Benson Goodykoontz is some kind of financial genius and he probably is a smart guy. I personally think that the anti-smoking sentiment that my half-brother has plumbed makes it possible that the Air Monitor would have done quite well under what I call the LCM theory of management. That means we would have turned a profit if the leadership were the clowns Larry, Curly and Moe who dorked around as the Three Stooges.

I read a financial analyst's report once that predicted the Air Monitor will have a public stock offering. The analyst said that was the only way the newspaper can come up with the money for the technology that walked through the door with Benson

Goodykoontz. The analyst said there was no way in hell that the Air Monitor revenues could handle the debt from all the gizmos we have. Maybe we're high-tech and maybe we're not. J.R. Tyson says we are and J.R. is a genius at the stuff.

The computers may be techy but the rest of the furnishing is tacky. But there are fax machines everywhere and the unblinking eyes of computer terminals blinking away as far as the eye can put up with looking at them. There are rows of television sets which allow us to tune in on about any television or satellite signal in our hemisphere. The highest tech, of course, is the smoke-detecting equipment.

The financial analysts all agree that we're a phenomenon, even if they can't understand how we got so large, so fast. A privately owned specialty corporation that dominates its market is rare in any part of America today and the Air Monitor stands alone in a field that has been dominated by financial behemoths for decades.

Take the old Capital Cities Communications outfit. It started out as a newspaper and broadcasting group owner in the middle of the 20th Century, then bought the ABC Broadcasting network. NBC has been gobbled up by a mega-corporation and spat out several times. The New York Times and Washington Post both have more subsidiaries than a smoker has coughing fits.

***

I try to pay attention to the big picture in affairs of finance, but I'm not really worried about it. My private goal of irony is to work my way onto the Smoking Abatement beat. The reporter who covers that gets OTA. That's no prize, but he or she also gets to go out with the Smoke Jumpers. The Smoker Jumpers are a bunch of fascist assholes, but I love action and there's always action with the Smoke Jumpers. I love irony even more. That's the real reason I want to cover Smoking Abatement. People who love irony will get a laugh every time they pick up the paper and see that the Smoke Jumpers are being covered by Robert J. Reynolds.

Yep, R.J. Reynolds, just like the tobacco-stained company that started out decades before Winston DeWeerd and I were even gleams in our parents' eyes. I guess I'm part of the smoker underground. As I said, I love irony. Almost as much as I hate Winston DeWeerd.

I once thought Winston might at least believe in what he is doing. Now I'm certain he doesn't give a damn. I shudder at the thought of Milano Nagurski, chained forever to an OTA satellite feed. I don't know if I could take the strain of that kind of imprisonment. I would borrow one of J.R. Tyson's machine guns and make a run for it.

The fraud of the Barranca Lopez tape is just as despicable as the Nagurski leash. Nobody at the OTA would have changed her mother's words from "hair" to "air" without the blessing of King Winston. Only Winston would be so corrupt as to allow it in the first place, then to make the murderous little bitch a national icon in the second.

I've tried to get some of my fellow Washington reporters interested in the Barranca Lopez story but no one will run it. I wrote a long and reasonably dispassionate story exposing the fraud of the Barranca tape but my good friend J.R. Tyson convinced me I would be unemployed if I sent it to the Air Monitor copy desk. I don't need the job for the money, but I want to hang around. I think there's a better chance of doing something about what's going on if I'm here, even at the Air Monitor.

I sometimes wonder if that's not more rationale than reason. At those times I am full of fear that Winston DeWeerd and I share enough genes that I'm a sellout, too. Maybe I just like to play at being a reporter and going to the receptions in Washington and enjoying the relationships that come to a healthy guy in a town where there are a division of women for every platoon of men.

Winston would be here for those reasons, if he were me. Winston has no morals or beliefs. If fifty-one percent of the people turned into militant vegetarians Winston would be dragging camera crews with him so they could watch him shooting cows.

Winston says his greatest public service has been the creation of the Smoke Jumpers. Great group of people. Hitler's

SS troopers would have quit the Third Reich and jumped right in with the Jumpers. Of course the Smoke Jumpers aren't an all-male club the way the Gestapo was. We've got women Smoke Jumpers, gay Smoke Jumpers, African-American Smoke Jumpers, lesbian Smoke Jumpers, Serbian Smoke Jumpers and Croatian Smoke Jumpers, just to name a few Jumper mixes.

Winston even took a lot of pressure off the nation's prison system by creating the Reformed Felon Smoke Jumpers. You'd rather smoke a nitroglycerine cigarette than get busted by these guys. They're based on a small island off the Carolinas. Some of the elite of America's crime wave proudly sport the white uniform of the Jumpers. Murderers, rapists and robbers, all armed to the teeth and given the best military equipment America has developed.

No wimps need apply to the Reformed Felon Smoke Jumpers. One Wall Street sharpie decided his black belt in karate would keep him safe in the unit. He had once made headlines by taking on three muggers, killing one and severely injuring the others. He thought it would be more fun to bust tobacco shipments and smokers than to work on his backhand at a minimum-security federal slammer in Arkansas for twenty years. He didn't fit in with his new crowd, most of whom thought financial futures were somebody else's pocketbook a couple of minutes from now.

The OTA says the Wall Street guy was the only person to ever desert the Reformed Felon Smoke Jumper unit. OTA said he was killed while trying to escape the island. A friend of mine at OTA says there wasn't much of the guy left when they brought him in for autopsy. My friend said whoever had shot and hacked him to pieces had been kind enough to cut off his penis and put it where his nose once had been.

Not all the Jumpers are the kind of people who make your neck hair tingle. There's one elite group of Jumper people who claim to have been heirs to the great tobacco fortunes. I call them the Quiche Jumpers. They show up at state fairs and air shows to demonstrate technological gimmicks like the OTA Tobacco Profile Satellite Network.

OTA's satellite program uses light analysis and a supercharged computer program. OTA says it will identify any tobacco patch of more than four square feet, no matter what other vegetation is mixed in with the Demon Weed.

I submitted a column to the Air Monitor Editorial Page in which I, wimpily, as usual, questioned whether there might be a bug in the Tobacco Profile Satellite data. I didn't do all that well in college science courses, but I looked up the parameters on one OTA demonstration at a football game in Virginia. It clearly showed my aunt Mabel's tomato patch as a secondary target for those who exterminate the demon weed. I had reservations about taking Aunt Mabel's tomato patch off the hit list. Her homemade tomato soup is a crime against humanity, but the thought of a Jumper helicopter Rolfing Aunt Mabel's garden was too much. Even for me. I've seen the Jumpers Rolfe a rebel tobacco farm in Eastern North Carolina. Napalm might improve Aunt Mabel's mincemeat pie, though.

Mincemeat comes to mind because that's what my department boss, Katricia Coyne, made of the column. She grabbed it out of the computer for "fact-checking" with the OTA. One of the desk guys said OTA admitted that there had been some problems with the chemical analysis program but that a task force of computer nerds from Massachusetts Institute of Technology had worked them out. It's possible that they really worked them out, since I checked for Aunt Mabel's tomato patch the next time I got a shot at a demonstration. It didn't show Aunt Mabel as a suspected target. I asked the Smoke Jumper satellite demonstrator, a pretty blonde woman from Durham, North Carolina. She bubbled that the satellites now report only tobacco fields. I got the idea that she probably refueled her brain by putting her ear next to an electric fan.

She said she was a distant heir of Buck Duke, one of the most hated men in America today. She gushed that she and her fellow Smoke Jumper tobacco-related kin are atoning for the sins of their parents. "Isn't it, I mean, wild! I mean, we're doing it, I mean..." That was the most coherent remark I recall. Personally, I think Buck Duke could have used the wind out of his descendant's ear to cure his tobacco. And I think Miss Airhead Duke and her

Quiche Jumper pals have some sins of their own to atone for. But that's going to have to wait.

For the atoning, I mean. Winston DeWeerd and the Congress love them. The Supreme Court loves them. The same nine justices who recently held that prison inmates have a First Amendment right to taxpayer-paid portable telephones refused to review a decision upholding Winston DeWeerd's Smoker Privacy Act. Some privacy.

It prohibits contact by mail or visitation with inmates in the Smoker Colonies. The lower court said the legislation was constitutional by the need to protect the public from dangerous criminals and the threat of harm inherent in smoking and smokers. At least the court didn't quote Winston's favorite line, that being that "all smokers are mass murderers."

CHAPTER 13

WEST YELLOWSTONE, Montana — Smoke Jumper units joined local law-enforcement authorities Saturday in efforts to root out a rebel group of pro-tobacco squatters reportedly living in the interior of Yellowstone National Park. "We will not rest until this nest of tobacconists is no longer a threat to the public or our facility," a Park Service spokeswoman told a news conference. The spokeswoman said a search continues for two Smoke Jumpers who left the Old Faithful Lodge by snowmobile to check out a citizen tip as to the location of the rebels. County officials said the Smoke Jumpers might have been killed in a gunfight with the squatters.

***

The environment. We all love the environment. I've never seen any place in North America's environment more beautiful than Glacier National Park. The national parks are still part of the environment, even if they've lost a couple of pitched battles with various Total Sensitivity groups.

Glacier was exempt from the foolishness. It's name was something from nature. The first to fall was logical, considering the times we're living in. Great Smoky Mountains National Park on the North Carolina-Tennessee border. The Park Service tried to explain that the Smoky simply referred to the haze that makes the Great Smoky Mountains even more beautiful, but the Total Sensitivity people and anti-smokers were not impressed. The Park Service dug in its heels at a truly sensitive name but decided it had seen the time to compromise. The time rolled around when thousands of militant anti-smoking groups blocked roads and started burning facilities. People who visit the half-million acres of what I still call the Great Smoky Mountains are in the Great Mountains National Park. The fact that all the "great" mountains — in the sense of large — are in the West doesn't mean anything to the militants. And the fact that the Great Mountains are still "smoky" at dusk and dawn is meaningless. Symbolism was what was important to them and symbolism was served.

Kings Canyon National Park in California didn't fare nearly as well as Great Mountains National Park. The Park Service caved in to Persons Canyon National Park with less than a whimper.

The Custer Battlefield in Montana had been spared some of the current humiliation back in the 1990s, when American Indians objected to the name as glorifying a white-eyed idiot of a commander who lost his entire command to the Sioux and Cheyenne. It's now the Native-American Victory Park. Tonto National Monument in Arizona fell before the onslaught of sensitive people. They objected to the name, which they viewed as glorifying the Lone Ranger's sidekick. Totally Sensitive Native Americans said a National Monument named Tonto was inappropriate because the faithful companion was never sufficiently assertive in his dealings with the Lone Ranger.

The silliness over names of parks and monuments was a walk in Persons Canyon National Park compared with the stress that accompanied the environmental movement. Anything that burned oil or gasoline was targeted.

With Winston DeWeerd's anti-smoking movement as the linchpin, the general environmental coalition shut down thousands of electric generators that burned natural gas. Then they laid down strict rules that flooded the streets with electric-powered automobiles. People are paying huge amounts every year for electricity, since there is a short supply and a huge demand.

The politicians and their special-interest groups thought it made sense. It somehow strikes me as a shade short of total insanity. A little like telling everybody to screw themselves to chastity.

Winston managed to exempt Montana from the total-electric-car movement. He quite logically pointed out that the distances between cities made electrics considerably more hazardous than the pollution that came from burning gasoline on the seemingly endless miles of Montana. New Mexico didn't have Winston's lock on the coalition and the winter death toll from travelers stranded in their cranky electric cars fell to only ninety-nine last year. I'm not completely against it. It was, after all, a twenty-five percent improvement.

The electric-car push brought a flood of people into journalism, whose practitioners are exempt from the provisions of the electric-car act. Rich people can pay a couple of thousand dollars pollution penalty every year and continue to drive their gas-powered automobiles.

I try to take a favorable view of it all, but it's tough. I think it's crazy. The collapse of the Soviet Union in the 20th Century brought a flood of oil into the world. The new Russian republics have more oil than the Middle East ever dreamed of and want to sell it. Everyone but the United States is buying it.

As I said, I love the environment and unquestionably want to see it saved, if it's really under the weather. I'd hate to see the environment go the way of our national senses of honor or humor. If we lost it completely then the best we could hope for on a delightful weekend afternoon would be a walk in Newark. I haven't agonized over it, but probably Newark is what the world would look like without an environment. It is pretty scary.

Winston and his followers were the key to the movement because they said they knew how to pay for everything and give everybody a windfall as a sweetener. Winston called it the Clean-Lung Dividend. People were ready for a dividend. The tobacco states would have killed for a sniff of one. More than half a million people lost their jobs in the tobacco-growing sectors of the economy and the departure of the Merchants of Death had ended about seven billion dollars that once rolled through the electronic cash drawers in tobacco country.

SMOKE JUMPERS

The math was simple, at least to Winston. He first laid out the skeleton of it when he was visiting some skeletal lung patients at a hospital. There were plenty of television cameras along for the trip and the lovely and faithful Cecilia Word was shepherding Winston's own video crew to record every golden phrase.

Winston swept his arm toward the emphysema sufferers in the ward and thundered: "This, ladies and gentlemen, is Marlboro Country."

"A non-smoking America will free these medical facilities to serve the ill, not those who have committed slow-motion suicide by their evil addiction to the Demon Weed," DeWeerd said.

Then he got into the figures. Winston said every environmental initiative for a pristine environment could be funded with the money from a non-smoking country. Winston mentioned the forty billion dollars a year spent on medical treatment for smoking-related diseases. He said the "productivity improvement" from a non-smoking country would be even more dramatic than the Clean-Lung Dividend itself.

Winston said one-hundred billion dollars a year would flow back to the nation's consumers in productivity gained from a nation which didn't have to clean up ash trays, air conditioners and computers polluted by the smoke of the Demon Weed.

He said the productivity figure didn't include the incalculable sums we would realize from generation after generation of clean-breathing children, children spawned by parents with no nicotine or tar on the cilia of their lungs. He pointed out that pregnant women who smoked had babies that averaged about six ounces less than those borne by non-smoking mothers. Winston said not even he could imagine the monetary value of the excess brain power to be gained from babies of non-smoking moms. Pressed for a guess, he said it would be "in the trillions of dollars."

Winston chose the lungers in the emphysema ward as the backdrop for his final word of the day, which turned out to be the most malevolent act of a malicious man. With the all-but dead people in the background, he made his proposal for the Smoke Jumpers, "a national force of anti-smoking men and women who

105

will save future generations from the tobacco ravages that have brought these benighted souls to the brink of the most painful death imaginable."

DeWeerd said employment in the new Office of Tobacco Abatement and its Smoke Jumpers subsidiary would be staffed by people whose jobs had vaporized as quickly as the contrails left by the departing Lear Jets of the cowardly Merchants of Death.

For a pittance of seed money, a paltry billion dollars, the OTA and its Smoke Jumpers would exorcise the Demon and the money would flow. It would be no time, he said, until the OTA and Smoke Jumpers would be more than paying their way.

We were going to breathe ourselves rich, after a little resuscitation from a vast new bureaucracy and a few thousand heavily armed goons.

Someone asked when the bonanza would crest. Winston said the ravages of tobacco were an accumulation of centuries of misbegotten addiction and would not be banished overnight. He pointed out that it took years for a former smoker to regain the heart function of his or her non-smoking equivalent.

"We must take the long-term view," DeWeerd said. Almost everyone forgot the classic description of the "long term." It was one of the only good things that ever came from the engaging but erroneous British economist, Lord Maynard Keynes. Keynesian theories that governments could spend their people to wealth form the firm background of the problems we still have today, but Keynes was not wrong about everything. He once was asked about the effects of something over the long term. He said there was no reason to worry about the long term. "In the long term, we're all dead," he said.

Winston had gone to Harvard and squeaked out with a degree in philosophy. There's no record of his taking an economics course, even if he is pretty much in the Harvard economics tradition of the gurus who came out of Cambridge, Massachusetts in the last half of the Twentieth Century.

The productivity improvement is hard to prove or disprove. Every computer in the country has to have a government-approved tobacco monitor. The monitor shuts everything down if the Demon Weed offends its nose, or whatever it is a computer smells things with. The monitor isn't foolproof. A friendly woman cop in the 911 Center in Charlotte, North Carolina, brought in some fried eggplant one afternoon and killed every computer in the Charlotte Emergency Communications Center. She explained she didn't know that eggplant and tobacco were cousins in nature's scheme of things.

Computers are now equipped with signs that warn us that eggplant and tomatoes can give a false tobacco signal. The warning label came a little late for the five children in Charlotte who died in a fire when the 911 Center was down. The anti-tobacconists soothingly tell us that good economics is served by the automatic tobacco shutdown for computers. They point out that second-hand smoke is more even more deadly to computers than people.

They're probably correct. J.R. Tyson won't allow smoking around our computers at home, even though he long ago took care of the tobacco shutdown programs. The sneaky devil reset my computer so it shuts down whenever it sniffs jalapeno peppers. J.R. says I'm going to kill myself with jalapenos. I wish I were a computer nerd, so I could shut his down whenever it gets an earful of that godawful country music he likes to listen to. But I'd have to pay somebody to do it and that would be illegal and uneconomic.

My half-brother is big on talking about economics. Somebody has to be writing it for him. One of Winston's classmates told me once that Winston probably figured the Gross National Product was operatic music, which he despises with a consuming passion. I didn't know Winston hated opera so profoundly but thought it was worth checking into if he loathed it. I even read a book about the great tenor Enrico Caruso. Quite a guy. Loved women, booze and cigarettes. The book said Caruso probably killed himself with the cigarettes, choking what might have been the greatest male operatic voice the world had ever known. Given Winston's sense of humanity I'm surprised he doesn't have a soft spot for smoking. After all, it killed Caruso.

The woman's call was at the normal time. Milano Nagurski went to a pay telephone at the same time every Friday. Today's message wasn't normal. Nagurski could only say "thank you" before he ran to his office to pick up his palmtop computer. He carried the computer tightly in his right hand as he sprinted into the underground. Nagurski had looked up the plans for the underground area and had calculated that the reinforced concrete · atop a computer store would stifle, or at least garble, transmissions from his tracking device. Experience told him that more than ten minutes off the air would bring out a ground-based Smoke Jumper unit to find him. Nagurski hustled inside the pay-telephone station and used a counterfeit identification card to dial up the number for the computer at the specialty metal shop. He specified the order and hit the keys angrily to override the computer's persistent questions about the strange order it was trying to digest. Nagurski ran up the ramp that led to the open air. He held his left arm defiantly in the air, extending his middle finger at the spot in the Heavens where the OTA satellite might be.

CHAPTER 14

WASHINGTON — A spokesperson for the Federal Communications Commission said Army censors probably violated the spirit of the First Amendment in altering government television footage of Libyan dictator Muhammad Qaddar. "It appears that footage from the Army satellites was altered to make it appear that Qaddar was smoking a cigarette," the spokesperson said. Senator Winston DeWeerd, D-Montana, deemed the dispute "much ado over nothing. Qaddar is a mass murderer and has that in common with smokers," DeWeerd said.

***

The jet-powered Bell helicopter cruised at two-thousand feet. Captain Lindsay Bruce hated the monotony of night duty with the Smoke Jumpers and the Georgia countryside did nothing to relieve his distaste. The instrumentation showed no probable targets. It had been the same the past two evenings. Not even a plume of nicotine from some diehard tobacconist's curing barn. There hadn't been a reading on the nine-million-dollar nicotine detector all week. Bruce had written a report on the machine to Smoke Jumper maintenance but nothing had been done. Four days with not one nicotine alarm was pretty hard to believe.

Bruce was beginning to wonder if the maintenance foreman might have smoker tendencies. The guy did, after all, have a yellow spot on one of his front teeth. He said it came from a nutrition problem when he was growing up in North Carolina, but you can't ever be certain.

Take the black Smoke Jumper captain, for instance. He

had spotless teeth. But Lindsay Bruce and his crew busted him one night when they were working motels. He and his boyfriend were both nude. The boyfriend was smoking one of those old Virginia Slims and the Smoke Jumper captain was trying to flush a pack of Camels down the commode. The crafty ones go for unfiltered cigarettes. The filtered ones are hard to flush.

Flushing works pretty well for the smokers. The nicotine monitors on the sewage systems will catch the flush and give an alert but the smokers know that Congress cut out the funding for nicotine monitors on every toilet bowl. The funding was in the budget until some idiot Congresswoman from New Mexico put in an amendment to require the detectors also pick up other illegal drugs, especially cocaine. Support flaked away, because the Supreme Court undoubtedly would hold that to be an invasion of privacy.

The squad dragged the Smoke Jumper captain away from the commode, but he broke free and put his pistol in his mouth. He said, "I'll be goddamned if I'm going to die as a guard in one of the Colonies," then pulled the trigger. It was just as well. The guy was killing himself anyway, smoking.

Lindsay Bruce couldn't blame the captain for killing himself, if the alternative was a lifetime job as a guard in one of the Smoker Colonies. Bruce knew he would never smoke and it would never come to that for him. But he had known several Smoke Jumpers who got caught with tobacco and it was a one-way ticket to the Colonies.

Busting a Camels smoker should have been worth a write-up in the Air Monitor but OTA put the lid on the bust. First of all, it was embarrassing that a Smoke Jumper captain, even one with perfectly white teeth, had been able to beat the random nicotine testing. Secondly, one of Bruce's troopers had yelled: "Drop the weeds, cocksucker!" The dead captain's gay lover had dropped them, all right, but the audio from the Smoke Jumper cameraman could have been pretty embarrassing if it had ever been played in public.

All Smoke Jumpers got sensitivity training. Getting caught calling anyone — even a smoker — "cocksucker" was not the kind of thing you wanted to come up at the next Gay Air Police meeting. To begin with the simple use of the term was a misdemeanor offense under the District of Columbia's new Hupersonkind Linguistic Sensitivity Ordinance. And the Gay Air Police was among the most effective volunteer groups the Smoke Jumpers had.

Bruce admired the way GAP volunteers would go in and break up smoker enclaves that the Smoke Jumpers couldn't get to. Those were becoming fewer under Winston DeWeerd's new legislation.

A speaker at the last staff meeting said smoking arrests were up twenty-five percent, thanks to the DeWeerd Law, which gives Smoke Jumpers the ability to enter private residences without search warrants. The smartasses in the media called it Winston's Nicotine No-Knock bill but Lindsay Bruce liked it. The press always oversimplified everything. The Smoke Jumpers don't just bust people who suck nicotine into their lungs. Smoke Jumpers are people who make things better for everybody.

Bruce seldom used the informal connection with the Gay Air Police, but they were there if you needed them. He had tipped the local chapter president on a smoking den at a Catholic Church in Alexandria, Virginia. The GAP guys went in and busted up the place like they were a bunch of drunk lumberjacks. The pros couldn't have done it better.

GAP didn't find any weed, but that happened sometimes even with the Smoke Jumpers. It could have been a bad reading that set off the monitor, anyway. Some yo-yo in the church kitchen might have burned some eggplant and eggplant could put out a plume that looked pretty much like what you got from a bunch of burning tobacco. Bruce hated eggplant. Bruce had lost a bunch of good busts because the addicts got rid of their cigarettes and would plop a batch of eggplant into a red-hot skillet. The murderous bastards were getting craftier all the time.

Bruce tapped the suspect nicotine monitor as he flew over a small subdivision north of Atlanta. The damned thing couldn't be working. There was no reading of any kind. Any subdivision ought to put out enough of a nicotine plume that Bruce would get to drop a dye packet to mark a house for the ground guys to check out. There were smokers down there. That was for sure. There always were. You'd think that at least some asshole among two hundred houses could have burned some eggplant.

The on-board instrumentation showed hundreds of blips from people and animals afoot in the neighborhood. Ashley Bunting, the navigator, was scanning the ground with his night glasses. He asked Bruce to make a second pass over the area. "Looked like two guys, holding a young girl. Both of the guys had knives. We could put down in the field where they've got her," Bunting said.

Lindsay Bruce fixed the young navigator with a withering look. "Anything else? Either of the guys have a cigarette?"

Bunting's embarrassed look told Bruce the answer was no. "We've got more important things to do than put down for every neighborhood crime. Call it down to the local cops," Bruce sneered.

They turned north and flew in silence for five minutes. Bruce couldn't suppress a triumphant grin at the first signals from the Vegetation Detector, a sophisticated machine put together by a former defense contractor in Dallas. The minicomputer in the Vegetation Detector took information from laser-activated sensors on the bottom of the helicopter and identified the chemical profile of what the lasers were looking at. "Looks like we got rebel weed," Bruce said.

"That's what the monster says," Bunting said, sweeping the countryside with his night glasses.

Bruce knew Bunting was still angry over the peremptory treatment he got when he wanted to put down and stop the rape. He thought some small talk might help. "Only good thing about Jumping at night is the Vegetation Detector works better then. Good pictures of the hot spots and no wind."

"Yeh," Bunting said, "all the high wind's up here."

Bruce banked the helicopter sharply and swooped down over the suspected field of illegal tobacco. He pulled up and hovered over the rows of trees in the field. Bruce had had enough of Bunting's surliness. His next words were spoken in the unmistakable tone of command. "Still getting the weed profile?"

"Yep. Stronger than before. That's what you expect when you get closer. We can't get a positive from here, though. Guess we ought to get the ground guys to go in and shred it," Bunting said.

"Screw the ground assholes," Bruce said, "I'm gonna Rolfe it."

"I don't know about Rolfing it," Bunting said. "We're not supposed to Rolfe it unless we're one hundred percent certain and I couldn't sign the Rolfe paper from what I know."

The Smoke Jumpers had converted proper nouns to other uses. A good opportunity to "Rolfe" something was a terrible thing for a Smoke Jumper to waste. The word Rolfe was linked with tobacco in 1613, when John Rolfe shipped the first Virginia tobacco from Jamestown, Virginia, to England. It was John Rolfe who brought Caribbean tobacco to plant in the fertile soil of Virginia. Smoke Jumpers had turned the Father of Smoking's name on its ear, of course. The ultimate Rolfing of a tobacco patch was done with napalm. A lesser Rolfing involved herbicides.

"What kind of animal signatures we got in the weed?" Bruce demanded.

"Just a small one. Probably a dog, or maybe a pig. These rural jerks love pigs. I still don't think I can go along with the Rolfe," Bunting said.

"You don't have to go along with the Rolfe. That's what we've got captains for," Bruce said. He moved the helicopter forward, set the target parameters on the Rolfe computer and hit the switch.

The napalm showered into the covering stand of trees, then exploded into flames so hot that the helicopter's tracking mechanisms went off their scales.

Bunting peered into the flames. "Bad news, Captain," he said, fighting to conceal the glee in his voice.

"You ain't meanin' to tell me..." Bruce said in disgust.

"Yep. Tomatoes. Friggin' tomatoes. You Rolfed

somebody's tomato patch."

"Serves 'em right, trying to hide them in the trees like that," Bruce snarled, hovering over the burning stand of trees. The heat bursts of the ripe tomatoes threw streams of red into the air.

"Kind of pretty," Bunting said.

He ducked reflexively as a bullet bounced off the bullet-proof glass in front of his face. "Get us out of here before they hit the rotor. Frigging rednecks and their goddamned tomatoes." Bunting slapped the Vegetation Detector in disgust. "You'd think for a couple hundred million those Texas assholes could build a machine that wouldn't give the same profile on tomatoes and tobacco."

Bruce had the helicopter at maximum speed. Another bullet pinged off the tail section. "Yeh, and don't forget the friggin' eggplant. Goddamned eggplant. Who the hell needs eggplant, anyway."

CHAPTER 15

WASHINGTON — An Education Department spokesperson emphatically denied an Atlanta television station's report that a yet-unreleased study showed a fifty percent increase in smoking by students and professors on federally assisted college campuses. The spokesperson said any increase in campus tobacco use would imperil federal funding and could lead to an increased presence of Smoke Jumper units.

***

Speaking to groups is not my favorite chore. People tell me I do it reasonably well, but I would have preferred to use some time today to try to run down a few leads on the Colonies. That was impossible because I had, months ago, accepted the invitation of a professor from George Washington University. He asked me to speak to his students about the old tobacco companies.

The students turned out to be a good audience. They paid attention to what I said, or at least appeared to. I told them that the tobacco giants saw the handwriting on the wall and fought for as long as they could to keep their markets in cigarettes. But they knew the trend was against them and they diversified so that their companies wouldn't sink or swim on tobacco.

I pointed out that different companies diversify for different reasons. Newspaper publishers, for instance, diversified because they couldn't spend all the money they were making back in the good old days.

The newspapers are still here and the dear and departed

tobacco companies are not. I said they were "dear" to me because the tobacco story has furnished good jobs for me and the rest of the people at the Air Monitor. I called them departed and then sketched the way the tobacco people fled the country when Winston DeWeerd threw in the first bill aimed at confiscating their total assets. Their total assets were something. They used to spend more than three billion dollars a year in advertising and promotion.

The students nodded knowingly when I talked about the old ways of doing politics in this country. The old tobacco giants, or the automobile industry for that matter, once could buy politicians at bargain rates. Then came the first Surgeon General's Report. The auto people still had a good run on their politicians but the tobacco people had to up the ante after that.

"When they grabbed their bags of cash and fled the country they were paying top dollar for politicians and they couldn't even buy them any more. They had to rent them by the hour," I said. Several of the students applauded.

That warmed me up a little more. "The Tobacco Barons of the late Twentieth Century knew how to profit from every end of the business, right up until the moment they split," I said. "American Brands, for instance, owned both American Tobacco and the Franklin Life Insurance Company. Loews Corporation owned both Lorillard and an insurance company called CNA Life. And a bunch of Britishers doing business as B.A.T Industries owned British American Tobacco and Farmers Insurance Group. Their love for tobacco didn't cloud their vision when it came to the bottom line. The tobacco company insurance companies all charged higher rates to smokers."

A slender young man at the back of the room spoke. "Damned slime," he said. I almost let slip that I believed personally that the tobacco companies were simply doing business the old American way, but decided not to take the chance.

I didn't use my favorite analogy on the students. That holds that the situation was a little like a venereal disease clinic running its own stable of infected whores. Besides, I probably have no business saying anything critical of whores, infected or wholesome, because I work at the Air Monitor. Everybody who works at the Air Monitor is a whore.

I admitted to the students that I'm a little hooked on the Washington scene. They know that everybody gets addicted to Washington. That's what creates monsters like Winston DeWeerd and the OTA and the Gay Air Police and the regular Air Police and the rest of them.

One young man, wearing the distinctive pink uniform of the Gay Air Police, asked me if there were any closet smokers at the Air Monitor. I detailed our random nicotine testing and told them what little I understand about the detection gear. I didn't tell him that I had quit smoking until I went to work for the Air Monitor. I don't think he noticed that I never really answered him.

***

I thought about the GAP guy's question as I walked off the campus. So far as I know, J.R. and I are the only closet smokers at the Air Monitor, but I'd bet there are a couple more, out of more than a hundred people. But not many more. Some of the staff people even believe that what they're doing is either journalism, or the Lord's Work. It's possible that writing stories exhorting children to turn in their parents for smoking could be the Lord's Work.

Anything's possible. Maybe the Great Nonsmoker in the Sky is the Supreme Smoke Jumper. After all, if it weren't God's Will there wouldn't have been Winston DeWeerd's law that outlaws what the old folks still think of as cigarette lighters. Of course they don't call them cigarette lighters any more. It's not illegal, but any neutral use of the word cigarette can make your neighbors and friends think maybe you're a closet smoker. If you have to call the devices anything, it's socially acceptable to refer to them as Mechanical Ignition Devices. There's no cigarette anything any more.

I once did a story about Joe Huff. Joe was one hell of a boat builder but he wasn't too politic in his advertising. Joe built those hundred-mile-an-hour wave-hopping boats. And in the ad, he called them what his father had called them when his father manufactured them. Cigarette Boats.

117

A bunch of militant anti-smokers from Little Rock drove over and torched Joe Huff's factory. They left a note. "All vestiges of the Killer Weed, no matter how small, must be dealt with."

I screwed up after we ran the story. I met with the Air Monitor editorial board and suggested we take a position that burning a boat factory over the word "cigarette" in an ad was a little extreme.

I couldn't have been very persuasive. The next day's lead editorial in the Air Monitor was a ringing endorsement of the arson job.

That wasn't all that surprising. What I didn't expect was getting called in four times in the next two months for random tobacco testing. It's not one of those pee-in-the-jar things like they used to do for drugs. An RTT is a full-body nightmare. You have to blow and blow and blow into a balloon to see if any cigarette tar dislodges from the cilia in your lungs.

Then there's the blood-letting, to check for traces of nicotine. That's not all that hard to beat. The nicotine test won't pick up anything on me. The one I hate is the skin scraping. The Air Monitor staff physician takes scrapings from your index fingers to see if there are signs of nicotinic acid on the skin. J.R. and I wear gloves when we smoke and we don't smoke but two cigarettes a day. We're ideological smokers. Neither of us particularly enjoys the habit, except for the feeling that it sets us apart from assholes like Winston DeWeerd and Katricia Coyne.

CHAPTER 16

A custom loathsome to the eye, hateful to the nose, harmful to the brain, dangerous to the lungs, and in the black, stinking fume thereof nearest resembling the horrible Stygian smoke of the pit that is bottomless. King James I of England (1566-1625)

***

I got back to the office and had my finger over the dialer to see if I could link up with the elusive Veronica French. It was my best shot, since the computer said she had called only five minutes earlier. Then I saw Ben Goodykoontz coming my way. He waved at me, then yanked on his left sleeve. It's a curious habit.

Ben comes by occasionally and tells me about computers. He likes for me to tell him about golf. I've tried to get Ben interested in talking about computers with J.R. Tyson, who knows enough to put me to sleep in two languages. But Ben doesn't like talking to J.R. because J.R. can't give him golf tips.

I talked about his slice. He wanted me to continue while he went into the computer room. Ben loves his computer room. We've got millions of dollars worth of computers, burping away in sixty-eight-degree comfort in a high-security area. High security at the Air Monitor means you have to use a plastic card key to get in. Even Ben has to have one.

Ben opened the door, then identified himself to the moron who's about seventy years old. I think he retired from the police force of East Fishfondle, New Jersey because of failing eyesight.

Then we got to the point where we got an electronic

119

patting-down from one of the hundred-thousand-dollar detectors
the eight-buck-an-hour guard keeps on his desk. The Air Monitor
contends that its anti-tobacco security in its computer room is the
best in the world. It probably is, but I've done a lot of reading and
I've never come across a case in which a crazed smoker broke
into a computer room and brought the system wheezing to a lung-
damaged halt with a volley of well-placed Lucky Strikes.

If you get into the newsroom you've already been "swept"
by one tobacco monitor. The whole thing is electronic. You never
feel a thing, although a couple of people on the staff have filed
lawsuits. They say the electronic sweeping gave them cancer.
Janie Osmond filed one suit, saying it probably gave her breast
cancer. She could be telling the truth. Janie has the biggest chest
of any woman on the copy desk.

The second lawsuit came from a former Managing Editor
named Walker Lansdale and we know it's a laugher. Walker's
lawsuit said the Air Monitor's electronic gadgetry gave him
cancer of the testicles. Anybody who's ever worked with Walker
Lansdale knows that Walker, like most Managing Editors, doesn't
have any balls at all.

Ben hired Lansdale, but grew to dislike him. Now he
hates his guts because of the lawsuit. Ben asked me if I despised
Walker Lansdale as much as the rest of the staff apparently had.

"No, I didn't despise him. I rose above that. I hated his
guts," I said.

I told him that Walker talked about having been a reporter, but he had never covered anything bigger than his
managerial ass. I pointed out that Walker went from college to
working a desk job at a newspaper in Denver and began his
inexorable rise into management by taking credit for guiding
reporters who survived his advice and counsel to get good stories
despite him.

I pointed out my best case, in which I broke the story on
a Mexican connection between the South American tobacco
growers and a longshoremen's union in Galveston, Texas. Walker
read me off because I couldn't nail the union president in the
scheme.

Ben appeared relaxed, at least in the context of relaxation as it applies to Benson Goodykoontz. It seemed to be a good time to draw Ben out on what he did before he took the national advertising community by storm.

"I've read your biography, Ben, but I've always wanted to know more about your background. I know for damned sure you never were a golf pro, but I've always wondered if you served any time as a reporter."

Ben's relaxed mood disappeared in a millisecond. "We'll have to talk about it someday," he said. His pager went off and he left at a trot.

It was obvious that my question had been disturbing to Ben, but I really didn't care. I was still pissed at the memory of Walker Lansdale. The Walkers of the world do that to me.

**

My college professors said it wasn't always thus. They said there was a time when newspapers were proud of their writers.

It was my damned luck to be born the son of Winston DeWeerd's father, and brought into the world when newspapers got prouder of their computers than of the people who write on them. I guess I've got to admit that the computers are better now than they were in the good old days, tho. There's one old coot on the sports desk who says he was covering football for a wire service in the early days of computers. He says one of his pro football stories didn't get on the wire for thirty minutes because the deskman he dictated it to hit the wrong series of keystrokes and the computer kept burping out a signal that said "Bad Header."

I took a survey of my fellow mostly male reporters and got a consensus that a bad header was probably an inadequate sex act. I use the word "mostly" because our Anti-Tobacco Music Editor, Bruce Dukakis, looked at me brightly and said, "I've never given one."

Bruce isn't all that bad a person, but he is so stridently "gay" that he tries everybody's patience. Our office tennis tournament wasn't any big deal until somebody pencilled Bruce

121

in for "Mixed Singles." The jokester thought Bruce would be insulted. Bruce liked the idea so much that he demanded that the Air Monitor have a separate tournament for gays and lesbians, with the winners meeting the best of the straights in sort of an all-Air Monitor Wimbledon.

I figured we might call it the Different Strokes Open. I got J.R. Tyson to bring up Katricia Coyne's computer file for me. I put a phony note from her in the Air Monitor electronic mail setup. The note said the Different Strokes Open tennis championship was a great idea and that all costs of the lesbian team would be underwritten by Snap-On Tools Company.

Katricia figures the note came from me, but she can't prove it. She was afraid to make too big a deal of it, because the Air Monitor internal computer security setup is her bailiwick and she was embarrassed that anybody could hack their way into her file the way J.R. did.

Even if the mixed servers never got down to playing, most of the computer people backed Bruce's petition. I've never figured out why computer careers attract so many gay people. Bruce Dukakis says computers are a little like music and art. They attract people who are sensitive and free of the tired old mores of the straight world. Bruce is pretty intelligent about anti-smoking music and he won a national award by spotting some outlaw pro-tobacco lyrics in a London heavy metal group's album. That made Bruce pretty highly regarded by the unforgettable Katricia Coyne.

Whatever the genesis of their talent, half the people inside the computer area wear little buttons that proclaim them to be: "Gay and Smoke-Free."

Gay is optional but smoke-free is everywhere. The little plaque on the door says every component of the Air Monitor computer equipment was built "in a completely tobacco- and smoke-free environment." The Air Monitor doesn't do business with anybody who won't certify that he/she/it or he/she/it's employees also are free of the demon weed.

It may work all right here in the good old USA but I happened to see a contract for a computer that came from Japan.

There was a small cigarette burn on one corner of it. Our management explained that the contract got that way in a fire in a bin at the Post Office. They've never explained just how the letter from the Japanese set off the nicotine alarm when the postman brought it into the business office. Pretty easy to explain, if you follow logic and not the Air Monitor's wishful thinking. The Japanese still smoke like crazy. I figure the cigarette burn was some Japanese executive's way of telling the Air Monitor that he signed its stupid no-tobacco pledge with a pen in one hand, a cigarette in the other and a smirk on his face.

I sometimes go into the computer room to try to escape the professional guidance of Katricia Coyne. You have to be a minority, an animal or a computer if you're going to escape Katricia's howling visage.

She started out in a marketing job, went to work as a researcher for Senator Winston DeWeerd and bumped right into a top job at the Air Monitor. Katricia was brought aboard by Walker Lansdale. He didn't mention her ties to Winston. He said her mission was to "sensitize" the staff "to the issues of women, minorities and the powerful anti-tobacco sentiments they represent."

One of my Male Chauvinist Pig fellows once wanted to bet me that Katricia couldn't write fifty words on her day at the orgy. I declined the bet. The only evidence would be to ask Katricia to write fifty words on an orgy with which she purported to be intimately familiar, which would either invade her privacy or abuse her limited imagination.

Katricia has no inventiveness that anybody has ever been able to identify. We've always wondered how even an idiot like Walker Lansdale could have thought she could sensitize anybody or anything, since she screams her lungs out at the first sign of disagreement from any of her many subordinates. I take a good deal of pleasure out of provoking a series of howls from Katricia, since it's such a sight to behold.

The hair shakes like it's Medusa's snaky "do" and if Katricia is really angry her eyes disappear into serpentine slits behind her glasses, which are about as thick as a package of today's hundred-dollar-a-pack bootleg cigarettes. An industrial-strength job of provoking Katricia generates what we call a screech-in. In a screech-in, Katricia whirls on her flat-soled shoes and lurches into the office of the new Managing Editor and screams about the incompetence and obstructionism of the idiots who work for her.

I hold the Indoor Air Monitor Record for screech-ins, having caused four of them in one day. My friend J.R. Tyson says I should have gotten just an assist on the third one, but Tyson always exaggerates his role in my misdeeds.

***

I wanted to work on the Smoker Colony information or keep after Ms. Veronica French. Getting her on the telephone had developed into a fixation with me. But J.R. asked me to go with him on one of his Lung Beat stories. J.R. Tyson never begs for anything, but one glance into his eyes told me a friend would go with him. So I went.

"I hate the Lung Beat," J.R. said as we drove to the Virginia high school for his afternoon story appointment.

J.R.'s work brings him into contact with a lot of emphysema and tons of doctors, which probably spurs his imagination. You need a lot of imagination to write about anything as horrible and slow-moving as emphysema, especially under the Air Monitor's coverage policy. The Air Monitor sticks sternly to the credo that emphysema is a criminal's disease and that the poor emaciated bastards who have it are getting the due of their criminal behavior. J.R. knows they asked for it, by smoking, but he has trouble lumping the poor bastards in with killers and rapists.

"We've got another Lunger Olympics today," J.R. said as we pulled into the parking lot.

"Wonderful. Frigging wonderful. I hope I won't embarrass you if I throw up," I said.

We went through the tobacco detectors, then the metal detectors to get to the Principal's Office. Six uniformed Smoke Jumpers were standing in the hallway. One of them had a withered little man on a leash. Another Jumper was carrying a locked box. It bore the international no-smoking symbol and was marked "Extremely Dangerous." I knew the ten-pound box contained the one cigarette that would mark the big finish of the Lunger Olympics.

J.R. has been through war and even survived one roll in the hay with Katricia Coyne, so he's not your average wimp who turns green at the sight of death or violence. But it bothers him that the Office of Tobacco Abatement's Education Services people take emphysema patients out of their beds and parade them in front of school children. J.R. got in trouble with the Air Monitor when he tried to question the Education Service big finale for its anti-emphysema program, the one he and I call the Lunger Olympics. It features the poor emphysema sufferer, running a hundred-yard dash against some kid selected at random from the school. The OTA calls it "anti-smoking involvement" but J.R. think it's a lot closer to torture.

Today's event was pretty much standard. The hard-muscled kid did the hundred in about twelve seconds and then stood at the finish line, hooting for the old lunger to finish. The poor guy fell to his knees and crawled the last twenty feet to cross the line.

The Jumper with the leash reconnected it to the patient's neck and handed him the cigarette. The old man looked almost happy for a second, then almost euphoric as another Jumper struck a lighter and touched its flame to the cigarette. The smoker pulled until the weed got to its sixteen-hundred degree temperature, grinning like an idiot as the nicotine and gases started working their way through his system.

The OTA Education Services representative continued her canned speech as the old man pulled on the cigarette. His shoulders heaved as he smoked. It was a little akin to watching someone try to breathe through a hundred-foot soda straw.

"One of the deadly elements he is ingesting is carbon monoxide. Carbon monoxide is picked up in the lungs about ten times as fast as oxygen, depriving the body of the oxygen it needs. If the CO level of the blood gets to thirty percent, the smoker may become nauseous, dizzy or suffer headaches."

The students cheered and the old smoker smiled and kept dragging.

The OTA woman continued as if nothing had happened. "At sixty percent or higher damage to the brain and heart occurs and death can follow in a matter of minutes. Tobacco is more addictive than either heroin or cocaine," the narrator said. Then she clicked her heels together, shot both arms forward and intoned: "To clean air!"

The students cheered and hooted. The lunger drew the cigarette down to its filter before the Smoke Jumper led him away.

"That's the second ugliest thing I've ever seen," J.R. said as we drove away. I knew what he meant. J.R. says the first ugliest thing involved the time Katricia Coyne dropped by the apartment and undressed while he was making her a Scotch and water. Tyson says he did what he had to do. He said it was like making love to a pine board with a chain saw running in his ear. Katricia screamed so loudly that the neighbors called the police to report a murder in progress.

The cops came before J.R. did and Katricia quickly donned her slacks and blouse. The cops left and Katricia stretched luxuriantly and asked J.R. if he had a cigarette. He was relieved. He had been afraid Katricia would want to complete the encounter, but the question about a cigarette told him it was a setup. Katricia had fired five people for suspicion of smoking in her first eleven months at the Air Monitor. Katricia had a special plaque from Winston DeWeerd for her efforts to combat smoking crime.

Some skeptics thought an amendment to the National Labor Relations Act was a strange way to fight crime. Winston's amendment gave employers the right to fire people for suspicion of smoking. The employees could be reinstated if they could prove they had been smoke-free for one year before the firing and every day hence.

Winston's big anti-crime package boomed through the last Congress with little debate. He and his coalition had to accept a compromise with senators from California and the northeast to get the bill through. The deal gave special standing under federal civil-rights laws to a gaggle of Winston's pet groups. He pledged that a separate national health insurance program would be funded from the Clean Air Dividend to cover victims of AIDS.

Winston and his ilk have been spending the Clean Air Dividend for years. We unbelievers view it as a Clean Air Credit Card with no limit and no intention by the holders to pay the monthly minimum, much less the balance. DeWeerd and his foundations and Sensitivity groups are forever telling us, fervently, that the Clean Air Dividend will rain money onto us when the last vestiges of the Demon Weed are expunged from society.

I knew that getting J.R. to fulminate about the Clean Air Dividend was a good way to get his mind off the ugly scene we had witnessed.

"How do you plan to spend your thousands from the Clean Air Dividend?" I asked.

J.R.'s face relaxed into something approaching a smile.

"I think I'll buy Winston a piano and chain him to it. It's time he had an honest job."

I laughed appreciatively. One of my favorite politicians from history is Harry S. Truman, the honest little political accident from Missouri. Truman once explained that his choice early in life was to go into politics; or become a piano player in a whorehouse. Truman said he didn't believe there was much difference between the two jobs.

"Can you find any statistics on the likelihood of our beloved government paying for the AIDS plague from our ever-decreasing smoker population?" I asked.

"I can find the OTA's, but they're bound to be bullshit," J.R. said.

We drove back into the Air Monitor parking area and went our separate ways after clearing security. J.R. had to sign a Minor Tobacco Event form. He apparently had been standing close enough to the old lunger at the school demonstration to catch some nicotine molecules in his cotton shirt.

I knew J.R. would come up with the figures we had discussed. When he is upset he loves to work his magic with the computers. A newsroom clerk told me that Katricia Coyne had been looking for me, so I went to the computer room to at least defer a meeting with my Beloved Supervisor.

I knew better than try to ask the computers for any Colonies information while Katricia was around. I once voiced a question about the Colonies to Katricia at a staff meeting and provoked Katricia into a full-body, on-the-spot screech-in.

Katricia is always pretty well hacked off, especially if I'm breathing the same general air. But when she really gets hacked she starts out with about fifteen seconds of what turns out to be a tortured version of the word "well." It comes out as a rolling WELLLLLLLLLLLL! that tapers off to a growl at the end when she starts spitting heartfelt invective.

A WELLLLLLLLLLLL! is a bad way to start any day. I had heard my first one today when I was back in the computer room, watching desultorily as one of the computer guys ran some statistics on tobacco production in the new South American Golden Leaf Coast.

I checked my Message Center from the computer-room terminal and saw that I was due to go to the Senate Office Building within an hour. I left by a side door and took a cab. Katricia had assigned me to cover a Winston DeWeerd event today and I wanted to avoid another conversation with her about my mission.

Katricia's way of assigning stories to me is borderline hilarious. She never worked in journalism before coming to the Air Monitor, but she speaks a little of the language. Katricia had used a little journalistic jargon to assign me to the story. "My sources tell me Senator Winston DeWeerd will have a news conference with a major announcement today," she intoned.

I didn't have the heart to tell her that anyone who has ever worked in the news business knows that there is only one source on a politician's news conference and it's an unreliable one. I've covered local politicians in a couple of states and have covered swell-headed politicians in Washington. I don't recall that any of them ever called me and said, "I don't have one other thing to do and I'd like to fool the rubes who sent me here into thinking I'm really performing some service. So, I think I'll have a news conference."

One of the beat reporters says Winston has the Air Monitor so deeply in his pocket that he believes we ought to carry a daily graph recording his quarter-hourly erections. I could go for it if we would chronicle the time he awakes every morning. We could put a standing headline on it and run it every day. We could call it: The Prick Also Rises.

Katricia knows I hate covering staged events almost as much as I hate Winston. Having to cover a Winston news conference is an eight-point-five on my personal bullshit scale. Which, of course, is why Katricia wants to make me do it. Something good may come out of it. Maybe Winston will answer my questions about The Colonies. He's never done it before, but hope, like smoke, springs infernal.

***

I was walking toward the building when my portable telephone rang. It was Cecilia Word, telling me the Winston event was a hearing, not a news conference. Cecilia said Winston would grace the news folk with a large announcement. Cecilia always says Winston has "something big." Then she lets go with that throaty laugh of hers. I laughed along with her. I've never understood how a vibrant, intelligent and beautiful woman like Cecilia is attracted to a slimeball of Winston DeWeerd's high ooze.

Even though I'm Winston's genetic half-brother, we don't know each other well at all. We never spent any time together, as kin. I knew his reputation on The Hill even before I got here. He was a legend in Tobacco Country when I was working there. Newspapers hadn't had much tobacco advertising for years but the North Carolina daily I worked for got the economic pinch when Winston harangued the Senate into a series of laws that made the cultivation and sale of tobacco difficult, then illegal.

North Carolina never knew how much it had always had in common with Mississippi. Where there was smoke, there was no hire. I don't know how many thousands of people lost their jobs when the tobacco companies went offshore. I could find out, but the Air Monitor wouldn't print it. Katricia would be happy to blacklist me in the industry if she could prove I had tried to find out subversive information.

I ducked into DeWeerd's office for a minute. Cecilia Word probably is a world-class bitch, given the man she sleeps with, but I can't repress a sort of grudging affection for her. There's something about the woman, outside of her phenomenal beauty, that is both mysterious and attractive.

I've read her resume. It says she came to Senator DeWeerd from somewhere in Georgia. She had a degree in something from what once was called Duke University and had worked as a researcher before she joined Winston's staff in the Biblical and bureaucratic senses. Winston's news release announcing her job said she was attracted to the Senator's office because her mother had died of emphysema.

Cecilia told me the hearing was in recess while Senator DeWeerd made a teleconference with some anti-smoking activists in Sri Lanka. "Maybe Winston ought to go to Sri Lanka and set up shop," I said. "It would be one way we could raise the average IQs of two nations."

Cecilia laughed heartily, then put on her business face.

"The Sri Lankans have a serious problem with youth smoking," she said. She said twelve percent of the schoolchildren between the ages of fifteen and twenty were regular smokers.

We chatted for a while about the sorry state of the world's economy. Cecilia said Winston DeWeerd was gaining support every day from the international anti-tobacco community.

I was pretty dubious about that. "I'm certain it's only a matter of a few weeks until Winston will be able to fund a Smoker Colony on the Moon and get rid of all vestiges of tobacco on the earth," I said.

"The moon is out of the question, but his message is gaining acceptance every day," she said. I shrugged noncommittally and walked to the door.

Her parting words chilled me. "I hear you're working on a story about Milano Nagurski."

***

SMOKE JUMPERS

I took a last look at Cecilia's five-foot-eight body and left to take my seat in the hearing room. The place was packed with Winston's people. The Chairman of the Board of the parent Total Sensitivity movement was flanked by five aides. A guy I recognized as the president of Totally Sensitive Lawyers of America was trying to get the big man's attention.

Cecilia appeared with a sheaf of papers for Winston and it occurred to me that Cecilia had managed to bring at least some semblance of order to Winston's Kennedyesque life. The pre-Cecilia Winston would hop into bed with any woman who appeared to have a fifty-one percent likelihood of possessing a vagina. The post-Cecilia version had that smirky and satisfied look but Winston's roaring libido appeared to be toned down to a whimper under Cecilia's capable control.

There were Winston sex-and-smoking jokes that predated my arrival in the press corps. My personal favorite is the one in which Winston's long-suffering wife, Virginia, tells Winston for damned certain that she is fed up with his fooling around and is leaving him the next time he pops into bed with some bimbo. The story goes that Virginia comes home early from her garden club meeting and finds Winston in their waterbed, in the tender embrace of a midget nymphomaniac. "I'm leaving you, Winston!" she screams. "Virginia...Virginia..." he soothes. "Can't you see? I'm just tapering off."

I could see from Winston's face that there was no joke afoot in the land. Winston had the same set to his tough-looking jaw that he had when he told a Capitol Hill news conference he was divorcing Virginia because his private investigator had obtained videotape of Virginia, lying in the sack with her tennis instructor. Nude. Smoking. Pulling on a cigarette and obviously enjoying the nicotine rush in the calm afterglow of sex. Winston said he could forgive her infidelity. But not the smoking.

He had kept the set to his face when he nodded soberly to Cecilia to start the videotape. As iron-balls political hypocrisy goes, it ranked right up there with one of the thousands of stories the oldtimers tell about Teddy Kennedy, the horny white-haired old whale from Massachusetts. A woman reporter said Teddy

131

Kennedy dedicated a center for sexually harassed women. She said he did it with a straight face and a tell-tale bulge at the front of his pants. Winston doesn't read much, but he was always a big Kennedy fan. Teddy was his favorite. Winston admired a guy who could pretend he screwed women in the name of chastity, and get away with it.

Today I could see that Winston was wound up like a politician about to get his first gratuity. Winston almost never disappoints my sense of him. "Last night," he said in his most sincerely outraged voice, "rebel tobacconists in Georgia fired on a Smoke Jumper helicopter on a peaceful mission. This is another in a series of illegal attacks by the merchants of death."

We were all taking notes like crazy. Winston used the "Merchants of Death" stuff so much that those of us abbreviate it. My Winston notes are full of "MOD" this and "MOD" that.

"Today, I am introducing a bill to confiscate the guns owned by any person who has a record of allegations of violations of the National Tobacco Abuse Or Production Act," Winston said. I made a note to get our Atlanta Bureau to check on the Georgia shooting. The Atlanta tobacco rebels had to be crazy, shooting at a Smoke Jumper helicopter. The Jumpers are mean bastards and they've got better equipment and armament than the Army or Marines. Winston has seen to that.

There had been a time when a bill like Winston's would have gotten the National Rifle Association and the American Civil Liberties Union in one of those strangely American unholy alliances. That time was past. The ACLU membership, meeting in the pristine splendor of a fine hotel in New York City's smoke-free zone, had decided five years earlier that the act of smoking was a violation of the rights of the killers, communists, Ku Kluxers and kooks that the ACLU loved so deeply. The NRA tried to fight Winston's bill but its clout on Capitol Hill had been diluted by the surprising growth of Smoke-Free Shooters of America.

SFSA membership rocketed after a tear-jerking story in the Air Monitor. Founder Cleon Biggs, a roughhewn business-man from Wyoming, told the story of a wilderness guide who developed lung cancer from years of close contact with cigarette-puffing hunters. Cleon Biggs said he had watched as the mountain man shriveled from a burly two hundred and twenty pounds down to a pitiful one-hundred thirty, and died with a fly-fishing rod in his hands on the banks of a trout stream. Cleon said the cancer patient was his father. I had been filling in on the Air Monitor copy desk the night the story came in and I had questioned the premise. I asked our Denver bureau to fill in some of the medical questions that any idiot might have. For instance, how much second-hand cigarette smoke can a guy inhale when he spends his days in the Grand Tetons and his nights sitting around a campfire. Katricia Coyne had stepped in and railroaded the story onto the Air Monitor's front page.

I was in a pack of reporters. I noticed that Cecilia Word was staring our way. Her flawless face appeared to be anything but serene. I looked over my shoulder to see what, or who, was disturbing Cecilia so mightily. Pierre Latouf waved jauntily my way and made a motion with his hand as if he were cocking a pistol.

CHAPTER 17

I kissed my first woman and smoked my first cigarette on the same day; I have never had time for tobacco since. Arturo Toscanini (1867-1957) Italian conductor

***

I wrote my Winston DeWeerd story. The desk editor said Katricia Coyne had slotted it for the lead item in every edition. Then J.R. Tyson and I left to hit the reception co-sponsored by the Air Monitor and the Anti-Tobacco News Network. It wasn't as if we were lucky enough to be invited. Katricia had made it clear that anybody who wasn't working, or dying, should either show up or expect to spend the rest of his or her career doing in-depth interviews for Little Lungs. Little Lungs is the weekly supplement we distribute to the grade schools.

The poor schmucks who have to work on Little Lungs get to interview children about smoking. Since the kids don't know anything about smoking, the only way to fill up the crap columns for Little Lungs is to get the kids to talk about how much they hate smoking. And all kids hate smoking. Little Lungs might be a cut above doing locker-room interviews in football. It's pretty grim duty.

J.R. and I cleared the tobacco alarms into the reception area and ran into the only person in the history of the Air Monitor who ever turned an assignment to Little Lungs into something with real journalistic impact, assuming there is such a thing as real journalistic impact.

I said hello to Kristen Price, who is now a reporter for one of the networks.

"Television agrees with you, Kristen," I said.

"Thanks," she said. She gave me a big hug and did the same for J.R. J.R. shuddered a little when he got his. He doesn't care much for the Kristens of the world. Kristen Price was an Air Monitor intern a few years back. She managed to piss Katricia Coyne at their first meeting. Interns who don't irritate Katricia usually get to tag along with regular staff members and do some semblance of real stories. But Kristen didn't show the proper respect for Katricia and it looked like she was going to get to go back to college with a clip file chock full of stuff like, "I hate smoaking becuz smoaking maked my Father croke whin he wuz ohnly thirdy yrs old."

But Kristen wasn't going to let Katricia beat her. Kristen figured she was going to be a big name in journalism some day and she persevered, even at Little Lungs. She was fighting to stay awake one afternoon, listening to a group of third-graders. Then the eight-year-old daughter of an Assistant Secretary of State blurted out: "My mommy and daddy smoke."

Kristen launched into the first recorded instance of investigative journalism in the history of Little Lungs. She discovered that the State Department's medical records indicated the Assistant Secretary had an absenteeism record that was roughly twice that for other Assistant Secretaries. That was enough proof of smoking for Kristen, whose story wound up on the front page of the next morning's Air Monitor.

She included comments from the Assistant Secretary, who said that he and his wife had indeed smoked an obligatory cigarette each while on a visit to the home of the chairman of the Japanese conglomerate known as Nicofuji.

Had they known their daughter was watching, he said, they would have declined the cigarettes, despite the possible consequences to the U.S.-Japan trade package being negotiated. He left town in disgrace, only to find that he had been declared persona non grata at the manufacturing firm he worked for before trying to serve his country.

I asked Kristen if she had kept up with the whereabouts of the poor Assistant Secretary.

"Who gives a damn?" she said, flashing that particularly caring smile that they teach people in some television school somewhere.

All of which goes to explain why J.R. and I fear Little Lungs Forever more than we did Short Term Brain Death. I left Kristen and mingled with some of the politicians, business people anti-tobacco hangers-on who populate such gatherings.

Any Air Monitor reception is non-alcoholic. The Air Monitor always insists on that because smoking and drinking have always been associated. Besides, there was one a couple of years ago where one of our circulation people got drunk and was Smoke Jumpered in the alley behind the hotel, holding a red-headed hooker with his left hand and a red-tipped Viceroy with his right.

The reception ended with this jerk black singer from Miami, who calls himself Smokey No. He gave us his new song, "Butt Kickers."

It's a real work of art. It's got to be, because Smokey No got a half-million-dollar award from the Office of Tobacco Abatement Music Division for its lyrics. Music Division says it is "an eloquent yet straightforward commentary on smoking in the argot of the Black Community." I can go along with "straight-forward." I have a little problem with "eloquent." I don't see anything of Edgar Allen Poe or Shakespeare in:

> *"Kick They Butts*
> *"Kick They Butts*
> *"Broads Who Smokes*
> *"Is a Buncha Sluts."*

It's pretty easy to drive me to a drink. Tonight it was a walk. Two hours of anti-smoking propaganda, thirty minutes of videotape and three and a half minutes of Smokey No had numbed my mind so thoroughly that I was having fantasies that I was in politics. I didn't want a drink. I *needed* a drink. And a smoke.

***

J.R. and I were picking our way through the creeps, tourists and crooks when we came upon two cops, wrestling with a bearded guy who was damned close to seven feet tall. The male cop was about J.R.'s size, meaning smallish, and the female was about the size of Smokey No's brain, meaning tiny. A gray-haired woman was lying on the sidewalk, screaming.

The monster had a purse looped over his left arm. I got the distinct impression it wasn't his, since the colors blended very nicely with the suit the gray-haired woman was wearing.

He was wearing the female cop on his back and was holding the male cop by the throat. The male cop was making feeble little swings with his nightstick. I felt sorry for him. His arms were shorter than mine.

Five people were nearby, all wearing the pale-pink uniforms of the Gay Air Police. They were scared to death. The group would make an occasional mass mincing movement toward the fight, then mince en masse backward.

I knew it would be best for everybody if I did something. J.R. Tyson is a martial-arts buff and the paperwork would take hours if I let J.R. handle the big guy. It takes a long time to explain how a monster of a Washington mugger loses his spleen, nose, throat and knees to a skinny little guy about half his size.

I moved in close. I guess he thought I had minced in close because he never even looked at me. He just said, "Back off, faggot."

It was a great shot. I had fought a couple of guys who were six-foot-six and had to pay attention to keep from hitting them below the belt. This one was a joy. I wanted to hit him below the belt. The punch didn't travel far, but it was the best left I could bring up. I transferred my weight perfectly and had all two-hundred and five pounds behind it. Straight at the big guy's balls.

J.R. swears that the burst of air from the monster blew the male cop's cap off, but I didn't see it. I was looking at the guy's eyes. I think he had come to believe I wasn't in the Gay Air Police.

I moved in a step and ripped him in the balls again with my left hand, then caught him on the nose with the best right I've ever thrown. His nose more or less disappeared and I came in damned close. I hit him eight or ten more times before he collapsed. The woman cop rode him down. She looked like a uniformed squirrel clinging to a chain-sawed oak tree.

The Gay Air Police crowd surged forward and started kicking hell out of the guy, which bothered me only because their technique was so poor.

The woman cop shooed them away, grabbed the victim's purse and then clamped the electric handcuffs on the guy. The gray-haired woman tried to grab her purse from the cop. It spilled open and a pack of Marlboros tumbled onto the ground.

One of the Gay Air Police grabbed the old lady in a choke hold, then let go when I started toward him. The male cop put his electric handcuffs on the woman, slipped the Marlboros into an evidence bag and it was over. I got their names. I wanted to check later to see if he got more time than she did. I knew he wouldn't, but hope springs infernal.

***

I convinced the Gay Air Police that we had to go to an important meeting and couldn't take them up on their offer to buy us a bunch of drinks. I wouldn't have been so nice, but one of them had recognized my face from a picture in the Air Monitor.

We found a cab, finally, and my right hand was throbbing so badly that I knew I had a good excuse to stiff J.R. on my share of the fare. I was saving my gumption so I could reach into my pocket for money for a drink. It took ten minutes before we got to our favorite Post-Brain-Death Bar, The End. J.R. paid the fare. He figured his hand felt good enough that it was a fair trade.

The End is a gathering place for the informal smoking underground. A comfortably seedy place to the north of Capitol Hill, The End has the best smoking connections in town. We always ask the front bartender for a spot in the French Room. It's a subtlety that plays on the name of Jean Nicot, the Frenchman who lent his name to nicotine. Smoking Jean was the ambassador to Portugal, who took the Demon Tobacco to France, linking his name forever to the genus Nicotiana to which tobacco belongs.

J.R. and I had handed over fifty bucks for ten weeds and coughed up two bucks apiece for the gloves, protective head

138

covering and gelatin mixture. I got the waitress to help me put on the right glove. I obviously had hit the big guy on the skull. I've got small hands and I know damned well that punch hurt me a lot more than it did him.

I got the waitress to help me put on the gel. It's mostly standard Vaseline but you can put it on your face when you smoke, then wipe it off when you're ready to leave. If you happen to get stopped by a traffic cop who does the Nicotine Wipe, you'll come up clean every time.

The French Room has a fireplace going during business hours for ditching the protective gear and cigarettes, in case the Smoke Jumpers come a'calling. They never have. I figure the management pays them off. The Air Monitor editorial page says the Jumpers are the essence of morality in law enforcement but J.R. and I are pretty certain the Jumpers and the OTA are probably the pacemakers in federal corruption. They don't have to explain anything to Congress, or anybody, thanks to Winston DeWeerd's legislative mischief.

Some of J.R.'s former Marine pals joined us at The End. J.R. was telling them I had been a hero before we got there. He told them how I had fearlessly stepped in and clobbered the big guy. He didn't say I jumped in because I figured J.R. might kill him and we'd spend the rest of our lives talking to the Metro Police.

Larry Flournoy is one of J.R.'s Marine buddies. Flournoy still looks like a Marine. Short hair and hardly an ounce of fat on his body. He's the only stockbroker I've ever met who could whip a bull and then sodomize a bear.

Larry asked me quietly if J.R. had ever told me the Iraq story. I said J.R. had talked about his time in the Middle East but hadn't told any war stories. I knew he had been on a sniper squad of some sort. Larry said J.R. should have gotten the Medal of Honor in Iraq. We're in an extremely anti-military society and I wondered aloud if the prevailing pacifism was the reason J.R. wasn't honored.

"Didn't have anything to do with this one," the man said. He went on to tell me the story. He said the five-man sniper squad had dropped in near Maximum Leader Saddam Omar Hassan's desert redoubt. They were about a mile away and trying to figure how they could shoot their way past a couple of hundred armed goons when J.R. saw the Maximum Leader, walking outside the compound. He said J.R. said, "I'll take him from here." Several people pointed out that John Wayne couldn't have made the shot with Jesus Christ as his Special Effects Director.

Larry said J.R. just smiled and kept adjusting his laser sight. J.R. squeezed off three shots and everybody was saddling up for the battle. They couldn't believe it when Hassan fell. Flournoy said he could have read the Air Monitor while the bullets were in the air.

That hacked me a bit. We don't get much respect at the Air Monitor. Our newspaper is definitely deplorable but it's big. Still, I was stirred. I asked why J.R. didn't at least get a medal of some kind, if not the nation's highest military honor. Larry Flournoy said J.R.'s long shots had to take down the French ambassador to get to Hassan and the French were supposed to be neutral in the war. The official story was that Hassan and the Frenchman died in a coup attempt at the hands of Hassan's inner circle. I was so impressed by the fact that J.R. Tyson had ended the war that I almost forgave him for pretending to pass out drunk and setting Katricia Coyne in pursuit of my body. Not completely, but almost. There's a moral difference between ending a justifiable war and trying to start an unthinkable piece.

Larry and the guys left and J.R. and I were surveying the room when my eyes fell on Barbara Savage. I knew I had found something more addictive than nicotine.

Her fair complexion shone, even in the dim light. The gelatin makes most of us look like drag queens or zombies. It made her even more beautiful. She had a halo of medium-length brown hair, blue eyes and sparkling teeth. She appeared to be about five-feet-eight, with long and slender legs that looked athletic, even at rest under the medium-length skirt. She was donning her smoking paraphernalia. She was elegant, even doing that.

She was with two other women. I guess my staring was

pretty obvious because she looked at me and smiled.

J.R. Tyson doesn't say much but he doesn't miss much, either. "You're dead meat," he growled, sipping on his bourbon and water between drags on the ersatz Camel Filter.

I'm a little less than remarkable on my approaches to golf greens, fistfights or women. In golf, I take one club more than I think I should, then try to take a relaxed swing. With fistfights, I usually try to talk my way out of it, then attack as if my life depends on it, once I determine there's going to be a hassle. I can't stand the sight of blood, especially if it's going to be mine.

Women are considerably more complicated than fistfights and almost as difficult to approach as golf greens. With women, I let my agile and fertile mind click off a couple of hundred possible sophisticated witticisms, then walk up and say something memorable. Like "hello." I'm better at golf.

She glanced at me occasionally. I was staring. I took the last drag on the phony Merit 100, got a fresh drink and stepped across the room to where she and her friends were sitting. My mind was teeming with sophisticated witticisms as I took the last step. I had narrowed it down to "hello" but never got it out.

She turned me to rubble again with that smile. The one that could grow flowers in the Arctic. "You're Rob Reynolds," she said, standing and holding out her hand. "I'm Barbara Savage and I hate Winston DeWeerd as much as you do."

Barbara is one of those people who could put a shark at ease. She had a business degree from Cornell University and worked for a consulting business that had something to do with foreign trade. She had been born in Montana, married too young, and ditched a worthless husband a couple of years back. "I kept his last name," Barbara laughed. "It's so much more memorable than Jones."

I guess my curiosity wormed its way onto my face. "Yes," she said, "daughter of Ed Jones. Winston's first political victim."

I couldn't believe it. I remembered that Ed Jones had two daughters. I remembered both of them were young. I didn't enjoy remembering that, especially with our knees touching under the table and those wonderful eyes glued to my face.

I asked about her father, the man Winston left as a Montana laughingstock in the race for Governor. "Dad is a proud man. Or was, at least. He still raises his sheep, but he never socializes any more. He just sits at home and drinks Scotch and smokes. God, does he smoke! He says anything Winston DeWeerd hates has to be a gift from God."

I took her home after we ditched and burned the smoking gear. She had a brother in one of the Colonies and was afraid her father was going to end up there. She really did hate Winston DeWeerd as much as I do. It was a beginning.

CHAPTER 18

LONDON — British newspapers, educators and historians are reportedly enraged by the action of the chief United States anti-tobacco agency to minimize the role of World War II leader Winston Churchill. Senator Winston DeWeerd said in a speech that research indicates Churchill was so strongly addicted to tobacco that American Office of Tobacco Abatement researchers believe that most of Churchill's writing was done by an aide. "Winston Churchill after a box of cigars and a bottle of brandy had more unimpaired ability than the Montana madman. Americans had best take a look at their anti-tobacco fixation," the London Messenger said in an editorial.

***

J.R. Tyson searched all the public databases for information on the Colonies. I knew J.R. could bust into the Office of Tobacco Abatement's private stock, but that would have to be a last resort.

"I can get in," J.R. said, "But there's no way to keep them from knowing we've come and gone. And there's virtually no way to keep them from knowing who we are, or at least whose password I used."

We looked over what we had.

"I didn't recall that the Colonies went up this fast," I said.

"Easy to build things when you're the one who prints the money to pay for them," J.R. growled.

The files showed that the three Colonies were built on

143

land nobody wanted. Land that wasn't near people. Winston DeWeerd got the appropriations moving and there was the promise of billions of dollars in savings. The lung benefit. The health benefit. The productivity benefit. The young-mind benefit. There were going to be so many benefits from smoking that it was going to be unbelievable. As usual, it was.

"I'd say they went up faster than a fundamentalist preacher grabbing a hundred-dollar bill," I said.

"Nothing's that fast," J.R. scoffed. "Maybe faster than a television preacher grabbing a fifty-dollar whore..."

J.R. tells me I tend to exaggerate, except when I'm writing news copy. Writing news for a living smothers your imagination under a blanket of things like, "He said" and "She said" and "The Office of Tobacco Abatement announced..."

Newspapers are that way. There are a lot of reasons why not much newspaper writing gets remembered past the garbage pickup, but one good one is the tons of attribution that editors throw in. A lot of it means less than nothing.

The Air Monitor has some editors who think the readers expect everything to come from some source other than the reporter. I personally am a mild-mannered agnostic but I've always wanted to do the story of the Second Coming of Jesus Christ. I admit I would feel good, knowing there was indeed a Supreme Being. But mostly I'd like to win the standing thousand dollar bet I've got with my pal J.R.

My side of the bet is that I'd be in someplace like Assbreath, Alabama, and I would file the story. A story like that wouldn't need any embellishment, so the simple fact of it would be the most important thing. And I'll bet the thousand and more that some jerk on the Air Monitor desk would add his two words of "attribution" to it and it would hit the newsstands reading: "Jesus Christ returned today, police said." Another thing we would have to do would be work our peculiar angle into it. If He declined to condemn tobacco right off, we'd have to find one. Maybe we could point out that Assbreath, Alabama, was one of the OTA's Model Smoke-Free Cities. Almost every town is, if it wants federal money. The federal money is the carrot. Of course, there's always the stick.

J.R. had piled up computer files on the Charleston, West Virginia, case.

"I wonder how many of those Charleston people are in the Colonies?" I said.

"We'll never know until we decide to violate a couple of dozen federal laws and hack our way into the OTA database," J.R. said.

"Do you really think they keep all that information in one database?" I said.

"No question about it," J.R. said. "Computer people usually have tunnel vision. They think they're so damned smart that they can make something foolproof. They don't realize that foolproof doesn't exist."

We read the stories about the stick and carrot routine that worked in Charleston. The problem arose when Charleston's stiff-necked realists refused to sign the Municipal Anti-Tobacco Compact that Winston DeWeerd hangs onto every piece of legislation that has anything to do with aid to cities. The sudden arrival of a special battalion of Smoke Jumpers and the sudden departure of every federal buck brought the hillbilly theorists back to reality in record time. The Office of Tobacco Abatement doesn't miss much.

J.R.'s searching had even pulled up some material from the OTA Youth Division, which mentioned the Colonies. Youth Division even publishes a book for religion institutions. The book tells kids that Jesus Christ would be militantly against smoking and would do the Old Testament routine on those who insisted on doing it. It's a pretty good stretch of logic, given the fact that Jesus hit the planet a bunch of hundreds of years ahead of the first matches and more than a thousand years before the first cigarettes.

If Jesus Christ were to return to one of the Colonies, the Air Monitor and a lot of the federal government would want to see his birth certificate. Hypothesize that He might light up a weed in sympathy with the benighted colonists. That would be a violation of Winston DeWeerd's Anti-Health Political Statements Act and they'd toss Him in with the rest of the puffers. Winston came up with this particularly venomous little bill after a group of professors at a little college in Vermont fomented a smoke-in to protest a Smoke Jumper raid on a pep rally.

Winston has explained time and again that there are no violations of freedoms involved in the summary disposition of people to the Colonies. The smokers are simply relocated so they can be with their own kind. Since smokers are criminals and their smoke is lethal, the non-smoking population is kept away for reasons of health and public safety.

"Does that line of thinking sound familiar to you?" I asked.

"Sure does," J.R. said. "I believe it's exactly the same kind of rhetoric that came from Southern sheriffs back in the 1950s when they were trying to explain that the Negroes really preferred to stay with their own kind."

The computer files contained a tortured explanation of the benefits of isolating a smoker from family. OTA said the average smoker regretted the harm his or her secondhand smoke had done and had an improved self-image when removed from pressures and people of the past. The OTA document explained that non-smoking family members are allowed to visit the smokers only by video hookups. The Office of Tobacco Abatement Criminal Rehabilitation Division, which runs the three domestic colonies, says face-to-face visits resulted in the handing off of cigarettes to smuggle to the outside world, where the going price is a minimum hundred dollars for a package.

The career smoker is allowed to ruin his or her lungs at will in a Colony life, OTA says. The career smoker is incorrigible and simply must be contained so he or she can't inflict the habit on others. Cigarettes are available everywhere, for free, or at least that's what OTA says. The announcements indicate that OTA holds its nose and buys them at arm's length from one of the new tobacco empires that sprang up with Colombian addresses.

It's not all that large a departure from tradition, when one thinks about it. The government was the first big buyer of the drug LSD, which put a couple of generations of kids into orbit. The

146

government even had a program once to give people syphilis, without the benefit of the fun part of getting it. The government lured companies into making asbestos, then stepped back and pretended horror when thousands of people died from lung disease caused by exposure to asbestos.

Some schmuck from Vermont suggested that OTA simply buy it's cigarettes for the Colonies directly from the old USA tobacco barons. It would cut the price, he said. But OTA stuck to its policy of buying weeds through a third party. OTA is a law-abiding agency and a Winston DeWeerd law prohibits OTA from doing business directly with the former Merchants of Death now prospering in their new digs across the waters.

There are a few non-smoking enclaves inside the Colonies, OTA says, for the Smoke Jumper guards who keep order among the dying criminals. OTA occasionally releases videos of the Jumper guards, all masked against secondhand smoke and keeping hawk-eyed vigil over the nicotine-crazed Colonists.

"I've never understood how the courts have let this go on," I said.

"Neither have I," J.R. agreed. "I guess it was the crime problem and the times. Smoker arrests were filling the jails, emptying them of bad guys, and people blamed the smokers, not the system."

We went through the information without getting much real information about the Colonies.

J.R. scoffed at the OTA document that said the Colonies were too dangerous for people to visit. "Difficult for an ex-Marine to believe he has to be protected from a few thousand smokers. They were passive people when they went there. I'll bet they're still passive now," J.R. said.

Neither of us even mentioned the idea of writing a story for the Air Monitor. Publications like the Air Monitor are happy to take the OTA grant money and pretend that the Colonies are something like a maximum-security ward for thousands of Charles Manson types.

I had an idea. "Let's see if we can find Happy Peeler. She might have be able to help us."

"I ran Happy in the computer a couple of days ago," J.R. said. He said the national database showed Happy Peeler had gone from Washington television reporter to a public-relations job in Asia for one of the old tobacco companies.

"Interesting career move," I said.

"Not when you consider that Happy's home was burglarized five times by various anti-tobacco groups and she was tired of nothing but death threats on her Message Center," J.R. said.

Happy had been the one exception to the OTA shroud on the colonies. She had managed to get inside the Texas Colony with one of those pocket-sized mini-cameras but her report wasn't very enlightening. Happy is a knockout blonde and was approached by a Smoke Jumper guard who immediately noticed that her clothing and hair bore no telltale scent of tobacco.

The dead giveaway, of course, was that the smoker "S" on her forehead wasn't the proper shade of yellow.

OTA denies it, but I got some names of Jumper guards assigned to Colony duty. I've checked their hometowns and former duty stations and it seems that they never seem to get reassigned to regular butt-busting duties.

"I get this compulsion to oil my guns every time I think about the Happy Peeler story," J.R. snarled.

"There are two of us who feel that way," I said.

"There are a lot more of us than that," J.R. said.

J.R. is right about more. I'm just not certain how many more there are.

CHAPTER 19

Winston DeWeerd drummed his fingers on the massive mahogany desk as the American Medical Association's witness droned through his testimony. Winston knew some people called him intolerant. They didn't know the goddamned half of it. Calling Winston DeWeerd intolerant was complimentary. A little like telling Hitler he seemed to be somewhat insensitive to Jews, homosexuals and gypsies.

He kept his face straight while the goddamned doctor droned on. He hated the goddamned doctors. Not as much as the goddamned lawyers, or the wimpy-assed politicians he spent his life with. But he still hated doctors a lot.

The goddamned doctors had their shot at tobacco. Their surgeon general put together a bunch of the clowns back when men were still wearing ducktail hairdos and women all had brassieres. In 1964 the wimpy assholes came out with a report that smoking was bad for health.

Winston chuckled at his recollections. If the yo-yos had been the Weather Bureau's commission on Montana weather they might pitched a tent in Cut Bank for a couple of years and then concluded: "It Gets A Tad Cool Up Here In The Winter." Their work wound up with a little line on cigarette packages that said "Smoking May Be Hazardous to Your Health." Not that "Smoking May Put Your Dumb Ass In A Sling..." or "Smoking Will Fry Your Frigging Lungs Harder Than A Republican's Brain." "May be hazardous..." Big frigging deal.

Winston made the requisite eye contact with the droning doctor and nodded as if he were in rueful agreement with the physician's conclusions on cilia. Winston's mind, freed by three martinis at lunch, was racing well ahead of the good doctor on the subject of cilia, the millions of waving threads that try to keep the lungs clear of foreign objects.

He wrote a note on his personalized paper and passed it to his press secretary. "Cilia, my ever-loving ass," it read.

The doctor was decrying the destruction of cilia by tobacco tars. Silly little assholes in a smoker, those cilia. Waving like a stoned hitchhiker in the good people. The ones who don't smoke. Harder than a horny pissant's dick in a smoker. Lying down in the muck and the yellow crud while every piece of crap in every breath piled up where the cilia used to wave.

DeWeerd wanted to scream instructions at the doctor. "Tell them cilia in a smoker is like whale shit in the Potomac!" But the goddamned press people would call it "rude" and would go interview some jerk ichthyologist who would say there hadn't ever been a recorded instance of a whale taking a dump in the Potomac.

Winston pretended to stretch his slender six-foot-two frame and stole a glance at Cecilia Word, his press secretary and mistress. The doctor was clearly the biggest boob. Cecilia, he thought, was the best set of them. Cecilia could get a group of press people together by a couple of calls. Winston figured a press release Cecilia handed out with one boob slightly exposed was worth a couple of inches of type. A brief brush from Cecilia's front was worth a two-column headline.

Winston DeWeerd glanced at Robert J. Reynolds, sitting at the press table and doodling on his copy of the good doctor's transcript as the witness droned on. One of the only press assholes who was always lusting to jump on him, Cecilia's tits or no, was his own half-brother, he thought.

Winston hunched his shoulders and assumed a thoughtful pose as the physician got to the end of his boring recitation. He was pleased to see that the news people became more attentive. Even his jerk half-brother.

CHAPTER 20

There was a note on the Message Center screen when I came in from my Saturday run. It said I had been called again by the slippery Veronica French. I had tried to return her calls from the newspaper so often I had come to believe she might be a wraith with a name that sounded like either a pretty woman or a beautiful sex act.

Veronica French obviously had her own Message Center because she answered with: "Hello, Mr. Reynolds. You don't know me, but I was married to Joe French. Possibly you remember Joe."

I laughed. "Call me Rob, please. My face and I remember Joe French very well. We'll forget Joe right after the Japanese forget Harry Truman." I could tell from the silence that Veronica French was one of those average Americans. I mean somebody who probably thinks Pearl Harbor is a fat Mississippi woman who sings gospel music. My analogy hadn't been all that good, since most Japanese probably forgot Harry Truman and the Hiroshima atomic bomb years ago. They own whatever they want of this country now, including almost all of Hawaii, so the past was way less than prologue.

"Well, you remember him, then," she said. It was a statement and a question and I wanted to put her at ease.

"I remember Joe very well," I said, "he was the toughest man I ever fought. I remember visiting him in the hospital after the fight. I was a lot closer to crying than he was."

"That's Joe French," she said.

"I couldn't find Joe in the database," I said. "What's he doing now?"

"Time," she said, "time in the Texas Colony."

That explained why she said she was Joe's ex-wife. I have always held that Winston's mandatory divorces for smokers to be one of the more venomous little pieces of legislation ever put together by Winston and his fellow serpents. Murderers get to sleep with their wives or girlfriends once a week. Smokers are cut off at the family tree.

There had been the possibility that Veronica French was a phony. Since the calls started at the paper, she could have been calling on one of the Air Monitor's Smoker Security checks. I discounted the idea now because it was a weekend and Veronica sounded like a live human being, even if she had slept through Harry Truman and Hiroshima.

The people the Air Monitor hires strike you as having slept through everything until yesterday. Security hires local teenagers to make the calls and almost anybody can identify their clumsy reading of the script. I say "almost" because a couple of people have gotten their one-way ticket off the staff by showing too sympathetic a response to people pretending to represent smokers.

I decided to activate the Stress Level feature on the Message Center. It costs twenty-five bucks a month, flat, and another three bucks every time you use it, but Stress Level is worth the money. You can double the price and ask for Stress Level and Probable Truthfulness, which I decided to do. My video screen started flashing with a message that read: "Stress Level High, Probable Truthfulness Indicator 95 percent."

The Probable Truthfulness Indicator is nice, but hardly foolproof. I hit it once on a call from Katricia Coyne, who was telling me I had to come to her apartment for an emergency meeting of the Tobacco Smuggling Task Force. It registered an 85 percent "Probable Truthfulness Indicator" on Katricia. I didn't really have any choice on going, but I went with the heart of a lion and the libido of an amoeba.

Sure enough, I found Katricia waiting for me, alone, with a glass of bourbon fast in her hand and a black negligee loose on her shoulders. I had been lucky enough to suspect the Probable

Truthfulness Indicator and had arranged for J.R. Tyson to ring me on my portable telephone. Katricia probably believes my story that the caller was a news source a little less than I now believe the Probable Truthfulness Indicator. The Message Center boiler-plate message covers Katricia-style calls, however. You can't get out of the Probable Truthfulness section without a warning that the indicator can't be trusted when the caller is intoxicated or psychotic. Katricia isn't always both, because I've never seen her drunk at work.

I got a warm feeling that the Probable Truthfulness Indicator on Veronica French was more reliable than it had been with Katricia. "How did Joe get arrested?" I asked.

"The Smoke Jumpers got him in the Buffalo Bust almost six years ago," she said. She said Joe French was bartender at a Holiday Inn when the Jumpers came in. They had found ten cartons of phony Camel Filters in his locker and he had been sent to the Texas Colony both as a convicted smoker and a convicted dealer.

"Was Joe a smoker?"

"Big time. Two packs a day. It almost broke us. He was dealing cigarettes to try to support his habit."

It wasn't all that unusual a case. I have covered a lot of stories involving people who couldn't afford the hundred-buck-a-pack price of today's cigarettes and went for one of the illegal connections to try to support a heavy nicotine problem.

History was on the side of the Joe French story. Queen Elizabeth I was taken with the charms of Sir Walter Raleigh, the guy who popularized pipe smoking in England. She was such a puffer that she required the ladies of her court to smoke a pipe at least once. She died in 1603 and James I became king. He hated smoking and Sir Walter Raleigh, in that order. English puffing was supposed to be at an end when King James tried to limit the tobacco supply from Virginia and the price of the Demon Weed rose until tobacco cost more than silver.

James had raised the duty on tobacco by four-thousand percent, thinking that would price the Demon Weed out of the market. King James could have been an economist for Jimmy

153

Carter. King Jimbob the Smokeless created a new smuggling industry and British farmers began growing tobacco for the first time. James did what every good politician does. He went for a piece of the action. James had his government take over the importation and sale of tobacco and made a ton of money.

I punched up the Buffalo Bust while Veronica French was telling me Joe's arrest had left her with one dead daughter, a young son and a bad job in the City of Buffalo Tourism Department. I managed not to laugh at the thought of anybody being gainfully employed in the Buffalo Tourism Department. The continuing economic crisis has hit places like Buffalo harder than others. Buffalo is old, cold in the winter and hotter than hell in the summer. The unemployment rate in Buffalo hasn't been below ten percent in my memory. One of the only bright spots in the local economy has been Canada, which gives Buffalonians a shot at the cigarette-smuggling market. King James lives.

The database on the Buffalo Holiday Inn bust showed it was, indeed, a big one. Twenty-five people arrested, twenty of them smokers and the other five both on smoking and dealing. The manager of the Holiday Inn had avoided a trip to one of the Colonies by doing a racing dive under the wheels of a Smoke Jumper transportation van.

I didn't have any appointments on my busy social calendar. I was waiting to hear from Barbara Savage. Veronica French was paying for the call, which is another neat thing about the Message Center. I didn't think it was worth paying Baby Bell to check out the Probable Truthfulness of her story of poverty. I figured anybody who would admit to working for the Buffalo Tourism Department wouldn't lie. I hit the Reverse Charges option and I could hear Veronica's voice relax a little. Her screen had told her that I was now paying for the call, if it was all right with her. It was all right with her.

Still, it was obvious that she was holding back. I couldn't blame her for being suspicious about talking with anybody from the Air Monitor, even if she made the call. After all, her husband was in the Texas Colony and the Air Monitor regularly editorialized that the Smoker Colonies were the only hope of saving hupersonkind from the ravages of the Demon Weed.

I decided to be frank. Maybe she had a Probable Truthfulness Indicator in her Message Center setup. I doubted she did, since she kept talking about how tough it was to make it as a single parent.

"I don't believe there is anything I can do for Joe," I said, adding: "If you can think of something, I'd be interested in hearing about it."

She started crying. You don't need a Probable Truthfulness Indicator to tell you when sobs like the ones I was hearing were coming from the heart. "I don't know why I'm calling you. You work for that goddamned newspaper that says Joe is a mass murderer," she said. She cried some more. I pointed out that the "mass murderer" crap came from our editorial page, not me.

It seemed to put her a bit at ease. "There's something wrong. There's something badly wrong. If you could look at the videotapes I think you'd know what I mean."

"Could you send them to me?"

She seemed surprised at such an inane suggestion. "Of course not. You know that they only play on the OTA monitor. The people from OTA say they'll erase themselves if they're moved more than twenty feet from the monitor." I would curse myself later for not believing that and thinking about what it might mean.

I knew that the Colonists were allowed one video visit a month with their families, but this was the first I had ever heard about the technical games. Reporters only get to see tapes the OTA releases. OTA has always explained that the privacy of the families and the inmates must be protected and that the tapes can be shown to outsiders only after a laborious process involving written releases from all parties.

It sounds like bullshit but we're so afraid of lawsuits that we have to go through laborious processes all the time, so I'll have to plead guilty to believing something that OTA says. It doesn't happen all that often, but I had never given this particular area much thought. Now that it had come up, it occurred to me that there was a certain stone quality to the tapes I had been allowed to view.

I had always thought the inmates were heavily coached, or were trying to curry favor with their jailers.

The thing that had puzzled me about the videos was the smoking. Even a convicted smoker can stop long enough to make a five-minute video, but the inmates were almost always smoking. It was a little like a child molester making a video for his mother while fingering an anatomically correct baby doll.

Veronica French had left the telephone to check an "Intruder" signal on the message center. It occurred to me as I waited that I could remember seeing only two videos in which the inmate wasn't smoking. And both had involved people whose bodies had been so ravaged by tobacco-related disease that they could barely speak.

She returned. The Intruder was a neighbor kid looking for a lost cat. She resumed telling me what a nice man Joe French was, down below the depths of his nicotine habit. She talked about how her son had never known his father except for the videotapes from the Texas Colony. Her voice cracked again and she started sobbing.

The crying made me feel rotten about what I was thinking, which was that the next-to-last thing I wanted to do today was go to Buffalo on my own credit card. I always rank abominable choices with next-to-last being the first one I mention. That gives permanent Last Thing primacy to the thought of hitting the sack with Katricia Coyne. There has to be some constancy to a man's thinking, or he runs the risk of turning into J.R. Tyson, George Bush or Jimmy Carter.

"I'll be there before midnight. I don't know about the flights to Buffalo at this time of day," I said. I told her I might bring Barbara Savage.

Veronica French was chary about anyone else coming with me. "She's not connected with...with..."

"With OTA? No, she's in business in the District. You can trust her."

Her voice gained some strength. "I hope I can trust you. The man from OTA says it's a felony to show an inmate videotape to an outsider."

"I've never heard of that one," I said. I admitted to her that didn't mean much. There are some pretty strange laws on the books, thanks to the Office of Tobacco Abatement and Winston DeWeerd. There is always the possibility that Veronica French had been presented with an OTA Special Tobacconist Rule-making.

The most egregious one of those in my experience had been the one in which the OTA Enforcement Division seized the home of a young woman in Barstow, California. Her husband had been sent to one of the Colonies, triggering the possibility of a Special Tobacconist Rule-making. The woman took part in a small civil-rights demonstration in San Francisco. The demonstrators, mostly academics, contended that the Colonies violate the Constitution. The woman had carried a little sign. It read: "Smokers Have Rights Too."

In no time at all, the woman was brought under the special ruling. The OTA investigators found she had failed to divest herself of stock in a mutual fund that owned a small piece of a Japanese conglomerate which had some ownership in one of the old American tobacco giants.

Veronica French thanked me about three dollars worth. I didn't need the Probable Truthfulness Indicator to tell me she appreciated my agreeing to come. I asked her to make a reservation at a hotel near her home. She said she would take care of it and thanked me about a buck-fifty more before we ended the conversation.

It had been an expensive call. She couldn't have afforded it, if anything she said about money had been true. I don't waste money but it doesn't really mean that much to me. I live on my Air Monitor salary, which isn't all that low.

I've done a lot harder work for a lot less money. I had my first job when I was fourteen and worked part-time even when I was in college. I guess I've always wanted to prove to myself that I didn't inherit anything from my biological father, other than a big trust fund. He never had to work and he wound up stoned and dead at a cocaine party with his new wife. He was forty. I was two.

My mother never harped about what an asshole he was,

but there is plenty about Conwood DeWeerd in the public record. Enough that I was proud to bear the Reynolds name of my mother's second husband.

Let's just say that Winston DeWeerd is his father's son. If anybody ever puts together an historical All-America Team of Real Pricks it's damned likely that my biological father and half-brother will be the only father-son act in the starting lineup.

I figure I'll kick back some day and let myself live the life of a rich person. I'll know when it's time. Until then, I haven't even told J.R. Tyson that the guy who shares the little condo is a wealthy man. J.R. knows, anyway, because of his computer hacking. J.R. can find out anything about anybody.

Our Message Center databases are completely separate, so there's no way J.R. could have stolen the passwords to find out about my finances, but he asked a question one afternoon that made it pretty clear that he knows about me. He said: "What would you do if you were the five-hundred and thirty-first wealthiest man in the country?"

"I'd find a roommate who didn't like Country and Western Music," I said. He has never brought it up again.

I called Barbara's portable telephone.

We were developing a wonderful, if strange, relationship. I had been busy at the Air Monitor and her business was doing well. She worked long hours at her office and was often called out of town on short notice. We hadn't staked any proprietary claims on one another but I knew we would get there. Someday.

It wouldn't be on the trip to western New York State. Barbara said an important client had come to town unexpectedly and she was going to have to work all weekend to prepare a presentation for Monday morning. I told her she missed a chance for an all-expense-paid trip to Buffalo. She said she always wanted to go to Buffalo. The Probable Truthfulness Indicator would have had cardiac arrest.

I left a note on the Message Center for J.R. Tyson, telling him I probably wouldn't be back until late Sunday. I didn't tell him any more than that. Some of the security geeks at the newspaper can hack into the top tier of the message centers. J.R.

can hack his way to the bottom.

I've always envied J.R. his computer skills. I can use the damned things, but J.R. understands them. If he were a slimeball, J.R. could probably be the head computer snoop at OTA.

I was thinking about Milano Nagurski's permanently attached tracking device as I tossed some clothing and shaving gear into a flight bag. I was wondering if my Air Monitor security badge was actually a combination tracking device and radio transmitter. I laughed at my paranoia, until I remembered a line I had read in a novel. The main character and his lover had been attacked mysteriously by a gaggle of bad people and all manner of strange things were happening to them. He had said: "Just because you're paranoid doesn't mean somebody's not out to get you."

I rank that for truthfulness right beside: "He who hesitates is management."

I removed the Air Monitor security badge from my wallet and tossed it on the kitchen counter. I went to the computer screen in the kitchen and took the icon to the Travel section of the Message Center. I was about to click on Reservations and Buffalo when I remembered that my credit cards were billed electronically to the computer at the Air Monitor. I relaxed my finger at the thought of Air Monitor Cash Management getting a look at the bills. Cash Management is supposed to be an employee benefit. It lets the Air Monitor computers pay my creditors the same way the Air Monitor pays its own: at the last possible moment. I had liked Cash Management until now.

I went to an Automatic Teller Machine down the block, which isn't the smartest thing to do in the District. I double-checked and triple-checked to make certain that several of our city's ATM groupies weren't standing by with a pistol or a knife.

An older woman walked up with a Rottweiler dog and used one of the ATMs. I watched her walk away with her money, then drew out a thousand dollars and caught a cab to the airport. I wanted to stop at The End and have a bourbon and a cigarette, but going through the anti-detection routine would take too long for just one cigarette. I still wanted to do it. I had never before realized how paranoia increased my need for nicotine.

Traffic was light and I got to the airport with no particular problems. It was a good thing I hadn't had a weed. The Smoke Jumper security area was well-staffed and highly motivated. They were using the vacuum on everybody. The tobacco alarm went off when they sucked the lint out of the pant cuffs of a skinny long-haired guy. He was wearing a tee shirt that said, "Ski Mississippi" and was looking downright cool until the alarm went off.

The Jumper in charge was a woman of about my size and build, which would have put her out of the running for the Miss America title if we still did that sort of thing. She slapped the electronic handcuffs on the guy and was dragging him to the Smoke Jumper security area like he had wheels on his heels. He tried to wriggle away and she hit the button on the handcuff control. The blue lightning around his wrists zapped a cockroach in the corner of the hallway.

The line stopped once more when the Jumpers found a couple of cellophane-wrapped Brazilian cigarettes, hidden in the diaper of a cooing and gooing eight-month-old boy. The big Jumper woman didn't even put the cuffs on the kid's mother, a skinny teenager who looked like a fugitive from one of those big rock concerts they had back in the Twentieth Century. The Jumper just grabbed the little woman by her unkempt hair and guided her to Jumper security. The airport security people came and took the diaperless baby, who had started screaming like a banshee. The Jumper stormed out to boss the locals around just as the kid let go with a perfect yellow stream that caught her in the eye. "Great shot," I muttered.

Ms. Smoke Jumper whirled toward me. "What did you say?"

"I said, you'll probably need a shot."

"You're right," she said, "you never know what a smoker's kid might have. They got no resistance, you know."

Maybe there is a God. Maybe He thinks we're such a bunch of losers that he just grants us small and ironic victories.

We landed in Buffalo at 8:15. It was warm and a stiff wind

was assaulting my nose with the scents of Lake Erie. People used to call Cleveland the Mistake on the Lake, at least until the Cleveland Sensitivity Caucus started raising hell. I still call Cleveland the Mistake on the Lake. I figure Buffalo as the Dump Beside the Sump.

People were pairing up with the departing passengers. I saw a short, full-bodied, brown-haired woman checking out the passengers. She smiled when she saw me and flashed a little handwritten sign that read: "I'm Veronica."

Maybe I still look a little like a boxer. More likely she had seen my picture on one of the Air Monitor's billboards. I'm a member of "the greatest anti-tobacco reporting team ever assembled," according to the billboards. They don't bother to say that we're the only anti-tobacco reporting team ever assembled.

I followed her to her car. She drove north. She seemed preoccupied. I said I appreciated her picking me up.

"I got some friends to keep my son. He's asleep by now," she said.

She asked me about my match with her ex-husband and I probably overdid my description of Joe French's prowess. She said she knew that Joe had been a pretty fair fighter. "He had been thinking about turning pro but he said you weren't as fast as the guys he would have to fight as a pro and figured he might have a rough time with people who hit as hard as you did...and did it faster."

I nodded my agreement, thinking all the while that Joe French would have been better off if he had gotten his brains knocked out for big money instead of pushing cigarettes under the table in the Holiday Inn.

I asked her how she felt about the government-sponsored divorce. "It's the only thing I can thank OTA for," she said. "It saved me from having to get a lawyer. Joe and I had been on the way to splitsville before he got convicted."

Veronica pulled into the driveway of a smallish house on a decent-sized lot. "Nice place. It would go for a half-million in the District," I said.

"Take it back and sell it. I need the money."

I got out and locked my car door. "Forgot something," she said, unlocking it. She reached into the small back seat and grabbed my flight bag.

I followed her into the house. I noticed that every window had the latest burglar-proofing — a combination of metal and glass that's expensive, but pretty much bulletproof and hammer-resistant. She noticed that I noticed.

"I couldn't afford it, but there's a Gay Air Police chapter in the neighborhood. It's less expensive than replacing the windows they broke after their weekend rallies." I nodded. I had written a couple of stories about the secondary violence visited upon families of people convicted in high-profile Smoke Jumper busts. OTA encouraged local newspapers and broadcasters to use the home addresses of people arrested by the Jumpers, on the theory that such exposure gave family members more reason to prevail on their loved ones to avoid the nicotine taint.

I had thought the story on secondary victims to be pretty much sympathetic, but Winston DeWeerd had inserted it into the Congressional Record, so I had to accept that it might have been harsher than I had intended.

Veronica French led me to a small office room just off the kitchen. The screen of an OTA tape player stood in a corner.

"Could I mix you a drink?" she asked.

"Bourbon and water, if you have bourbon and don't use water from Lake Erie," I said.

She laughed winningly. "Erie water would dishonor the bourbon." She mixed two similar drinks and flipped on the OTA-issued player. "Burglars rammed the front door a couple of years ago and took everything electronic but this thing," she said.

"Why would they leave a marvelous piece of transistor-ized machinery, put together by nonsmokers in a smoke-free environment," I said, trying to smile subtly. Some people tell me I do "subtly" about as adroitly as Attila the Hun did "gently," since I sometimes show my pleasure with myself when I think I've gotten off a good line or a trenchant comment.

Her smile was easy, for a change. "My cousin is a cop and he figures the bad guys are afraid of the OTA when they aren't

162

afraid of the regular police."

"Guess that proves some of the bad guys can read the newspapers," I said.

She opened a file cabinet and took out several videotapes.

"These are the ones I wanted to show you," she said.

***

The man on the tape was Joe French, all right. Tall and muscular and with the big hands that had tattooed my face that night in Syracuse. The setting was comfortable, but plain. Just Joe French and his filtered cigarette, together on a blue armchair. The smoke was a halo around his craggy features. The yellow S on his forehead seemed to burn into the high-resolution monitor.

The only evidence that prison had changed Joe French inside was in the subtle part of the body. The eyes. The dark brown eyes that had bored in on me in the ring were strangely subdued. Prison must be hell if it can extinguish the fire in a guy who can fight like a tiger with a couple of busted ribs punching into his lungs.

The voice was strong and the hand movements and eye contact were what the television consultants would give a good rating. He said he appreciated the OTA taking him and people like him out of the Larger Society. He said he now believed that smoking was the greatest curse ever visited upon the Human Race. He paused to take a drag on the ersatz Winston and his expression changed to one of abject shame. "I wish I could quit and return to the ones I love, but the demon is part of me and I fear I can never give it up."

Then he began sobbing. The camera came in close on the tears, rolling down his spare cheeks from those lightless brown eyes.

I felt this involuntary movement that I always get when I experience a sudden moment of sadness. It's a sort of a noiseless gulp that starts low in my stomach and spreads to my throat. It usually ends in a shudder. When it doesn't, I cry.

I was afraid I was going to have to stifle a sob when Veronica French froze the videotape.

"Do you see anything strange about that?" she said.

I appreciated the interruption. I wasn't going to get to cry in the home of a strange woman with a strange videotape. "You've got to remember that I just fought Joe and talked with him in the hospital. I didn't really know him and we were both young. So I'd have to say it's strange, but not unbelievable."

She rewound the tape and inserted another. The setting was the same except Joe French was smoking a non-filtered cigarette. The S on his forehead seemed more prominent than it had been on the last video. My habit was asserting itself and I was envious of the nicotine, carbon monoxide, arsenic and assorted radioactive particles that were abusing his lungs and circulatory system.

Joe was saying he had been told that his mother had died recently and that he regretted he had disappointed her, even as a child, by his involvement with the Demon Weed. He broke into great sobs and the camera operator again moved in close on the lachrymose stream, zigzagging down the stubble of his beard.

Veronica froze the picture again. She sounded like a biology professor I had in college. "The tears. Everything is right, or at least not wrong, except for the tears."

I told her I didn't understand. "Did Joe French cry when you beat the hell out of him?" It was not really a question. She continued.

"Joe French didn't cry when his daughter died. Joe French didn't cry when he got sentenced to the Colony. Joe French didn't cry when his Labrador Retriever died and, god, he loved that dog."

Her eyes glittered with anger as they searched my face for agreement and understanding. She saw what she was looking for. "Joe French crying once is unbelievable. Joe French crying twice is impossible. Joe French does not cry."

I looked at the eyes on the still OTA tape. The eyes were lusterless. The tears were real only in the physical sense. The eyes and the tears belonged to a man neither Veronica nor I had ever met.

"What are these bastards doing?" I said.

Veronica French fixed those drowning-pool eyes on me.

164

"Somebody has to find out. You have to find out."

I had a king-sized version of the sinking feeling I last got when I stepped into the ring with Muhammad Uhuru, who weighed three hundred pounds and moved like a ballerina. I wanted to ask Veronica if there was a cigarette in the house.

CHAPTER 21

Fernando Phillips had to look at six monitors, thanks to the goddamned cutbacks. The idiots were always watching the videos. There was an old lady in Thibodaux, Louisiana, who watched the latest video of her ex-husband damned nearly every hour she was awake. She had even sued to try to overturn the mandatory divorce. The Supreme Court refused to hear the case.

She wouldn't be getting many more tapes from the old boy. He was a two pack-a-day inmate in the Nevada Colony and was getting that distinctive pallor that usually was the first sign of lung cancer.

Phillips was thankful he didn't have to pay attention to the tapes. He just had to watch the people watching them. There was one red-headed woman in Rhode Island who had the tape player in her bedroom. Her ex was a pack-a-day guy at the North Carolina colony. The record on her so far was screwing four guys in one shift. She was a joy to monitor. He even took some of her videos home for his friends to watch. Everybody wanted to meet Rhode Island Red. Everybody wanted to get a copy of the tape.

The bimbo had been a real bonanza. Fernando Phillips averaged taping one great sex scene a shift. One of his friends had introduced him to a little creep from Maryland who turned out porno videos. The creep paid a thousand bucks for an average screw scene and fifteen-hundred for a screw scene that had a little eating somewhere in it. He'd pay two thou for a couple of queers going at it. He said the fags paid top dollar for porno. It was a no-risk deal. The only people who paid to watch the damned things were creeps and there wasn't any way to track it back to OTA Surveillance. Nobody knew there was an OTA Surveillance.

SMOKE JUMPERS

He hated it when the poor bastards watched the video-tapes. The pictures from the Colonies displayed in a little box at the bottom of the screen. You sometimes had to move the box so you could see what was going on.

You could move the lens like you were some kind of Hollywood hotshot. That made it a lot better if you were taping something on the side. Especially if you were trying to take a couple of fags. Some of them jumped around the room like they were horny kangaroos.

Fernando Phillips stopped watching the other five monitors and paid rapt attention to the one from Buffalo. Procedure said you better be sharp when they were watching the tape. Sometimes they watched the videos and talked to fellow smokers on the telephone. You could get some good leads to pass along to the Smoke Jumpers. On a good night you'd see a bunch of them smoking. They thought it was a protest, or some shit like that. They were just a bunch of goddamned criminals.

You could just call for the nearest Smoke Jumper unit and get to watch them run around when the goddamned Jumpers rammed through the door.

Phillips turned up the sound and hit the record button on the primary monitor out of Buffalo. The Buffalo broad was worth running the backup for, even if nothing was going on. She had a guy with her. She wasn't a slut like Rhode Island Red but one of her tapes had brought a cool five thousand. It was too bad that he couldn't tell the management how they could make some money, so they could get back to buying good equipment.

In the good days every monitor was recorded, every hour of the day. But the damned budget cuts had made his job difficult. He had to watch and jump around the monitors with just one video recorder and the one backup. He had to use the backup to do his private stock.

No matter. This one was going to be good enough for a promotion off the night shift. He figured he'd wind up in foreign surveillance. Watching just one satellite picture. Maybe even one from one of those nude beaches where the old tobacco barons frolicked. That was good duty. You didn't have to pay attention.

167

He knew he'd miss the porno money but he was tired of working nights all the damned time.

He couldn't believe what he was getting out of the Buffalo feed. He adjusted the camera to home in on the guy's face, then punched a couple of keys on his computer. The Central Processing Unit found a match for the face within two seconds. The identifying data came up in a millisecond. Robert J. Reynolds. Air Monitor Reporter. The computer said Reynolds was the half-brother of Senator Winston DeWeerd. It said that fact was not publicly known. A crawl of red text moved in loop across the screen. It read: "Politically Sensitive." He cleared the background screen with an angry tap. He didn't need a goddamned computer to tell him it was politically sensitive.

Fernando Phillips wasn't going to screw around and call in the Smoke Jumpers on anybody even halfassed or halfbrother connected with Senator DeWeerd. He didn't want to spend the rest of his career watching satellite sweeps for kids smoking in high-school parking lots.

If it had anything to do with Senator DeWeerd, it was big. Every jerk or jerquette in the chain of command would want a complete report. Then the jerk or jerquette would bump it up one notch, where the bigger jerk or jerquette would want a complete report. Everybody would keep getting informed, writing a report, then nudging it up the line until it finally got to the Secretary. Whatever it was, it wasn't going to be fast. But that wasn't his problem.

Phillips punched the red button to activate his section chief's mobile receiver.

"You got big trouble with the Buffalo bitch," he said.

CHAPTER 22

Veronica French turned off the OTA video monitor. Her eyes were glittering with anger and excitement. She stood at her full five-foot-three and shook her little fist at the screen.

She turned toward me. "Can you help Joe?"

"I don't know. I'm going to try."

She took my glass and poured me another drink.

She filled me in on life on the fringe of a convicted smoker. She got a small check every month, so long as she agreed to stay on the books as Joe French's outside contact. It wasn't big money, but it covered the house payment. I told her I had never heard of such a program, which was difficult for me to believe. I've been through the four-volume budget reports that OTA submits to Winston DeWeerd's committee every biennium.

"Washington welfare programs are strange things," I opined.

She agreed. She said the money was computer-deposited to her account on the first of every month. She had balked, at first, on the direct deposit because she couldn't afford the forty-dollar monthly service charge the banks ding everybody with.

OTA agreed to add the service charge to the total of the monthly grant.

I wanted to change the subject but Veronica wanted to give me a complete rundown on her small triumph over the bureaucrats and their computers. She said the first check came in the right amount but the second didn't show at all.

It took four hours at her Message Center to run the problem to ground. I was getting the impression that Veronica had the tenacity to bring the next convention of Totally Sensitive

169

Gay and Lesbian Sunbathers to Buffalo in January.

"The idiots had been using a bank in the Cayman Islands and there was some problem with something they call Clearance Codes. I told them to straighten it out and they did."

The Cayman Islands. An OTA-sponsored check from the Caymans was almost inexplicable. One of the most modern new cities in the world is in the Caymans. It sprang up as New Winston-Salem to house some of the executives and money that once resided in North Carolina.

Veronica French wanted to know about me. I told her the short version of the story. As usual, I left out the part about the growing millions in the Trust Fund. Veronica was so money-conscious that I felt a twinge of guilt about the millions I never thought about. If I didn't have them I'd probably think about them.

She told me she, too, had been an adopted child. She said her brothers and sisters had been calm and conventional people. Not at all like herself, even though she loved them. I was suppressing the inward smile when she started walking toward me.

I like eye contact when I talk with people, hassle people, fight people, or vie for position in the Freeway Follies. Some people had called me a walking Privacy Invasion because of the way I pay attention. Most of those people have something in their orbs they don't want you to see. Sometimes my attention leads me astray. This was one of those times.

I hadn't really made a full-body appraisal of Veronica French since she picked me up at the airport. Until now. The eyes led me to make it, of course. The eyes were tossing off sparks from a fire that's older than flame.

There was a new Veronica French in the room. The breasts that had seemed to be rather limp and uninterested now appeared to threaten the fabric of her blouse. Legs once lumpy under the blue slacks looked muscular and vital. The smallish shoulders I thought to be permanently drooped were now square, exquisite and strong.

It was a little like watching a Shetland pony transmogrify

170

into a short thoroughbred, except looking at any thoroughbred, tall or short, never gave me an advanced case of Terminal Insensitivity Syndrome. Which is what Veronica French was bringing me toward at the moment.

Lots of people have Terminal Insensitivity Syndrome but few of us are brave enough to face it. Only my friends and I know its name, since it's my very own Syndrome. J.R. Tyson has tried to borrow it but I won't allow that. J.R. wanted to call his rip-off version of it Terminal Insensitivity Tyson Syndrome, which is doubly insensitive, once you make an acronym out of it.

I discovered Terminal Insensitivity Syndrome when I was covering a convention of Totally Sensitive Gay and Lesbian Nude Sunbathers of America. It was one of those easy stories, where you just write about people as they are and it's more entertaining than anything the writers come up with for the yo-yos on the talk shows.

Glynda Vincent, a totally tanned and long-legged New York model, was the keynote speaker at Totally Sensitive Gay and Lesbian Nude Sunbathers of America. Ms. Vincent made the speech memorable when she shed her elegant gown and stood nude at the podium. She said, "There is no reason why men and women of sensitivity cannot shed their clothing together without the specter of carnal behavior rearing its ugly head."

An Associated Press reporter named Nick Coughran was sitting beside me. Coughran has to be credited with an assist on developing the Terminal Insensitivity Syndrome. Coughran is a heavyset bearded guy who wears thick glasses and a smile. He writes like an angel but is a closet devil off the printed page.

Coughran tucked his chin into his chest, glared at his fly and commanded: "Down, Specter. Down, Boy." I laughed out loud and Glynda Vincent pointed at me with a silver Cross Pen, proclaiming me to be Terminally Insensitive.

The convention-goers hooted at me and started shedding their clothing to support Glynda. The television reporters loved it. Glynda Vincent leaned over me and whispered into my ear. "You are the most disgusting man I have ever met."

I whispered back. "I'm happy you think so."

Ms. Vincent's brand of Sensitivity takes a lot of commitment and Veronica French didn't help even a bit when she slipped onto the couch beside me. There was tiny bit of Glynda Vincent in her, all right, because she unbuttoned her blouse and shrugged it to the floor. I kissed her on the mouth, then on the thrusting and newly elegant breasts. She relieved me of my pullover shirt in a second, then her hands went to my belt. Her fingers were at once frantic and wonderful. She straddled me for a minute after she freed the center of my Terminal Insensitivity, then leaped to her feet to help me remove the rest of my clothing. I wondered fleetingly when she had palmed the condom, which she put in place with a sure sweep of one hand. It was like watching a surgeon cut a hangnail.

She kissed me and mounted again, working me inside her, trembling, swaying and moaning: "More...More..." I arched my body, lifting her off the couch and gaining only a tiny bit of extra penetration. It wasn't much, but it touched off an almost-inconceivable rush of movement that drove me back into the softness of the couch.

She spread her thighs and tore at the couch's fabric to try to lower her body. "Bedroom," she said hoarsely, leaning backward and holding my shoulders. "Don't take it out," she commanded. She leaned backward and wrapped her legs around my hips as I stood and carried her toward the bedroom. She started to climax and I lowered her to the floor with a roughness that wasn't intended.

She didn't give a damn. I joined her at climax. Our thrashing propelled the OTA video monitor on its rollers toward a corner of the room. Its electrical plug came out of the wall and slithered across our clasped hands. The machine hit the wall with a thud and made an almost inaudible honking sound. I might have wondered if the honk meant something if Veronica and I had been sipping tea at opposite ends of the couch. But the horniest item in the room was bucking and grabbing underneath me.

Her hands and lips were all over me when I rolled onto my back to try to catch my breath, thinking seriously that it might be time to give up my token rebellion of two cigarettes a day. I squatted, put my arms under her and carried her into the dark bedroom. Veronica's wonderful fingers were restoring the vitality of the center of my Terminal Insensitivity. She whispered. "Do it again. Do it again."

Charlotte Gay sent me an admiring letter from Raleigh when she saw the video. I never heard from Glynda Vincent. Maybe she lost her Cross Pen at the beach.

***

Veronica and I lay, spent, in what people once called a queen-sized bed. One of the Total Sensitivity groups — I forget which one but I think it was Totally Sensitive People for Nomenclature Neutrality — objected to King Size and Queen Size. They said the names implied that men were larger than women. Having never met Veronica French's sex drive, they were confused about the relationship between physical size and absolute dominance.

Reason had been running a competitive race with Totally Sensitive People for Nomenclature Neutrality when the anti-tobacco people joined the issue. King Sized was a phrase from the discredited tobacconist past, they said. The King was dead from that moment but the Queen was still alive. At least until the Gay Air Police came down on the side of change, supporting the anti-tobacco point of view and objecting to Queen Size as "another in a series of historic, subliminal, slanders on gay people everywhere."

I've always been under-whelmed by things subliminal. But I'm obviously somewhat incorrect. Virginia Slims cigarettes used to sponsor tennis tournaments on the theory that the subliminal connection between its slim weeds and championship ball-knockers would sell cigarettes. The cash registers proved that subliminal worked.

So, to be correct, Veronica and I lay, spent, in a Medium Bed, which is smaller than a Large Bed and larger than a Standard Bed. To be completely correct, only Veronica was spent. I was in Chapter Eleven. I was wondering if Joe French had been sleeping with Veronica when I broke his ribs and if she let him get the bandages off before her fingers worked him into a sexual frenzy. Veronica was lazily fondling me when she did something totally out of character. She let go.

Nonsmokers have an incredible edge over even casual smokers when it comes to the sense of smell. Veronica noticed the odor before I did, confirming the truth of her story that she hadn't smoked since she joined Joe French in a cigarette on her honeymoon. Poor Joe probably figured smoking was the only way he was going to get five minutes of rest.

"Something's burning," she said, jumping out of bed. I smelled it, too, and followed my nose into the family room. Veronica let her experience override her superior sense of smell and ran to the kitchen. My nose led me to the cabinet where she kept the Colony tapes. I opened the drawer and jumped backward, my eyes and nostrils burning from the oily, chemical smoke. The tapes were dissolving to an ugly black ooze.

I yanked the drawer off its runners and tossed it out Virginia's back door. Her son's baseball bat was standing in a corner. I grabbed it and attacked the Office of Tobacco Abatement video player. The shoddy plastic of the OTA machine was no match for the little metal bat. I kept on crushing the plastic with a free-swinging style until I found a platinum-colored metal box, located behind a prism in what obviously was supposed to be the "eye" for the remote-control device.

Veronica cringed when I knocked the box out of its moorings, set it on its side and split the metal with a stroke that Paul Bunyan would have admired, even after his story was banned because the Totally Sensitive Green People objected to lionizing anybody who felled trees.

Veronica French caught the idea quickly. She fell to her knees and pried away the few splinters of metal of the box. She ran her nimble fingers over the tiny surveillance camera. Given my experience with Veronica's fingers I was surprised that it didn't grow into a full-featured Home Entertainment Center.

"Does your Message Center Environmental Sweep ever give you a radiation alarm?" I asked. "A minor one, every time I use it," she said. I peered at the tiny machine and saw the telltale international sign that identified the atomic battery. I held the almost-microscopic lens about a foot from my face and spoke

174

clearly and slowly.

"I'm going to find you. I'm going to find every goddamned one of you and you're going to be sorry," I said. I put the camera apparatus on the floor and was raising the bat when Veronica stopped me.

"Shouldn't we keep it...as...as...as evidence?"

"You're right," I said, dropping the bat. I asked Veronica if she had a security box. She did. I checked it and saw it was nicely lined with lead. She put the device atop her most important papers and memorabilia.

"Remember that if you open the box, it's possible that some OTA satellite somewhere will be able to home in on it again," I said. The Space Agency has never tried to recruit me, but it doesn't take a rocket scientist to know that even today's television signals don't travel through lead.

I wanted to be certain she understood. I don't think the Space Agency has ever tried to recruit Veronica, either. "If there's anything in the box that you might need, take it out now," I said.

She unlocked it and her wonder-fingers shuffled through the papers before she pulled out a six-pack of condoms. She shut the box before her Divorce Decree could blossom into War And Peace.

"What do we do now, Rob?" she asked, moving close and bringing me to Terminal Insensitivity Syndrome Condition Yellow.

I stepped backward before my brain did a Ted Kennedy Purge, which shuts down all reasoning and concentrates control in the Center of Terminal Insensitivity. A comedian who comes to The End now and then was doing his political routine one night and started off on Ted. He said Ted's biographer asked, on his deathbed, if there was anything in his life he would like change. He said the Senator's last words were: "I'm sorry I never screwed Madonna."

I laughed then. I laughed more, two days later, when I looked in the history files of my computer and read about the untalented bimbo of the last century who called herself Madonna.

If what I read was true The Massachusetts Erection was one of the few people she missed.

Veronica dropped the package of condoms and was doing a two-hand assault on my good sense. She took me to a Terminal Insensitivity Syndrome Condition Ted Red before I gave up. I hustled her to the bed and pounded her frantically. Her neighbors must have thought someone was killing her, unless they were, by now, inured to her screams of delight. She climaxed three times before I exploded on her fourth, wondering in the solitude of the end if a platoon of Smoke Jumpers was going to stride in to relieve me of Veronica's condom.

Veronica stripped it off and tossed it into the commode. If she had been a pickpocket, she'd be a millionaire. "You've got to stop this and *think* about what we're going to do," she said, scoldingly.

"You're right," I muttered. "Sometimes I don't know what comes over me."

We dressed quickly and I told her to pack enough clothing to keep her and her son going for a couple of nights. She brushed past me and started reaching again. I retreated toward the door out of an abundance of caution. I was so sexually depleted by now that Glynda Vincent probably would enjoy asking me to spend the weekend.

I kept a wary eye on the driveway, expecting to see the green Jumper van squeal in at any moment. I could see J.R. Tyson's headline for his personal version of the arrest story. "Smoke Jumpers Jump Reporter Jumping Ex-Wife of Smoker Once Jumped By Jumpers."

***

We picked up Veronica's son, who was a nice-looking child of about seven. It occurred to me that there might be a fifty percent seduction rate in the second grade somewhere if the kid inherited his mother's sexuality.

Bryan French was polite. He shook my hand earnestly and hopped into the back seat. He told his mother he had been to a movie with his friend. Then he asked: "Did Mr. Reynolds make you scream all night, Mommy?"

"Of course not, Bryan. Mr. Reynolds is just a friend." When you cover Washington, you come to have a grudging admiration for adroit evasion. Veronica hadn't told a complete lie. She had, after all, moaned a good forty percent of the night away. The kid couldn't grow up to be a great reporter if he didn't learn to phrase his questions more expertly.

"Too bad," Bryan said, burying his nose in a comic book. I wanted to say a little prayer for everybody who had a daughter in the second grade.

***

I stopped at a car dealership and asked Veronica which of the Japanese-made cars she liked. She said she didn't know zilch about cars. Bryan recited the strengths of a gleaming four-door sedan. I used the credit card for my Trust Fund and bought it. I tossed their luggage into its substantial trunk and drove toward Canada. The on-board computer in the car gave me the address I wanted and I stopped at a Financial Service Center. I withdrew six-hundred-thousand dollars, converting most of it to Veronica's name in a separate account and got a credit card in her name.

I got a hundred one-thousand dollar bills for myself. I figure a hundred thousand is about the difference between a nut-case and a paranoid. I was wondering what I was going to do to the hidden Smoke Jumpers I had threatened on the hidden camera. And, of course, wondering what the Jumpers were going to try to do to me.

I got a mental image of myself on a prancing horse, dressed as General George A. Custer at what the old folks call the Little Bighorn. I could hear myself yelling: "Take No Prisoners." I wondered what Custer would have said, had Custer discovered that Sitting Bull had recorded him on a spy camera. It didn't make me feel better when I went through the possibilities and concluded George probably would have said exactly what I had.

I explained to Veronica how she could put the Buffalo house on the market once she and Bryan were safely in Canada. Most foreign governments have consistently turned down OTA's efforts to treat smoker crimes as real crimes and OTA probably wouldn't think it worth the fight to oppose the funds transfer from the sale of the house.

Veronica was so distracted by the cataclysm in her life that she only fondled me four or five times on the way to the border. Maybe sudden wealth is a killer to a person's sex drive, the way smoking is supposed to be. Maybe she was climaxing on her own at the knowledge that she would never again have to try to get a convention to come to Buffalo.

I parked short of the Customs office. I kissed Veronica, who maneuvered me out of Bryan's line of sight, then plastered her body to mine. Her thrusting hips drove me into the molded fender of the car. I tilted her head backward with my index finger. Her head leaned back, dead still, but the wonderful grinding continued. "Be careful," I said. "I'll get in touch with you. They'll be monitoring me, I'm sure." I gave her the name and telephone number of a friend in Montreal. I told Veronica to call her when she was settled someplace.

She seemed interested in the female contact. "Your friend in Montreal...I mean...do you...is she...like..."

"No, we just worked together in Raleigh," I said. She appeared to be disappointed.

"You were serious about doing something for Joe, weren't you?"

I said I was quite serious, but hadn't decided what I could do. I didn't tell her I wouldn't be able to think clearly until her devouring sexual needs were on the other side of the border. She transformed to Mother French when she called Bryan out of the car.

"Say goodbye to Mr. Reynolds," she said.

"Come and visit us, Mr. Reynolds," Bryan said, warmly. "I'll bet you can make Mom scream all night the next time."

I wondered if there was an all-male second grade in Canada. It would just delay the inevitable, I guess. I watched until she cleared the Smoke Jumper checkpoint, regular Customs and drove into Canada. I hitched a ride back to Buffalo on an eighteen-wheel truck. The driver gave her name as Debbie Morrison. She was a handsome and rough-talking woman who was about forty. She said she was a part-time trucker and a full-time rancher and lived near Calgary. She had been parked at the border while Veronica and I said our good-byes.

She flicked on the interior light and looked at me with interest. "I was thinking maybe you'd be some fun to go drinking with but you look like you've been rode hard and put away wet."

"You got both of those right," I said.

Debbie Morrison roared with laughter. "I got to drop my load by eight o'clock. Too bad you already dropped yours."

"It was a coast-to-coast overnighter," I said and she chortled again.

Debbie said she hated hauling into the United States, because of "the smoking bullshit." She liked to smoke a cigarette now and then and had been afraid to try to hide any in her truck. She wondered if I knew where she could buy cigarettes in Buffalo.

I told her I didn't, but I had heard that the area around any university was always a good bet.

A Country and Western station was playing on Debbie's in-cab stereo and the announcer broke in with a bulletin story. There are several reasons I hate C&W radio. One is the music. The other is that I'm afraid the announcer may break in with a bulletin and it will mean World War III has begun and I'm going to be dead in thirty seconds. Country stations aren't all that big on news.

It wasn't World War III. It was a report that a Smoke Jumper raid on a suspected tobacco den at a University of Texas dormitory had ended with ten students dead, apparently from gunshot wounds.

"Any bunch of people who go out of their damned minds over smoking the way you people have ought to get their butts kicked," Debbie Morrison said.

We exchanged telephone numbers and she let me off on a feeder street near a Holiday Inn. Veronica had described the neighborhood. It was the Holiday Inn where Joe French had worked.

***

There were no cabs around. I checked with the desk and

179

found that the next airport limousine would come around in an hour. I called the Air Monitor to volunteer to go to Austin to cover what the television set in the lobby was calling the University of Texas massacre. Katricia Coyne screeched that she had the situation completely under control and that I should come to work on schedule on Monday. She sounded almost as under control as the federal budget.

Rebuffed but not humiliated, I went into the bar and found a fan in the night bartender. He was a big guy, about six-foot-four. I thought I recognized his face. I was about to say that when he beat me to the punch.

"I know who you are," he said. "You're Robert Reynolds of the Air Monitor."

"Guilty as charged, and you're Bentley Benning," I said. "You played tight end for the Bays."

He corrected me. "Close catcher."

"Right," I said. I'm not all that much of a sports fan and I get corrected frequently when I refer to team positions by their pre-Total Sensitivity names. I've read so many of the old sports books that the old names stick with me. I don't call them insensitively on purpose. The knee-biters get downright hostile when I screw up and say something about somebody who screwed up at Shortstop, which is now sensitively referred to as Mid-Fielder.

I told Bentley Benning I would never forget the leaping catch he made to propel the Buffalo Bays into the National Football League playoffs against the Denver Wind. Benning had risen from five Cleveland Mist defenders to grab the pass. He bulled his way into the Final Area with three Misters trying to bring him down. The Final Area is what I still call the End Zone.

Bentley Benning was proud. He was obviously one of those ex-football players who has to tell people he once played for the Bays and then gets to watch them try to pretend they remember him.

Bentley said he had been a fan of mine since he started reading the Air Monitor. He said he was a fan even before he fouled up a knee and had to leave pro football. He said he had read every word I have ever written. I made a mental note not to pick a fight with him. Bentley Benning was a monstrous man, for openers. I've fought big people before, so that's not the clincher, but I figure anybody who has read every word I've ever written has a high tolerance for pain.

He got my bourbon and water, then leaned over the bar, speaking in a conspiratorial whisper. "Something big coming down in old Buffalo, huh?"

"You never know," I said.

"Got something to do with Joe French and that big bust here." He checked to both sides to make certain no one was eavesdropping. I ask questions for a living. This was not one.

"You're a pretty observant guy," I said. "People like you are good to have on the side of what's right. I hope you'll be careful so we don't tip off any of the bad guys."

He glowed with pride. "I'd never do that. I really don't know much. Like I told the two guys from OTA Undercover, I haven't seen Joe's old lady in here but I understand she has a couple now and then at a joint up in Niagara Falls."

"I hear she never stops at a couple," I said. I asked him how he knew Joe French's ex-wife. "They showed me her picture," he said.

I wanted to know how he knew the agents were from OTA. "I know you know more than you're telling me," I said, as he preened, "but I just want to make certain you're not talking with the bad guys. These smokers are pretty slippery."

"You're damned right," he whispered. He appeared somewhat chagrined. "I should have made them show me some credentials. I hope I didn't screw anything up."

Bentley Benning's eyes were flicking back and forth between me and two middle-aged guys in business suits. They were sitting at a table in a corner of the room. They looked to be drunk. Benning leaned across the bar again. "That's them over there. I bet you're here to talk to them about the story, right?"

I whispered back. "There isn't any OTA Undercover. That would be against the law. I'd bet those bastards are from the Cayman Tobacco Combine." I was telling the truth, more or less.

about the OTA not having an undercover division, or at least a legal undercover division. I knew it was improbable that OTA would let a little thing like the law keep it from doing The Right Thing. Bentley Benning was highly irritated at the thought that two Merchants of Death might be in his bar, impersonating OTA undercover agents. I knew I had best move before he did. Bentley didn't strike me as the kind of person who put things off.

"Cover me," I said.

"Gotcha," Benning said.

I walked to the table. The two drunks from OTA were deeply involved in watching a small video screen. I had assumed they were soaking up the bad news from the Austin massacre but the guys were shoulder-to-shoulder, obviously to mask the screen from passersby.

One of them looked okay as a fake undercover guy. His partner couldn't have gone undercover in that great bar scene in the old movie Star Wars, where all the monsters were drinking it up in the intergalactic hotspot. He was completely bald and had a shriveled left ear. His face could have launched a thousand upchucks.

The bald one moved slightly and I saw the video picture. Veronica French's face was a study in absolute bliss and a large fellow with dark-brown hair was on top of her. I recognized him from his marvelous physique and the mole on his left shoulder. My doctor has been after me for a couple of years to let him remove that mole.

They froze at the sound of my voice. "Under cover?" was all I said.

The bald one jumped backward and swung at me with his left hand. He screamed, "HAH-YUH!" I thought it might be a karate move OTA teaches its people at lunch once or twice a year. It was pretty funny.

I clubbed him in the kidney with a straight left that turned him around. Then I smashed his nose with the right and put him to sleep with a combination. It worked all right, but I didn't feel the zing I expect from my right hand. Another two days in bed with Veronica French and I might turn into an accountant.

The blond guy stood and started back-pedalling, trying to get to his ankle holster. I went for him but stumbled over a chair. He put a table between us and had the gun in his hand. I figured I was deader than Smokey No's brain. My life was flashing before my eyes. It was pretty boring until I got to the part about Charlotte Gay. I was hoping to fast-forward to Veronica French before I died. Then I saw Bentley Benning flying through the air like a javelin on steroids.

Benning cleared three tables in flight and crashed into the OTA guy. He plucked the gun from the floor and spiked it beside the guy's head, then did a little dance that shook the floor. He plucked the gunner from the floor and airmailed him across the room. The OTA man didn't touch anything until his head broke the kick paneling at the bar. He could make a case for some frequent-flier miles, when he came to. That was going to be a while.

"Fun deal," Benning said.

"Great move," I said. He did his little dance again.

Everybody in the bar was cheering Bentley. I picked up the OTA video player and tossed it into my flight bag. I left a thousand dollar tip and caught the airport limo while Bentley Benning was calling the police. I noticed my hands were shaking. I wanted a cigarette.

CHAPTER 23

Dean Dean Deering was known variously among the University of Texas ninety-five thousand students as Three D, Double-Dean or Dean-squared. Dean Deering had been Collier Smythe's choice for Dean of Continuing Behavioral Improvement. He came to the Austin job from a top administrative position at the Smoke Jumper Academy near Butte, Montana. Deering had been the guiding force behind the widely applauded detector system that isolated nicotine abusers by sensors in the sewage system. He was not only technically adept, he had laid down the combat-training regimen that made the Smoke Jumpers probably the finest military strike force in the history of America.

Deering went to the Smoke Jumper Academy after early retirement from a dead-end career with the FBI. He got to know Winston DeWeerd when Deering was agent in charge of the FBI's office in Butte. His rise to the top of the new federal smoke-fighting agency was not even slightly hindered by the FBI files he had slipped to Winston DeWeerd in Winston's race to become governor of Montana.

Dean Deering had become Commissioner of Agriculture under Governor DeWeerd, was out of work for a few months after Winston became a United States Senator then came to Washington to help set up the Smoke Jumpers.

Dean Deering had told interviewers he had been an anti-smoking zealot since his youth. He said he believed he could have been a world-record sprinter had it not been for the lung damage caused by his parents' second-hand smoke.

Dean Deering took to the Smoke Jumper job with his customary blend of fanaticism mixed with political astuteness.

But in Winston DeWeerd's second term, Deering had enough of Washington, with its endless traffic jams and tedious people. He told DeWeerd he had always wanted to work in Texas. DeWeerd forged the link with Collier Smythe, the nationally acclaimed anti-tobacco firebrand who was president of the UT Austin campus. Deering had flourished under the relationship, even though Collier Smythe was a boss who never gave any credit to subordinates for ground-breaking work. Collier Smythe, for instance, had taken complete credit for the UT anti-tobacco informer network without ever mentioning Dean Deering, who had fought all the political battles in the academic bureaucracy to get it started.

DeWeerd, and only DeWeerd, called Smythe "Collie." Today the man DeWeerd called Collie was a snarling Doberman. Collier Smythe hated bad news and Dean Deering was, he knew, about to bring him some more of the product he despised second-most. Right behind smoking.

***

Deering replayed the Cilia Hall problem in his mind as he waited for the meeting to begin. It should never have gotten to be a problem. It was just a standard raid. Dean Deering had presided over hundreds of them. The problem with this one was its site. It was at Cilia Hall, the place named in honor of the waving lung-protecting fibers that form the first line of defense against air pollution.

Collier Smythe had borrowed the idea for naming the new residence area Cilia Hall in one of Smythe's frequent public-relations ploys to boost his image as *The* primary anti-tobacco activist in academe. Any student who signed up for the cut-rate residency at Cilia Hall agreed they would submit to random smoke-testing on the first Monday of every month.

A member of the informer network formally known as the UT Secret Smoke Jumpers Auxiliary had tipped Deering that some residents of Cilia Hall were taking nicotine-masking drugs on the Sunday before each month's test. Deering's laboratory people were working with OTA Labs in Washington and Baltimore to come up with a new chemical test that would isolate the

185

nicotine-blocking agent. Ordinarily that would be good enough, since the presence of anything deemed to be a nicotine-blocking agent was illegal. It was a misdemeanor, all right, and Deering thought anybody testing with test-blockers ought to be guilty of a felony. But it would be good enough to get the person tossed out of school, with forfeiture of all fees paid and a lock on transfer of any and all course credits.

It got worse. The student said a significant proportion of residents of Cilia Hall had rigged a basement fan system to gather the air from the energy-efficient building and clean it through a special series of filters, most of which had been pilfered from the Science Department.

Dean Deering did not see the situation as a standard piece of undergraduate rebellion. Particularly worrisome were recent figures which indicated that the smokey denizens of Cilia Hall were among the better academic achievers on campus.

Millions of dollars of financial aid from the OTA was at risk if the situation got out of control. Deering was particularly interested in the aid figures since his entire department was funded by an OTA grant, which had been lovingly pushed through Congress by Winston DeWeerd. DeWeerd had even come to Austin for ceremonies heralding the beginning of the grant. Deering had a picture of himself, standing respectfully in the rear of Senator DeWeerd and Collier Smythe.

The newly hewn "Cilia Hall" sign was in the background. It was a beautiful piece of work. The sculptor who had done it had labored for months to create what was almost a hologram of waving, hairlike cilia. The Cilia Hall sign was a visual anthem to good health worldwide. The thought that a bunch of air-brained students might despoil that image set Deering's square jaw in an expression of rage. Even worse, it jangled his nerves. He reached involuntarily toward his shirt pocket before he caught himself. It was evil. Dean Deering wanted a cigarette. He grabbed his ballpoint pen and made some marks on the report in his hands.

Deering now knew that it had been a mistake to call in the Smoke Jumpers for the Cilia Hall raid. It had seemed a good idea at the time. The television pictures of the handsome Jumper men and women cleaning the environment of Cilia Hall of the scruffy and disreputable killers who abused tobacco should have been a watershed event in the national anti-tobacco movement. Just one wrong move by a Smoke Jumper captain had turned Dean Dean Deering's plan on its ear. The captain explained that his squad had come onto the Tobacco Den in the bowels of Cilia Hall and mistook a calculator in the hands of one of the students for a gun.

The captain didn't help matters with his explanation. The television cameras zoomed in on his stony face as he said: "The room was so full of evil smoke that we couldn't see clearly. The students really killed themselves."

Dean Deering had moved in to try to take control of the media but the harm had been done. Almost every daily newspaper in the country and most of the radio and television outlets had questioned the level of force employed in Cilia Hall. Worse, a couple even questioned whether an entire battalion of Smoke Jumpers should have been called in bust a seedy and weedy bunch of student tobacco abusers. Only the Air Monitor had managed to come down on the side of Right. And the Air Monitor endorsement had been somewhat wishy-washy, saying only that the public should wait until all the facts were in on the Cilia Hall "incident."

Some media outlets were referring to it as the Cilia Hall "massacre." The word "massacre" was one that Collier Smythe could brook only when it related to a good drubbing on the football field as administered by the University of Texas Preservationists. The Preservationists were heir to a proud football tradition once established as Longhorns and every member of the team wore the international no-smoking sign on his chests as he did battle on the gridiron. It had been mere weeks since Preservationist quarterback Billy Fred Morris's pass hit Close Catcher Lopez Grenado on the diagonal slash to bring victory over the Texas A&M Minerals.

The University had not yet released the names of the dead students and Dean Deering knew there would be another media firestorm when the names came out. Quarterback Billy Fred Morris had been one of those mowed down in the malignant haze of the room in Cilia Hall.

***

Deering flipped his eyes warily toward Collier Smythe. He wondered privately how Collier Smythe had missed the tobacconist tendencies of Billy Fred Morris. Smythe had, after all, spent hours with Billy Fred and had even taken the handsome young man with him as window-dressing for speeches and appearances before various Total Sensitivity groups.

Smythe had the best developed tobacco sensitivity Deering had ever known. Collier had once bounced an assistant professor at a faculty gathering when his Roman nose caught the faint odor of tobacco. He had smelled the cigarette through the bag the professor had wrapped it in. Deering thought that Smythe's nose might be the reason Senator DeWeerd called him "Collie." Deering was lucky that Smythe had not seen the involuntary hand movement, which he often referred to as "smoker's giveaway." He couldn't understand how Smythe had missed identifying Billy Fred Morris as an enemy of public health.

***

Collier Smythe required an agenda for any meeting. An agenda was the emblem of an organized administrator. Smythe could sniff the exotic bouquet of extraordinary wine from the page of a well-done agenda. Page. Not pages. No agenda could be more than one page. To slop over to a second page was the mark of a truly second-rate person.

A professional agenda began with something necessary, but less important than the raison d'etre of the meeting. The truly important item could be next, or one more Roman Numeral down the line. Collier Smythe insisted that his agenda always bear Roman Numerals, which were so much more cosmopolitan than simple numbers.

Collier Smythe called the meeting to order and went, quite logically, to Roman One, which was a report on the enrollment situation. The national economic malaise was magnified in Texas. The Texas economy had suffered along with the nation and then got its private shock from the massive oil exports on the markets from the Soviet Union.

Every oil-patch town in the state had its localized version of the story about the Houston vice sweep which netted six prostitutes, four of whom tested as virgins.

Even the mighty University of Texas Austin campus was having to recruit students. Collier Smythe found it grubby and undignified and was gratified that there were splendid little people in the Administration to handle it. He paid no attention to the report. Roman One was never really a worthy item.

"And now," Collier Smythe intoned, "what progress does Continuing Behavioral Improvement have to report on Roman Two?"

Dean Deering had loved being Roman Two on the meeting agenda, until Friday. Friday was the day the students expelled the raiding Smoke Jumpers and campus police and barricaded all entrances to Cilia Hall.

Deering cleared his throat. "We continue to negotiate with the residents holding Cilia Hall..."

Collier Smythe interrupted. "Get the hell on with it!"

Deering gulped. Collier Smythe never used profanity. He continued, speaking swiftly. "The students demand that the Smoke Jumpers involved in the, the, the incident, be prosecuted for murder."

Collier Smythe nodded. Deering continued while his master's grace was in bloom. "They demand amnesty from any charges, including any anti-tobacco statutes, for any student in or appurtenant to the Cilia Hall problem."

Collier Smythe again conveyed his assent with a nod. Deering made a mental note that the word "problem" was the only acceptable way to make a future reference to the Cilia Hall situation. Smythe had fired the University public relations chief when the first headlines trumpeted word of the "Massacre In Cilia Hall."

Dean Dean Deering could sense that he had developed some elbow room with his crisp and businesslike presentation of the student demands. He had to capitalize on it before Collier Smythe's surly mood reasserted itself.

"They appear to be positioning themselves for a pro-

189

tracted period of time of involvement in the Cilia Hall problem,"
he said. Deering could see that his tortured words for a long siege
touched Dr. Smythe's affection for good euphemisms. Smythe
himself had been the moving force behind changing the Mass
Communications degree to Significant Informational Network-
ing Exchange. He was credited with being first among the
nation's educational icons to ban the hated "Bachelor's" degree
and replace it with a "Primary" degree. Dean Dean Deering knew
that the bitch who ran the awful little school in New Jersey
claimed that Smythe had stolen the idea from a cocktail-party
conversation in Washington, but the idea had caught on nationwide and Collier Smythe and his school were heralded as leaders
in the national sensitivity movement. Deering doubted the
woman's story. He knew that nothing good had ever come out of
New Jersey except an empty bus.

"It would be viewed as insensitive if we took Cilia Hall
by force," Collier Smythe intoned. "We must allow them the time
frame necessary for purgation of the emotional trauma involved
in the untimely demises associated with the Smoke Jumper
battalion's ill-conceived incursion," Smythe said. Deering
scribbled "wait them out" in the margin of his agenda.

Smythe's question chilled Deering, who was hoping
Smythe would declare Roman II at an end and move on to Roman
III. "Is there more from Continuing Behavioral Improvement?
Anything at all."

Deering gulped. "Yes, doctor. They want us to allow
pizza and beer deliveries." Smythe smiled. Everyone but Deering
smiled with him. "Acceptable," Smythe said. "Young persons
will, after all, be young persons." Deering didn't need to note
"young persons" on his agenda. His job had been imperiled in the
first month when he used the insensitive phrase "boys will be
boys" to describe a riot by students involved in the UT African-
American Heritage Program. It hadn't been fair. Deering wasn't
a Southerner and had no sociological background to sensitize
him. How had he been expected to know how those touchy black
bastards would react to being called "boy?"

"And they want something else," Deering said. He felt

relieved. The awesome burden was about to slip from his shoulders.

"What, pray, would that be?" Collier Smythe asked. He was still smiling.

"Cigarettes," Deering said, watching Collier Smythe collapse into the synthetic fabric of his immense chair.

CHAPTER 24

I got home late. Too late. I could hear J.R. Tyson's snoring. I rejected the impulse to wake him and tell him about my trip to Buffalo. I knew J.R. would immediately jump out of bed and pull out several items from his gun stash in case the Smoke Jumpers decided to come and get me. I would have to stay up with him and I didn't figure the Jumpers were going to have the moxie to kick in the door of two of the people who work for the voice of the anti-tobacco movement.

Besides, I had to wash my golf clubs and get a little rest. I had an 8 a.m. interview and then there was the obligatory monthly Monday golf game with Benson Goodykoontz, the funny little guy who is our publisher at the Air Monitor. I couldn't imagine anything that would insulate me from the Smoke Jumpers better than being in the company of Ben Goodykoontz.

Benson Goodykoontz takes me to play at his club, which is nationally acclaimed for its membership-testing program. Everybody who can pay the hundred-thousand-dollar levy to join Healthcrest earns the right to be tobacco-tested when using the club facilities.

Healthcrest's fame was achieved when the nicotine monitors in its urinals disqualified Clarke Douglas. Douglas was relieving himself after posting a six-under-par sixty-six for a three-stroke lead in the U.S. Open. Douglas admitted smoking a cigarette before facing the news media. He contritely explained that he had developed the habit for the Demon Weed on a two-month tour of Japan. His fame and his enrollment in a smoking abatement program saved him from the criminal charges that sent his caddie to the Nevada Colony. The Smoke Jumpers on duty during the Open found a carton of Japanese cigarettes in the caddie's locker. The caddie said they belonged to Clarke Douglas but Douglas denied that.

There once was an Arnold Palmer golf club in a display at Healthcrest but it was removed when Benson Goodykoontz pointed out that he had seen old tapes of the great Palmer in his early days. The days when Palmer would stride up the eighteenth fairway, smoking like a chimney.

Healthcrest has a championship eighteen-hole course, though. Benson Goodykoontz and I can't play at my club because I don't belong to one. I came to town as a two-handicap golfer but have slipped to about a four. About the only time I play, except for vacations or out-of-town trips to the old Tobacco Country, is my monthly match with Ben Goodykoontz.

One reason I cherish the scheduled game with Goodykoontz is its effect on Katricia Coyne. I could say it drives her nuts, but with Katricia that's not a drive. More like a knocked-down nine-iron. Driving Katricia nuts is definitely part of the short game, or would have been before the knee-biters descended on the United States Golf Association, the Professional Golf Association and the networks. People for Sensitive Stature Nomenclature in Sports didn't win a sweeping victory, probably because they were outside the umbrella of the Total Sensitivity umbrella organization. But most of the network commentators now babble about the "approach game." It finesses the problem for the people who need a stepladder to get out of a divot.

My monthly game with Ben Goodykoontz started when I was in his foursome in a media tournament. I helped him cure a screaming slice by adjusting his stance. The golf pro at Healthcrest hates my guts, because Member Goodykoontz loves to tell the other members that I did something for him that the pro couldn't. Goodykoontz doesn't hit the ball very far, but it's usually in play, thanks to me.

Katricia Coyne tried to take a screaming slice out of my ass the first time I signed out for the rest of the day, listing "golf with the boss" as my reason. When she found out that the appointment was with Benson Goodykoontz she decided not to dock me a day's pay. Katricia is pretty well-developed as a nut-case but she's not stupid.

Goodykoontz insists that I call him Ben when we're playing golf, which is nice, because I call him Ben anyway. I've never been able to understand the corporate types who call each other Mister. The secretaries at the Air Monitor call their bosses Mister all the time. I've also never understood how anyone can work with a person all day and enjoy him or her always using Mister or Miss or Ms. A Raleigh story may illustrate it better. There was a secretary at the Raleigh paper, for instance, whose boss was a dork named Richard Rodgers. Everybody called him Dick, except for his secretary. She appeared to be offended if you called and asked to speak to "Dick."

She would say: "I've have *Mister Rodgers* call you back."

J.R. Tyson swears he was crawling around a singles bar late one evening and heard Rodger's secretary tell a traveling salesman that she was a lonely divorcee. J.R. said the guy perked up a little, even though she was pretty homely. He said she snuggled up to the guy and said she really liked to dance the slow ones. J.R. said they kept drinking and the guy was liking her better and they were getting friendlier until she got in his face and proclaimed: "What I'm really looking for is a big, stiff Mister Rodgers." J.R. said the salesman walked out, making tiny circles around his temple. I guess some respectful habits seldom die hard.

***

I wrote up the interview, which hadn't turned out to be much of a story, and drove out to Healthcrest to meet Benson Goodykoontz. I put my golf bag on the conveyer that takes it through the tobacco detector, then watched the attendant pick it up and put it on the gleaming golf cart once it had been declared smoke-free. I love Healthcrest's golf course as much as I detest the trendy stupidity that swells its membership rolls. Playing at Healthcrest sometimes make me think I ought to tell the Air Monitor to shove it, move to a golf spa in the South and start working on building my game and depleting my trust fund.

The attendant said Mister Benson Goodykoontz hadn't

arrived, so I went to the pro shop to wait. My pal, the pro, was sucking on a cup of coffee and screwed up his face the minute he saw me.

"You been giving any good golf tips lately?" he said, glancing at his assistant pro with a sneer.

"Nope," I said, "I guess that's about all you and I have in common."

The assistant pro tried to suppress his smile but couldn't keep it all off. His boss wanted to tell me to wait outside, but Benson Goodykoontz's guests are treated with respect at Healthcrest. The pro almost strangles because he has to call me Mister Reynolds when Goodykoontz is around. I tell almost everyone else that I prefer to be called Rob. Mister Reynolds is fine in this case, since it's a hemorrhoid to a pompous ass.

Benson Goodykoontz and The Bookends arrived before we could swap any more insults. The Bookends are a matched set of goons who travel with Ben every time he steps outside the Air Monitor. They're both former Smoke Jumpers and are among the few civilians in the District of Columbia licensed to carry handguns. The Bookends are both six-four and each weighs about two-forty. They both have brown hair, cropped close. They always wear running shoes, which makes them appear goofier than normal when Ben has to go to some ritzy Washington function. When Ben Goodykoontz has a good round he can shoot below their aggregate IQ, which means he has to break one-hundred.

The Bookends use one of the Course Security carts when we play. Course Security is able to get an exemption from the government's antipathy toward anything that burns gasoline, except for the Smoke Jumper vehicles, of course.

Everybody else at Healthcrest has to ride in an electric cart, which is fine with me. I'd just as soon be in something slow and let the Bookends race off like Rommel to head off an attack by a bunch of tobacco-crazed terrorists.

The Bookends showed up early in the Air Monitor's life. I wasn't around at the very beginning but I've looked into the computer and read stories that said Benson Goodykoontz narrowly escaped death when a hit squad shot up his car on Pennsylvania Avenue. The stories said the hitmen were never arrested but that the trail of evidence led to the Cayman Tobacco Combine, which wanted to silence the media voice against the Demon Weed by killing its head.

Ben Goodykoontz is a funny guy to make a symbol of. He's about five-seven and a hundred-fifty pounds of nervous. Energetic, but nervous. I grudgingly admire energetic, which I'm not. I don't care for nervous because it gets on my nerves. Ben never stops moving. Ben always wears a long-sleeved shirt, even in the heat of a Washington summer. He does so, I guess, so he can pull on the left sleeve of it. He's forever pulling the left sleeve down around his knuckles.

I've seen him step back from the ball when he's standing on the tee box to yank the left sleeve down. When I can get him to finish with his hands high and toward the hole, he'll usually admire the flight of the ball, then drop his left hand and yank on the sleeve with his right.

He tries to mingle with the staff people and once showed up at a pool party, dressed in a swimsuit and a long-sleeved shirt.

J.R. Tyson once theorized that Ben could have a problem with skin cancer, but I refuted that, pointing out that Ben never wears a hat. J.R. fell back on a theory that Ben is a compulsive masturbator and transfers his attention to his left arm when there are people around. J.R. is better at writing and computer hacking than he is at theories to explain Ben's cuff fetish.

"Let's go tear this course apart," Benson Goodykoontz said, yanking on his left sleeve, which had moved up slightly when he donned his golf glove.

"Have a good round, Mr. Goodykoontz," the pro said. "You, too, Mr. Reynolds." The Bookends opened the doors for us and we went to the first tee.

Four women had teed off ahead of us. Three of them were attractive and the fourth was a handsome, fortyish blonde whose face I had seen often in stories about various charity bashes. Ben hit his tee shot about two hundred yards after the women hit their second shots to the huge green. The Bookends muttered "nice shot." I waited until the women were on the green before I hit. Everything felt right. All the neurons, synapses, or whatever it is that controls a golf game were in sync and I mashed the ball three-fifty, coming to rest just at the front of the green.

Ben breathed "Wow..."

One of the Bookends said "Nice shot." These guys would have munched popcorn and said "nice bite" every hour if they had been watching the lions eat the Christians.

I came within a hair of pitching it in for an eagle. Ben conceded the putt for birdie. He sank a twenty-five-footer for a bogey. "Nice shot," one of the Bookends said. He could have spent the night with Veronica French and said "not all that bad..."

The second hole at Healthcrest is a monster of a par five, five-hundred-forty yards. What the television announcers call a "yawning" fairway bunker ends about two-fifty off the tee. It's so wide and deep that it could hold Katricia Coyne's paranoia. Well, almost.

The smart shot is to hit a stiff two-iron or a wimpy three-wood just short of the fairway bunker, which leaves another long shot and a short pitch to the green if you meet all three perfectly. This was one of those days when I felt lucky.

I had recovered some strength from my evening in the Veronica French Sexual Olympics. So I pulled out my driver. Benson Goodykoontz shook his head as if to say "no way." I took it way back and unwound perfectly. The ball carried the bunker with about five yards to spare, hit hard on the fairway and took off. The drive wound up at three hundred yards. I had thought the women had cleared the green but their two carts were in the rough and out of my sight.

The cute blonde riding with the society lioness drove her cart to my ball, got out and did an elaborate little victory dance over it. Her yell of congratulations echoed off the trees. "FAN-TAS-TIC!" she screamed.

Bookend Number One muttered, "Nice shot."

I probably could have hit it three-twenty if I hadn't spent the evening with Veronica.

I thought about a two-iron for the next shot. I changed my

mind while the women sank their putts. I went up one club and hit a three-wood that bounced through a trap and rolled onto the green, stopping a foot from the cup. The blonde braked her cart and ran onto the green, doing her victory dance again. This time she ended it by unbuttoning her blouse and swishing her boobs over the ball. I was thinking she would be more fun to play with than Ben and the Bookends.

Bookend Number Two was looking at her as if she were narrating a public-service video on abstract art.

"Nice shot," he said.

"What did you hit?" Ben yelped, pounding me on the back in excitement.

"That was my Walker Lansdale Club," I said. I think Ben enjoys my ribald brand of humor. He might as well, because it's the only brand I've got. I'm pretty certain he was one of those who was happy to see Managing Editor Walker Lansdale leave the Air Monitor, even though he hired the dork. Ben mistook Walker's businesslike demeanor for quiet thoughtfulness. The first time I met the man I told J.R. Tyson that the newsroom was going to be run by an empty five-hundred-dollar suit. We all make mistakes and Walker was one of Ben's.

"I love it," he said. "Okay, what the hell is a Walker Lansdale?"

I showed him the three-wood. "You'll notice it's got a thick head and a limber shaft."

He was still chuckling when he hit his fifth shot, which caught the bunker I had bounced through. He got a seven and I had an eagle three.

"You must have played this weekend," Ben said. I started to make a joke about the mind-boggling number of strokes that had marked my weekend, but thought better of it. There was the likelihood that the Air Monitor and the Smoke Jumpers would come after me over the Buffalo trip. I didn't need to make any smartass remarks to Benson Goodykoontz on a subject that probably was going to rise up and bite me on the scrotum.

The Air Monitor has a pretty strict ethics code, which is pretty ironic when you consider the harm we do. One of the real killers to employment is to become "compromised" with a news source. I knew there was a videotape somewhere in OTA that could be viewed as compromising unless the viewer happened to be deaf, blind and/or a member of Totally Sensitive Sex-Addicted Persons.

The people who wrote the ethics code somehow managed to forget that the Air Monitor is a complete compromise on its own. It hired Katricia Coyne, a zealot of no talent or experience whose entire background was a compromise. The Air Monitor regularly massages stories to fit its journalistic niche, which is the bashing of anything remotely associated with tobacco.

It was a beautiful day to play golf and I reminded myself there would be plenty of time to fulminate about the Air Monitor, and larger concerns once we got off the beautiful Healthcrest layout. One reason I love golf is the total attention it requires, or at least allows. I thought about Joe French's dead eyes and phony tears only a couple of times. I thought about Veronica French's attentions and pleas only a couple more. I knew I had a lot of thinking to do, but there would be time for that later.

At the moment I was knocking the eyes out of the ball and had Benson Goodykoontz for a cheering section. The Bookends had vented their emotions for the day. They wouldn't even grunt when I hit a great shot.

One of them occasionally would say something complimentary when Ben did something right. But the monsters were good to have around for the occasional drive that strayed somewhat off course. Both Bookends had binoculars. I guess they needed them so they could spot the Cayman Tobacco Terrorists at long range. Anybody who can spot a terrorist sniper at a mile can be trusted to watch the flight of a little white ball. Just don't ask them to describe it.

The sixteenth hole is a par five of five-hundred-seventy yards. It bends slightly left and huge trees hang over each side of it. It's a beautiful piece of work and I was ready to attack it. I was four-under par on the round and Ben was on his way to beating the Bookend IQ figure. If his putting held up he might even shoot ninety-five.

I had crushed another drive on sixteen and Ben made a joke, which isn't all that typical for Benson Goodykoontz. "Looks like you've got a Walker Lansdale to the green," he said.

"I think Walker would be too much club," I said, grabbing a two-iron out of the bag. I was still laughing when I noticed both Bookends were staring into the trees to our right. Healthcrest is secure, with high fences, electronic motion monitors and an active patrol operation that keeps our growing quota of national riffraff from coming in and relieving the golfers of their wallets.

I saw two flashes of motion in the brush and trotted toward the edge of the tee-box. The Bookend on the driver side of their cart said, "Now" and yanked his nine-millimeter pistol out of its holster. I saw the barrel turning toward me and swung the two-iron. The head of the club caught the barrel and the shot intended for me whizzed through the canopy of the cart. I brought it back and hit him in the throat with the leading edge of the clubface.

I didn't intend to kill him. I didn't intend not to kill him either. I knew I had killed him because blood spurted from his nostrils and mouth. His reflexive thrust knocked Bookend Number Two out of the golf cart. Number Two fell to the ground, taking a shot at Benson Goodykoontz as he tumbled. Ben grabbed his left arm and collapsed on the seat. I squatted beside the cart and picked up the pistol dropped by the dying Bookend.

My hands were shaking. I wished J.R. Tyson were with me. J.R. is the gunslinger in our neighborhood.

Bookend Number Two leaped to his feet and squeezed off another shot that hit the cart above my head. I dropped to my face and shot under the cart, hitting him in the ankle. The shocking power of the nine millimeter round knocked him to the ground. I saw his ugly face staring at me under the cart and fired again.

Benson Goodykoontz came to my side in a staggering run. He was pulling on his goddamned left sleeve, which was soaked with blood.

I moved quickly around the cart and got the pistol of Bookend Number Two. It wasn't my smartest move of the year because the people in the bushes opened up. I made it back to

Ben's side and handed him a pistol. "Do you know how to shoot?" I asked.

"I hope I can learn," Ben said.

"I think there are two of them," I said. "If we can stay alive for a couple of minutes there's bound to be some help coming our way."

I snapped a look over my shoulder. I could see golf carts from every hole, careening toward the clubhouse. I figured there were twenty or thirty portable telephones, all calling 911 to quell the first non-golf shootout in the storied history of Healthcrest.

I had an idea. "If I can get to the gas pedal and turn the rear end of the cart toward the woods we can get out of here alive. The clubs will soak up the bullets." Goodykoontz nodded his head vigorously and I reached for the accelerator.

Then I saw something that froze my hand and my blood. It was the two carts from the foursome ahead of us. The women were coming to help, zipping down the fairway on the side the shots were coming from. They would be in the line of fire from the gunmen within seconds. They had to be nuts.

"We've got to get these guys before they kill those crazy women," I said.

Ben nodded assent. "My guards carry extra clips," he said.

"If we need extra clips those women are dead," I said, leaning to my left and squeezing off three shots in the general direction of the gunfire. Ben moved to the back of the cart and shot once. He ducked back as three shots ripped into my golf bag. One of them beheaded my Walker Lansdale Club, which pissed me off even more. It doesn't really have a limber shaft and I love that club.

I peeked over the seat and saw a medium-sized man in a business suit run to cover behind a tree. I could tell he and his partner were working their way nearer. The women were getting closer all the time. I squeezed off a shot at the guy behind the tree, then ducked when there was a sudden fusillade. I didn't hear any bullets and realized that the guns were of smaller caliber than the ones we had been hearing.

I stood and fired into the woods. There was plenty of covering fire. All four women were plinking away with their purse pistols. The guy behind the tree moved to return the fire, giving me a chance to put one into his leg.

Ben said, "Nice shot." I didn't tell him I was aiming at the torso.

We could hear sirens in the distance. That didn't mean all that much, since the District and environs are so crime-ridden that you suspect you're losing your hearing if you don't hear sirens. I couldn't get a good look at the guy I had shot, but I saw his hand motion toward his partner and he half-ran, half-hobbled back into the brush. The only sound on the course came from the little pistols of our female saviors. All four of them emptied their clips into the trees. I had never before been so happy that Washington was such a dangerous place that society women violated the Handgun Control law and packed heat.

Benson Goodykoontz looked like hell. "Let me see that arm," I said. I started to unbutton his left sleeve and he tried to resist. I was about to let his fetish prevail when I saw the platinum sheen of the watch.

"You sonofabitch," I said. I knocked the gun out of his hand, just in case, and ripped the sleeve off his shirt. The watch on the slender wrist seemed to glow with malignance.

"I've seen that before," I said, twisting the injured arm.

"I know," Goodykoontz moaned. I twisted the arm until he screamed. I didn't want him to say another word.

The women must have to drive through two-clip neighborhoods to get back to their mansions. They had reloaded and were still firing into the brush. One of them screamed, "I hit the mother, Adrienne. I got the sonofabitch right in the ass!"

Benson Goodykoontz screamed when I extended his arm in front of me and raised the pistol. I've got to admit I enjoyed letting him think I was going to shoot him. His howls tapered to whimpers when I stretched his arm onto the seat of the golf cart and fired one shot into the OTA surveillance device. The bullet broke the watch at its continuous metal band. The watch part of it spun over and knocked a hole in the seat. I identified what appeared to be the transmitter and blew it into a million pieces. I was hoping the OTA jerk who monitored Benson Goodykoontz lost his hearing to the muzzle blast.

"As I said, I've seen that watch before. Limited edition, isn't it."

Benson Goodykoontz held his injured arm with his right hand and nodded. "Milano and me. Just me and Milano Nagurski."

***

The women were chattering about the shootout. One said she had studied nursing and took a look at Ben's arm. She pronounced it a flesh wound and said he would be fine. Goodykoontz never took his eyes off his wrist.

Lynda kept asking if I had seen her shoot the shooter in the butt. She was so excited that she was shaking her breasts the same way she had in glorious commemoration of two of my better shots.

"Great shot," I said, hoping I did it better than the Bookends had. "Just out of curiosity, how do you manage to get handguns on the course."

"Well, in our purses, silly," Lynda said. "They just check for tobacco. The detectors don't pick up guns."

"Only in America," I said. I helped Goodykoontz into the cart and drove back to the clubhouse. The women flanked us in their carts. They still held their shining automatics. I believe I had misjudged them. I think these were three-clip females. I wondered what kind of hardware they carried when they went to downtown Washington. Designer machine guns, probably.

Lynda had called her husband. At least I figured it was her husband. She was still so hyper that we could hear every word.

"George, I shot a man at Healthcrest...No, I didn't kill him...No, he wasn't trying to do *that*, George...you think every man in the world is trying to get in my pants...He was trying to kill Mr. Goodykoontz and his nice young friend...Yes, George, the one who drives the cheap car...The one who hits it a mile...George, they killed Mr. Goodykoontz's guards, those two big men, you know..."

I had been in agony over what I feared was going to

happen. The OTA would flex its symbiotic relationship with the police, declare the Bookends to have been agents of "foreign tobacconists," install a new tracking device on Benson Goodykoontz, discredit me with the unique videotape of my evening with the unforgettable Veronica French and go happily on its mission of promoting public health.

It hadn't occurred to me that Lynda and her partners didn't know I was the one who took down the guards. I turned to Ben and said: "That's our story. The shooters killed the Bookends."

He looked at me blankly.

"The Bookends. Your goddamned guards..."

"Oh, sure," he said. He was still looking at his left wrist, turning it so he could see it from other angles. It was as if he were seeing it for the first time. "Okay," he said again. His voice strengthened and he looked me in the eyes. "I'm free. I guess I'm free."

"You're free of them," I said. "Now you've got me to deal with."

He nodded again. "I'm still free. Until they kill us. They'll kill us."

We were coming up the Number One fairway and Lynda was still talking on her portable.

"No, George, I'm sure they were both white. You're such a racist...Yes, George, I ought to be sure...I'm the one who shot him, George...Yes, he was, too. He was completely bald, like Simon Christopher...The stockbroker, Simon...He looked like Simon but Simon has two ears. He just had one...No, George, I didn't shoot his ear off...I told, you, I shot him in the ass...He was on the fence. George, you should have seen the look on his face. It was all bruised. It was a hoot!"

Completely bald, bruised face and one ear. I could get J.R. Tyson to run the probabilities and see if they were higher than a billion to one on what I was thinking about. But it wouldn't be necessary. The butt-shot shooter was the OTA guy I put to sleep in the Buffalo Holiday Inn. Chances were he had a new partner today. Bentley Benning had done a much better job than I had. I made a mental note to stop at the Holiday Inn again so I could leave Bentley another thousand-dollar tip.

CHAPTER 25

I have little use for redundancy. Writers should be unshakable in their belief that the word redundant means "unnecessary" or "repetitious." Short midget. Slimeball television minister. Wet water. Crooked politician. That kind of thing.

But I knew Benson Goodykoontz to be a modern redundancy man. Ben loved redundancy and preached redundancy. The entire Air Monitor computer setup was redundant. If we needed one computer to put out the paper, we had two. Just in case the first one broke down. Our foreign bureaus filed their copy by satellite transponder, but we had an option on a second satellite as redundant backup. Ben had two guards and I thought it was a good bet they were equipped redundantly.

"There are two more nine millimeters in the limo, aren't there?"

"Of course," Ben said. His tone implied he found it difficult to believe I had asked such a stupid question.

I could see the parking lot outside the pro shop. There were no police cars there, yet. I stood on the accelerator and zoomed away from the women. Lynda had called someone else and was telling them about her miracle butt-shot and the other three were babbling on their portable telephones about their adventure on the dreaded sixteenth hole.

I took the turn into the parking lot in a wide skid and stopped at the trunk of the limo. "The guns, Ben, get the goddamned guns."

Ben didn't understand why, but obeyed. He opened the trunk and produced a brace of black nine millimeters. I threw our guns into the trunk and slammed it. "Into the car!" I commanded.

He jumped in and I shut the door. There were several pillows in the back seat. I lumped them together and put them on the floor, atop about a week's worth of old editions of the Air Monitor.

"Do you remember how many times you shot?"

Ben said he shot twice. Bookend Number Two had fired twice.

"Put four into the pillow." He obeyed quickly. His eyes lit up as he pulled the trigger.

I put my redundant Ruger against the pillow and squeezed off seven. I remembered Bookend Number One put a shot through the canopy. I had no idea how many shots I had fired, but seven seemed a nice number. An odd number. Not the kind of number you would pick if you were the kind of person who thought redundant meant "two of them."

Benson Goodykoontz understood what I was doing. "We need to hide the pillows and the newspaper," he said, "there's an opening to the trunk."

He pulled it open and I tossed everything into the trunk.

We got back into the cart and drove to the pro shop as the first of about twenty police cars vaulted over the speed bumps and skidded into the parking lot.

The police lieutenant apologized profusely to Ben. "I'm sorry, Mr. Goodykoontz, but there were so many mobile 911 calls all at once that they bombed the communications computer before we could talk with anyone and the backup system didn't work." Ah, sweet redundancy. Maybe there is a God. And maybe He doesn't have a backup. I hate the idea of a redundant Deity.

CHAPTER 26

The police officers took our redundant Rugers. The lieutenant apologized to Ben again, saying he regretted having to seize them as evidence. But the law was the law, he said. I waited until the ambulance took Ben away, then went with the lieutenant to his office.

I gave a lengthy statement. I didn't mention that I was four-under when the bastards ruined my round and I didn't mention killing both Bookends. I did mention that the shooters shot the head off my three-wood when they were trying to kill Benson Goodykoontz. Beheading a great three-wood ought to be a high misdemeanor.

They sat me down at a computer that was supposed to allow me to draw a sketch of the attackers. I could have done a great job on Baldy One Ear, but didn't, because I hadn't really seen him. I did what I could on the guy I had seen. I'm pretty certain his mother couldn't have recognized him from my work.

Then I was invited in for a cup of coffee with the Chief of Police. The Chief said I should come out and get a look at his anti-tobacco training program. I asked if he had applied for an Office of Tobacco Abatement grant and he admitted he had. He said the grant had been pushed back by the budget constraints that came after the latest economic bad news. He said a little news coverage in the Air Monitor might turn the trick.

He asked if I knew Senator Winston DeWeerd personally. I replied that I knew him quite well. I've covered too many crime stories to think that the cop computers wouldn't reveal my dirty little genetic link with my half-brother. I thought my answer was just right. The Chief would believe I had too much class to brag about my kinship to Winston. For the moment, he seemed very impressed that I knew Winston in the flesh.

We had another cup of coffee and emerged from the Chief's office into a sea of news people. I have always hated to be part of those reportorial mob scenes. They don't do any good for the poor bastard at the eye of the hurricane and don't do much good for the hurricane, either. But I was there, so I did what the politicians do. I started talking and generally ignoring the questions.

I praised the bravery of the four women golfers who had, I was certain, saved our lives. I praised the quick response of the Chief and his men and women in blue. I said Benson Goodykoontz and I had every confidence that the Chief would bring the perpetrators to justice with a continued application of the intelligence, sensitivity and professionalism they had demonstrated in the first hectic hours of the investigation.

I knew the reporters from the Air Monitor wouldn't let me go without asking about the Cayman Combine, so I said that the Chief was investigating every possible lead, including the possibility of a foreign hit squad.

I glanced at the chief. I could have shot the Pope at that moment and the Chief would have testified it was self-defense. I was hoping the Chief's people weren't as good as I had told the world they were. There was an outside chance one of them might want an explanation of the bullet hole in the roof of the Bookends' golf cart, the one Bookend Number One got off just before I notched his Adam's Apple with my trusty two-iron. The gunmen had hit Bookend Number One. I hoped he hadn't quite died from the crushed larynx when the first round hit him.

I hoped the autopsies on the Bookends would be done by a graduate of the Sri Lanka School of Medicine who had to hack into eight more bodies before he called it a day.

I had to remember to wash the hell out of my two-iron. There was a complete likelihood that it had some of Bookend Number One's skin on it.

One dork from a radio station asked me what kind of round I was having when the attack interrupted it. I wanted to tell him I was four-under and was hitting the ball so well that Lynda would have shaken off one bra size before I holed out on eighteen.

But I've been covering politicians too long to fall into the trap of answering a question that's going to make me look like an asshole. I said: "I really don't care about that. Two men are dead and the assassination squad is still out there."

A woman from a suburban newspaper asked me about our three-clip heroines. I hoped my expression told her that she had asked the question I would have asked. I admitted ruefully that I hadn't even gotten the last names of the brave women, but said I was certain Benson Goodykoontz and I would be dead were it not for their heroic action. I said I hoped we could, in some small way, repay the four. The woman reporter was taking notes like crazy and the other reporters had stopped interrupting.

I pointed out that no men had come to our aid. I didn't point out that most men couldn't get their pistols onto the course as easily as women because some of us still don't carry purses. The female reporter appeared to appreciate the imputation of cowardice to the men on the course with us.

She pressed for elaboration. She liked what I was saying and wanted me to say some more of it. "Can you summarize your feelings about these women?"

My half-brother probably gave me grudging admiration for my answer. "I think they are the bravest, most selfless people I have ever met." I meant every word of that. I felt that little gulp in my stomach when I said it. I added: "There is little doubt that Benson Goodykoontz and I owe them our lives." I didn't say that Lynda's method of celebrating great shots could make golf the premier draw for male television watchers. You need to be sensitive when you're on television.

CHAPTER 27

I left my car at Healthcrest and drove Benson Goodykoontz's limousine toward town. I discarded the bullet-riddled pillow and papers in the dumpster behind a Sensitive Stop restaurant. Sensitive Stop is the chain name that came after militants from Totally Sensitive Gays And Lesbians promised to burn one Dairy Queen a day until a non-offensive name was forthcoming. Sensitive Stop signs blossomed like welfare programs in election years after Dairy Queens in five cities went up in flames. The Chairman of the Board admitted in an interview that he thought Sensitive Stop was a stupid name but he didn't have time to hire a consultant to find a better one. He didn't want any more flaming Queens of the Dairy variety. Personally, I believe he should have taken the heat and let them torch a couple more stores while he hired a consultant. Sensitive Stop makes me think maybe they serve hemorrhoids.

I was wondering how I could get rid of the two pistols. Then I saw a convertible parked outside a supermarket in a rough neighborhood. You can get rid of the Democratic Party if you can gift wrap it and leave it in a convertible in Washington.

I parked a few cars away, tossed the pistols onto the floorboard of the convertible and went into the store. I bought a package of gum and watched as a pair of scruffy teenagers tried the doors of a Cadillac, then looked inside the convertible. One of them grabbed the Rugers and they sprinted to a van. It had New York license plates. I know I should be ashamed, but two more pistols in the hands of New York or Washington riffraff is like throwing two jiggers of acid into the Potomac. My only hope was that the Rugers would wind up in the hands of some J.R. Tyson type.

Unlicensed guns are illegal in most states now and thieves make huge profits by selling illegal guns to normal people. Which isn't to imply that J.R. Tyson is anything approaching normal.

Besides being a country and western music fan, a computer hacker, and a reporter, J.R. is a gun nut. He inherited some money from his grandmother and blew most of on two machine guns and a couple of automatic pistols. J.R. bought them in Idaho, where they are still legal, but brought them back to the ten-foot-square safe room in our place in Washington, where they're not legal. He had to convert the machine guns so they would fire automatic, which is illegal to the third power.

J.R. and I almost got busted one afternoon when we were shooting on a friend's farm in northern Virginia. I was blazing away with an old Colt .44 magnum that's got as much power as Veronica French in the nude. Well, almost. It's a hell of a gun.

J.R. was firing the nine millimeter Ruger he says is the best handgun ever made. We were wearing ear protection and we didn't even know the helicopter was there until the rotor blast hit us. Ten Smoke Jumpers leaped out and took up positions. They were all carrying the latest Colt machine guns. Four of them peeled off and ran into the woods. J.R. and I lowered our guns but held our ground. The four Jumpers came back with a young guy, a young girl and a package of ersatz Camels in an evidence bag.

Then they searched us. We didn't have any cigarettes. They checked the computer and found out that neither of us had any history of any tobacco-related infractions. The computer also told them, of course, that we worked for the Air Monitor. The leader of the band said regulations compelled him to tell us that handguns were illegal. He was very polite. He snapped to attention and said, "To clean air..." before he jumped into the helicopter. I wanted to vomit.

***

I called J.R. and told him to meet me at the newspaper. I could have taken a cab back to Healthcrest to pick up my car but I needed somebody to talk with. He had seen me on television and wanted to know the full story. I told him I would tell him later.

I got stuck in a traffic jam and called Barbara Savage while it was unwinding. I had a slight feeling of guilt about Veronica French, even though sex had not yet become a part of my relationship with Barbara. I knew it would, someday. We were comfortable with each other and we both knew we would wind up together in the best way. I told myself I had nothing to feel guilty about. That made feel worse. I contemplated flipping the bird to a dork who tried to cut across three lanes of traffic to get in front of me. He was driving a pickup truck, of course. Some things change and some don't. From what I read, the people who drive pickup trucks are the same today as they were in the Twentieth Century, when they were responsible for most of the accidents and fully half the freeway shootings.

J.R. Tyson is a country boy at heart and once asked my advice on buying a pickup truck. I counseled against it. I told him that not everybody who drives a pickup truck is an idiot, but that sooner or later every idiot drives a pickup truck. J.R. started paying attention to the drivers menacing him on the road. He admitted I had it right.

Barbara Savage said she regretted not seeing me over the weekend. "How was Buffalo?" she asked.

"It was quite interesting," I said.

"I'll bet it was unforgettable," she joked.

"You could say that." I felt so guilty that I had a sudden craving to buy a pickup truck. I could trade my sports car for one of those little foreign-made pickups and put a sticker in the rear window that says: "American, Sensitive and Proud As Shit." The pickup that just cut me off had that one. Or I could put down five-hundred bucks for personalized license plates. I was wondering if "SCUMBAG" had been spoken for. I thought about how many people deserved "SCUMBAG" more than I do. I felt better.

I told her I would see her soon. I asked her if she had watched television news or listened to the radio. She said she had been busy and asked why I asked. "They tried to kill me and Benson Goodykoontz on Number Sixteen at Healthcrest," I said.

"Are you all right?" she said. The genuineness of the

concern in her voice brought me back to guilt. It was a short trip.

I moved past the cause of the traffic jam and stood on the accelerator. A Smoke Jumper van had curbed an ancient bus. The Jumpers had six people on the ground. One Jumper woman was leaping up and down, brandishing a package of cigarettes in delight. Her celebration dance reminded me of the one Bentley Benning did after he crunched the undercover OTA man in the Holiday Inn. It occurred to me that guilt was a luxury I couldn't afford at the moment.

I parked Benson Goodykoontz's limousine in the Publisher Only slot. J.R. Tyson was waiting. I checked the limo one last time to see if Ben and I had left anything incriminating in it. Finding nothing, I got into J.R.'s car and buckled the elaborate harness that's supposed to keep us safe.

CHAPTER 28

J.R. turned out of the parking lot and uttered one sentence. "What the hell really happened?"

I took a deep breath and told him the story, starting with the Veronica French telephone call that took me to Buffalo. J.R. is what people mean when they use the word "unflappable." He has an analytical mind that people discount because he looks like he should be breaking horses in Wyoming. He's a better reporter than writer and he's a pretty fair writer. If he had gone into lawyering, he would have been one hell of a prosecutor.

He could have been a great defense lawyer only if he was certain the client was innocent and it would be difficult to hide guilt from J.R. Tyson. He has a photographic memory and can play back anything you ever said to him. He even remembers the inflections you used. The mega-memory J.R. has keeps him from being sensitive in the generally accepted sense of our day, which involves forgetting things that are uncomfortable to remember.

I tried to hit the major journalistic high points of the Buffalo foray. I told him about Veronica French's suspicions about Joe French's tears. I told him I was certain Veronica was correct: that Joe French was probably under the influence of a potent drug when he made the videos. I told him about the OTA's bugged video player. J.R. asked: "What made you suspect it was bugged?" His eyebrows arched at my evasion but I plowed on with the story.

I told him about the two guys in the Buffalo Holiday Inn who told Bentley Benning they were undercover investigators for OTA.

"OTA's not supposed to have undercover people," J.R. said.

215

I knew J.R. knew I knew that. I knew J.R. wanted me to ask what compelled him to tell me something we both knew I knew.

"Right. So what's your point?" I said.

"Could be easy enough to nail the bastards on that," he said.

I had been lusting for some difficult way to nail the bastards because I knew it couldn't be easy. Since the statement came from J.R. Tyson I figured his solution had something to do with a computer or a gun. "How do we nail them? Shoot them? Or do we shoot them and then let you do a computer analysis?"

"I sneak into the OTA computer and get the expense account reports for anybody who had a trip to Buffalo over the weekend," J.R. said. If I had said it I would have looked so smug that somebody in a pickup truck would have put a couple of rounds through the passenger-side window. J.R. doesn't do smug.

I was with him, at least on the nub of it. "You must be saying the OTA has its own version of our credit-card thing at the paper..."

"Sure. Even better than ours. Their communications gear even has a little keyboard that lets them plug in their meals and drinks and things as they go. Sends it right up to one of their satellites and the money goes right into their bank account."

I asked J.R. how he came to know this gem of intelligence.

"You remember Marcia from the Waterfield Bar?"

He knew damned well I remembered Marcia. She was a junior accountant for Office of Tobacco Abatement. She was about five-five, blonde and striking in an unusual way. J.R. and I had stopped for a couple of drinks in the Waterfield one evening and had noticed poor Marcia's plight. She had been surrounded by six or seven male accountants, all of whom were trying to stimulate her sexual appetite by impressing her with their intimidating knowledge of accounting procedures.

J.R. said, "She needs help," and I agreed. I knew it would be better for all concerned if I did something before J.R. did. A few people have gotten seriously hurt by looking at J.R.'s spare frame and deciding to push him around.

I waded through the crowd and winked at the hostage when I got to the fringe of the bespectacled bevy of bean counters encircling her. She widened her eyes, then put on a smile that told me she was happy to see me, whoever I was. I could have been wearing a tee-shirt that said "Sensitive Serial Killers of America" and she still would have smiled and invited me with her eyes.

I elbowed my way in, embraced Marcia, apologized for being late and led her away from the group of Certified Pubic Accidents. It felt good. I'm not the kind of person who can stand idly by and watch a woman being gang-geeked.

She whispered her thanks, then gave me a big stage kiss while the Certifiably Pubescent Assholes did a group calculation on the probability of their surrounding another woman with knockout legs. The leader of the band was a brown-haired guy of about six-feet and one-hundred forty pounds. He set sail for a brunette who had just walked into the bar. The rest of them herded in behind him. "The tall one is the Judas Geek, right?"

Marcia laughed. "I believe so, and the Judas Geek smells like a Judas Goat, too," she said.

I had thought Marcia and I might be on our way to a close relationship but we were just pals from then on. It only took about five minutes, though, for her to develop an affection for J.R. Tyson. We spent the evening drinking. She wouldn't take her eyes off J.R. or her ears off anything he said.

She told me before she left town that she had never met anyone who combined J.R.'s intelligence, dry wit and knowledge of computers and software. I'm pretty certain she had developed a close relationship with J.R.'s hardware, too, until she was shot in one of our Washington drive-bys. She recovered, sold her furniture and caught the next airplane that would get her back to Tigard, Oregon, where street crime is more likely to be an occasional drive-by groping.

I told J.R. that I indeed remembered Marcia. I recalled for him that we had planned on taking her to The End for shank-of-the-evening cigarettes until she told us she was an accountant for OTA.

J.R. shifted lanes to avoid a freeway confrontation. One of the little electric cars the government loves had run out of juice and was blocking theright lane. "Marcia told me all about her job," J.R. said. "We sat down at her place one evening and I helped her neutralize the security codes so she could get into her office computer without leaving home."

"Of course, you remember them all," I said.

J.R. laughed. "Sure, but that wouldn't do any good. They probably change them every week or so, but I hid a shell program in the OTA computer that would update her home system every time they changed. We're as good as in."

I've tried more times than I can remember to avoid admitting awe at J.R.'s phenomenal memory. He could probably give me an exact count. Along with the dates and the amount of awe I tried not to admit. And he could quote me as having said, "Ah, bullshit. No way." Or whatever I said at the time.

A memory like J.R.'s can be a burden. Whenever he gets horsey about it I point out that it's not likely that I could hit the sack with Katricia Coyne, but might be able to forget it if I did. The memory of making love to Katricia might subdue even Winston DeWeerd a bit. It devastates J.R. Tyson, since he remembers every screeching moment.

"About the video player..." J.R. said.

I went ahead and told him the whole story of Veronica French. I told him I had the miniature video player I took from the two creeps in the Buffalo Holiday Inn and would show him the tape later. It never entered my mind that it might be scant hours from its premier showing at sleazeball theaters near and far.

CHAPTER 29

Fernando Phillips was a deacon in a small Baptist Church in suburban Chevy Chase. He hated doing business with the video connection but the money was too good to pass up. Fernando viewed his surveillance job with the Office of Tobacco Abatement as an extension of the Old Testament God's Will that people be protected from themselves. One of the fruits of God's zeal against the Demon Weed was the videos Fernando could sell to the video connection. Fernando Phillips loved the OTA job. Especially the retirement plan. If smoking could hold on in America for another ten years he and Maybelle would be on their new farm in Tennessee. Fernando called the farm Rhode Island Rolling Acres in honor of the leggy redhead who was the staple of his sideline. Phillips regretted that he could never disclose the genesis of the name and thus gain a lasting victory over those people who believed that staunch Baptists didn't have a sense of humor.

Phillips told Maybelle that he picked the name Rhode Island because the farm was rather small — only two hundred acres. Maybelle would have come unwound if she had known the name was a play on his pet name for Rhode Island Red — the lusty ex-wife of a smoker who rolled and howled with at least one guy on a bad surveillance shift and four on a good one.

Fernando Phillips knew that Maybelle wouldn't have made them give up the farm, even if she knew. Maybelle had often praised God for bringing Fernando the gifts that allowed them to buy it. "I know the money is manna from The Almighty and that's all I need to know," Maybelle had said.

Maybelle's appetite for worldly things had become voracious under the steady flow of unexpected grace from the

Almighty. It had turned out to be a mixed blessing. Maybelle hadn't let Phillips have his infrequent sexual pleasure lately because she was pouting over a car. Maybelle was tired of the cranky and slow electric car and wanted to move up a gas-powered one. Thanks to the Lord, they could now afford it.

Fernando couldn't tell her that a Grade Two OTA Surveillance Agent driving a gas-powered car might as well paste a sign in the rear window that read CROOK. So he told Maybelle that electrics were environmentally benign and combatted global warming. Maybelle's environmentalist tendencies had been killed by stranding after stranding in her cranky little electric.

Fernando wouldn't have anything to do with a whore, which would have been Unholy, but the chilling of Maybelle's typical glacial frigidity had forced him to seek the sexual attentions of Felicia Fallon. Felicia wasn't a whore but she liked flowers, quick dinners after work and exotic perfumes. Felicia was a somewhat unholy woman but even a man of God had to have some release, especially after he had spent a shift watching Rhode Island Red joyfully attaching her magnificently heaving body to her partner's penis.

Phillips felt the stimulation in his pocket. It was coming from the Buffalo bitch's tape. He could see Felicia's eyes widening when she watched the bitch and the Reynolds guy, going at it on the floor. He could imagine Felicia's breasts starting to heave and her legs tightening and relaxing in harmony with the delicious encounter noises from the couple on the tape. This one was so good it might get Felicia aroused and into her Medium Bed without a gift. He had picked up some earrings, just in case.

Phillips knew that pornography was a mighty force. He had even joined Totally Sensitive People for Sensitive Entertainment but Maybelle had pronounced the membership a bunch of perverts. The few meetings he had gone to didn't help much. Surround sound of tranquil music and heavenly pictures of beauty didn't stop the quickened breathing that always started when Rhode Island Red shed whatever small piece of clothing she happened to be wearing at the time one of her friends came by.

SMOKE JUMPERS

Fernando Phillips knew there had been virtually no risk to selling the other videos to the creep but this one had at least a marginal amount. The guy was, after all, that Reynolds fellow from the Air Monitor and the readout had said he was Winston DeWeerd's half-brother. Phillips would never do anything to harm Winston DeWeerd, who was the Washington denizen he admired most. But Maybelle's pressure for the car was too strong.

Phillips hated to be around the creep, who probably had never set foot in a church of any kind in his entire life. The creep was in a foul mood and wanted to steal the tape for a thousand. Phillips had to bargain and haggle like a rug merchant. The creep offended him mightily, saying goddamn this and goddamn that with every other breath and using the f-word.

He wanted to strangle the creep. They had watched the tape once and the creep said it was thirty seconds shorter than it was. They had to sit through it again with their stopwatches running. The creep appeared to get a kick out of watching Phillips squirming while Reynolds and the out-of-control brunette had at one another.

The creep always smoked. He always offered Fernando Phillips a cigarette. Phillips sometimes took one. He did so tonight. The draft from the unfiltered Pall Mall lookalike weed burned his lungs but calmed him. At least a bit. The pressure at the front of his pants didn't go away, though. He had to control his breathing. He hated for the creep to look at him with that knowing smirk, as if Fernando Phillips were some garden-variety pervert.

Phillips finally sold the tape to the creep for twenty thousand dollars. He put the church's two-thousand in a separate pocket of his wallet.

The dickering over the Buffalo bitch's tape had taken so long there wasn't time to drop by Felicia's apartment. He would hide his copy of the tape at home and take it to Felicia tomorrow. Tonight Maybelle would be waiting. Wanting to talk about the church and her damned car. Tonight, Phillips mused, Maybelle was going to get his pledge for the car only if she sought it religiously. After she assumed the missionary position.

221

He laughed aloud at his joke. Fernando Phillips would never understand how people could think firm believers had to be devoid of a sense of humor.

CHAPTER 30

J.R. Tyson and I picked up my car and returned to the condo. I knew it wasn't the best place to be but it was where J.R.'s computer was. I checked the security system and found no indications of an intruder. Paranoia is enough of a burden even when you don't have people from a worldwide bureaucracy trying to kill you. I hit a key to unblank the screen of J.R.'s computer and motioned toward his chair. "Sit and do good work," I said.

"In a minute," he said, disappearing through the door.

He returned with two pistols and his treasured machine guns. "Don't leave home without one," he said, sitting down at the computer.

J.R. having fun is not the most animated sight in the world. J.R. concentrating on a thorny problem at the computer is about a thousand percent less lively than two elderly pissants making love. It seemed that hours had passed since J.R. sat down and started tapping away. It was actually about fifteen minutes when I saw J.R. raise his hand in the grand motion of a concert pianist and hit the Enter key one last time.

He shipped the data to my computer so we could go look at it together.

He had tracked the two OTA expense accounts from a cab from OTA headquarters on K Street to the airport. One OTA man bought an Air Monitor at the airport. They flew to Buffalo and rented a car, arriving at the Holiday Inn after they stopped for coffee. J.R. had cross-indexed several in-room telephone calls from the motel bill. One was to OTA headquarters, another to a bar in Baltimore. J.R. said the Baltimore call had been cross-

223

billed to a surveillance account.

There was a hospital bill for Jerome Jenkins. J.R. pulled up a picture of Jerome. He didn't look nearly as scary in the OTA personnel shot as I remembered him, probably because he wasn't looking at me over a nine millimeter pistol in the OTA portrait. The hospital charges had continued through today. I had another twinge of admiration for Bentley Benning's cross-table lunge at Jenkins. Bentley had broken both of Jenkins collarbones, his right arm and several ribs. I imagined one of Benson Goodykoontz's dead guards looking at the hospital rundown on Jenkins' multifarious ailments. "Nice shot," I muttered.

"How's that?" J.R. inquired.

"Private Bookend joke, I guess. So we know Jerome Jenkins wasn't at Healthcrest. What about Baldy One Ear?"

"Interesting," J.R. said, nudging a key to bring on the next batch of data. J.R. Tyson narrated while I read the screen. "The expense account identifier belongs to Hedrick B. Hanley. Hanley is a ten-year OTA employee and did five of those on the Smoke Jumpers in the Carolinas. He's six-four, a former Georgia football player and an expert marksman, according to OTA." J.R. sniffed when he said "according to OTA." Tyson is so expert with a gun that not many people live up to his standards.

"You've screwed up your bits or over-bitten your bytes," I said. J.R. hates it when I try to make computer jokes. "The guy we're looking for is about five-ten and ugly. He doesn't shoot as well as I do."

"There couldn't be many people who don't shoot better than you," J.R. said, "but I didn't think about sorting it that way. I just pulled up the guy's ID picture. Not your man." The picture began materializing slowly on the screen, starting with the nose and letting the face build around it. J.R.'s sense of computer drama would be a pain in the ass to a lot of people but I don't object to a little showing off.

The flat nose materialized, then the mean eyes, then the bald head. The hairless head was accentuated by only one ear. "That's our boy," I said. "The nose will be a little flatter today. So who is this guy? Or who is the other guy? Do you know?"

J.R. Tyson peered over his half-rim reading glasses. "That's what took so long. I tried to do a match in the OTA's Employee Identification System and came up dry. I ran it through the National Criminal ID Base and got it."

The words "got it" heralded a new burst of information under the picture. The man was Dean Stanley, convicted in Gallatin County, Montana, of killing a 33-year-old school-teacher, then eating his heart. Stanley had been transferred from Montana jurisdiction to a federal prison in Illinois.

"So how did Mr. Dean Stanley get out and join the world's greatest anti-tobacco agency?" I said. I avoided making a joke about the Smoke Jumpers being a heartless agency. I can control myself, sometimes.

"That's the best part," J.R. said. "According to the Justice Department, our cannibalistic Mr. Stanley is still in custody. He's supposed to be an inmate volunteer guard at the Texas Smoker Colony."

"I should have made the cannibalism connection in Buffalo," I said.

J.R. looked puzzled. J.R. hates puzzled. "How could you have known?" he said.

"I saw him go to the buffet table. I should have figured he was stopping at the finger foods."

J.R. Tyson smiled. "One of these days medical science is going to figure out how to give you a sick-ectomy."

J.R. Tyson and I have known one another long enough that we often think of the same thing at the same time. Usually it's something minor, like identifying the proper moment to run out and get a drink. The situation we had was something other than minor.

We both stood up and headed toward our bedrooms. "You're thinking what I'm thinking," I said.

"Yeh. It's time for us to do our sheepherder routine and get the flock out of here."

We loaded the cars and came back for one last sweep. J.R. had his computer in his arms when the telephone rang. I picked it up.

The voice on the other end was tremulous. "This is Ben. They're here. At the hospital."

"Who?"

"Smoke Jumpers. Not in uniform but I recognize them."

"Where are you?"

"Infant Person Life Entry Zone."

One woman at the Air Monitor said I was a trogdolyte just because I refuse to abandon insensitive language. I still refuse to call the Maternity Ward the Infant Person Life Entry Zone. Totally Sensitive Persons for the Rights of the Newly Birthed had somehow managed to become offended by Maternity Ward because "ward" could be construed to convey dependency. As in "ward of the state." The hospitals brought it on themselves. Back in the last century they started referring to "death" as a "negative patient outcome."

"Stay in the Maternity Ward," I said. "J.R. and I can be there in ten minutes."

Benson Goodykoontz's voice took on a new moment of urgency. "Hurry. Please hurry. I don't want to go back."

***

J.R. had put his computer in the car and had disappeared back into the vault. I yelled for him to hurry up. The telephone rang again and I answered. I was afraid it was Ben again.

"Mr. Reynolds, please," the woman said.

"This is Rob Reynolds. I don't have time to talk right now."

"I want you to know that I killed him. He was a sinner, just like you. A smoker, too. He reeked of the Demon."

"Who the hell are you, lady, and what the hell are you talking about? You killed who?" I know I should have said "you killed whom" but proper grammar sometimes deserts me under pressure. J.R. Tyson came through the door, carrying the rest of his guns and saying, "It should be `whom'?" I considered letting J.R. finish the conversation with the crazy woman if he was going to be so goddamned picky. I put it on the speaker so he could suffer with me.

"My husband. Fernando Phillips."

"What the hell does this have to do with me? I'm a reporter at the Air Monitor."

"I know," she said. "I recognized your face from the billboards. I caught Fernando watching that unholy tape of you fornicating with that squealing slut. He threw me on the floor and had his way with me. His breath smelled of tobacco. He was an animal. It was horrible!"

My finger had been poised to hang up but I wanted to hear more. So did J.R.

"What did Fernando Phillips do..."

She interrupted before I completed the sentence. "I knew I'd have to tell. He ripped my panties off and just shoved his way in. He even tore me. I'm a little dry. He was watching that video while he was doing it and he kept saying, `Squeal, Maybelle. Squeal, goddammit.' It had to be the Tobacco Demon, don't you think?"

I got to finish my question. "What did Fernando Phillips do for a living?"

Maybelle Phillips told me the unholy beast had worked the night shift at an OTA office before his life ended at the point of her butcher knife.

"You should call the police," I said.

"I will," she said, "but I wanted to call you first to let you know I'll be putting in for the Smoker News Tip of the Month," she said. The Air Monitor sponsors a monthly competition for the person whose news tip about smoking tends to promote good health and an anti-tobacco atmosphere among the public. It pays ten thousand dollars and the newspaper gets more than that in free publicity.

"It sounds like you've had a very strong entry," I said, hitting the button to disconnect. J.R. smiled at my double entendre.

"One down," I growled to J.R. as we ran down the stairs.

"Yeh," he said, "only about two thousand Smoke Jumpers to go and we're home free." J.R. Tyson can be so coolly logical that I could murder him. Maybe I should just give him a cigarette and fix him up with Maybelle Phillips.

***

The Air Monitor was on the road to the hospital. I had a brainstorm and took a hard left into the parking lot. J.R. Tyson followed. I parked beside Benson Goodykoontz's limousine. J.R. started unloading his car. We tossed everything except the guns into the trunk.

"Good idea," J.R. said.

"Why go to battle on two skateboards when you've got a tank," I said.

One of the Air Monitor guards trotted up. He stopped trotting when he recognized my face. "Oh, it's you, Mr. Reynolds," he said. Saving the boss's life tends to burnish your image with the fellow hired hands.

I tossed him the keys to my car and motioned for J.R. to do the same. "I'd appreciate it you would take care of these cars," I said.

"Yes sir," he said. He said he would send them to the carwash and put them in slots where he could watch them.

"Mr. Goodykoontz appreciates your good work," I said before I put the limo in reverse and stood on the accelerator.

J.R. was fiddling with the keypad on his portable telephone as I drove.

"I know you'll be careful about using the telephone," I said.

He grinned. "Damned careful. If I can find a secure channel, I'll call some of my old Marine friends."

"Good idea," I said. That was an uncharacteristic level of understatement. J.R. does understating and I tend more to overstating. Averaged out, we are able to achieve an acceptable level of objective mediocrity that can be a real plus when both of you work in journalism.

J.R. found his secure line and was giving directions. I had never before heard the singular sound of command coming from the man. He hung up and smiled.

"We'll probably be outnumbered and outgunned but I got six people to back us up. By the way, what are we going to do?"

"Good question," I said. I was thinking about it when I skidded the limo to a halt outside the sign that proclaimed I was near the hospital's Infant Person Life Entry Zone. Every hospital in the District has metal detectors and nicotine alarms at every door. The nicotine alarms come from an OTA grant and the metal detectors grew out of sheer terror.

J.R. and I left our pistols on the floor of the limousine. We passed through the detectors without a setting off a beep. A guy wearing running shoes and a suit was standing to our left. His eyes told me he recognized us and I saw his head turn toward the little microphone that masqueraded as a lapel pin.

J.R.'s kick broke his jaw before he could utter a word. I started to say "nice shot" but decided the Bookends had suffered enough.

J.R. frisked the unconscious Smoke Jumper and came up with a Czech-made plastic pistol. "Not much shocking power in this little devil but it beats nothing," he said, stuffing it into his coat pocket.

We walked into the Maternity Ward that thinks it is the Infant Person Life Entry Zone. It was packed but there was only one man in the place old enough to be Benson Goodykoontz and he weighed two-fifty. "He has to be here," I whispered to J.R. Tyson, who shrugged.

A door opened to my left. I heard the crying of a newborn and saw Ben walking out, wearing the greenish garb of a doctor. It fit. The Air Monitor's advertising slogan is "We Deliver."

We walked toward the door just as the unmarked green Smoke Jumper van circled into the driveway. I looked to my right and saw four men trotting down the corridor toward us. I figured we were going to have to make a run through the Maternity Room when I saw the Addiction Center. Addictions are to medical people what oil is to Saudi Arabia; what television is to scumbag preachers; what sunshine is to Florida; what crime is to lawyers; what mountains are to Montana; what trees are to dogs. Important. I hated the idea of trying to blend in with a bunch of addicts, but I knew the room would be full of fractious people.

You can collect up to fifty-thousand dollars if you can show up at an Addiction Center and sell them on an addiction they've never met before. One woman tipped a national health chain on possible sexual-stimulation addiction linked to electro-magnetic fields around appliances. She negotiated for the standard fifty-thousand and her own electrical generator.

I knew we would have to declare something to get past the receptionist. I turned to J.R. first. "You're chewing gum," I said. "And you, Ben, you're peanut butter."

"Just for the record, what's your addiction?" J.R. asked. "Sex, of course," I said, putting on my most licentious smile.

We lined up at the counter. "Chewing gum," J.R. said. She made a note. "Gambling," Ben said, casting a defiant look my way. I thought about taking peanut butter but decided to hang in with sex. It doesn't stick in your throat, at least not the way I do it.

"Sex," I said. The receptionist looked interested. "You gentlemen go in and someone will bring you the necessary insurance forms," she said. She buzzed open the door and we walked in. There were a hundred people in the place. One woman who looked to be about forty was rubbing a Gideon Bible across her crotch and trying to keep her writhing down to an acceptable minimum. I wanted to ask, but there wasn't time.

I was hoping the Jumpers would queue up in confusion but they pushed their way in. I looked at them with horror in my eyes and screamed: "I know those brutes. They're all addicted to GANG VIOLENCE!"

It was akin to one of those scenes from what they once called Cowboy Movies before an unstoppable melange of Total Sensitivity Groups got into the act and forced today's movie-goer to sit through Historic Agribusiness Entertainment. The crowd rose as a wave and swept toward the front door. Everybody except one guy in an expensive suit who screamed: "Here! Pain! I love pain!" He was the only pain freak in the room.

Those Jumpers who weren't trampled were crushed against the wall. I sprinted to the front of the line and led the crowd out the exit of the Maternity Ward. I got off a pretty fair right on the jaw of one of the undercover Jumpers outside the door and J.R. busted his partner's knee. Ben kicked my guy in the ribs before we all jumped into the limousine.

"Nice shot," I said. I've never seen Benson Goodykoontz with such a wide smile on his narrow face.

The Smoke Jumper driver tried to get on our tail but the crowd was in the way. Three Jumpers with automatic weapons climbed atop the van. I was ducking when I heard the single reports of rifles. I looked in the rear-view mirror and saw the Jumpers tumbling to the ground.

"Your Marines landed," I said. J.R. Tyson just smiled.

CHAPTER 31

I drove toward the last place I would have looked for us if I had been the Smoke Jumper captain in charge of the hit squad.

J.R. was inspecting the plastic pistol. "Would your Marines meet us at the Air Monitor?"

"I suspect they would," he said.

I looked at Ben Goodykoontz in the front seat. "Ben, are you willing to play this out to the end?" He nodded vigorously and put his fingers to his lips. "Let's burn it right down to the tip of the filter," he said, laughing uproariously. One more OTA hit squad might turn Ben into a comedian.

I parked the limousine in Ben's reserved space at the Air Monitor. J.R. and I unloaded the guns, both of us checking the guard closely to make certain his attitude hadn't changed. There appeared to be no problem. You would have thought that every shift of Air Monitor reporters showed up with the Publisher in a pilfered doctor suit and unloaded an armory out of the trunk of his limousine. The guard looked longingly at J.R.'s machine guns, then resumed fawning over Benson Goodykoontz. All that assuaged my fear that the OTA might be waiting inside the newspaper.

I told him there were six new guards coming to join us and told him to let them in with no security checks and without telling anyone else in the newspaper.

The voice was accommodating. The words were not. He said, "Whatever you say, Reynolds."

J.R. winced when I dropped his machine gun. I tagged the guard hard in the gut with a left, kneed him in the crotch and slammed him against the wall. "How many?" I whispered. I stepped back, barely avoiding the stream of vomit from his mouth. I punched him in the gut a second time and slung him into the wall again.

"Two," he whimpered. "Just two."

"Where?"

"In Mr. Goodykoontz's office. They say they have to arrest him for violating the Tobacco Act."

"They're not going to arrest him. They're here to kill him."

He sneered. "They wouldn't do that. They're just soldiers in the fight against the Weed. They don't kill people."

"I'm going to bet your life on that," I said. I had to bang him in the stomach again to make him change clothing with Ben. Ben used his key to get us into the private elevator to the penthouse and office on the top floor.

The elevator door opened to an empty reception area, which wasn't all that unusual since the receptionist was known to have a long-standing practice of taking her break time in the intimate embrace of one of the photographers.

"You first," I told the guard. He balked and J.R. prodded him with the Ruger. "The man said you go through the door," J.R. growled.

"They aren't killers," the guard said. He walked slowly to the massive mahogany doors, then stopped.

"Open the doors," I whispered.

The Air Monitor guard stepped back. "You Smoke Jumpers in there, pass your weapons through the door. I've got the District Special Weapons Team here and they're going to start shooting if you don't."

I had to admire the quick thinking, even while doubting that anybody would be afraid of the Special Weapons Team, which was put under a Sensitivity-In-Force Order two years ago. SIFO was dreamed up by the District government after a bloody shootout that took the lives of ten civilians, one of whom was the Executive Secretary of Totally Sensitive Persons Against Police Brutality. The last trial conducted under the SIFO guidelines saw a man with a machine gun sentenced to two years in jail. The cop who shot him was fired, tried for what they called attempted personslaughter and got five years.

I decided to sweeten the deal. "Tell them we'll turn them over to the Smoke Jumpers for discipline if they hand over their guns. Otherwise they're dead."

He did as he was told. Within a minute one door opened and someone kicked out two pistols.

"Lie face down on the floor and open the doors. Both of them," I said. The doors swung open and J.R. and I jumped inside.

Baldy One Ear looked up from the floor and recognized me immediately. His howl echoed off the rich paneling and he tried to jump to his feet. "He's mine," I said, stepping in front of J.R. Tyson.

I always got a shameful amount of pleasure out of besting somebody else in the ring, but it was a sense of triumph in combat, not jubilation over hurting the other guy. I had never punished anyone before. I punished the hell out of Dean Stanley. J.R. Tyson assisted, yanking Stanley to his feet several times so I could continue the beating. It ended when I knocked him spinning and he fell, face down, on Benson Goodykoontz's desk, which is somewhat larger than the average American car.

I kicked him in the rear end. A growing red splotch formed on his khaki pants as he screamed. Healthcrest Country Club three-clipper Lynda had been absolutely correct. She had indeed shot him in the butt.

"My turn," Benson Goodykoontz said, and kicked hard at the red splotch. Stanley howled again and tumbled off the desk, landing on the mark of Lynda. He rolled onto his stomach and passed out. Ben pulled Stanley's shirt up to his neck, ran his finger's under the armpit and yelped with joy at what he found. I figured it was a gun or some other lethal weapon, but Ben jubilantly displayed a package of phony Merit 100 cigarettes and a Zippo lighter.

Stanley's Smoke Jumper companion made a move for the door but J.R. downed him with one clubbing motion of his gun. Tyson took the unconscious man's electronic handcuffs and communications gear, then put the cuffs on the Air Monitor guard.

Ben admired efficiency. He looked at the digital clock on his desk and clicked an imaginary stopwatch when J.R. snapped the cuffs on the Air Monitor guard. "Thirty seconds," he said. "Amazing."

He smiled at us and flipped a couple of cigarettes up in the package. We could see that he had done the offering flip a couple of thousand times before he became the head of the voice of the anti-tobacco movement.

"Join me in a smoke?" he said. Ben took one, rolled the wheel of the Zippo and pulled hard on the yellowish filter.

"Don't mind if I do," I said. J.R. took one and we all lit up.

The nicotine alarm on the wall started to hum. Ben put a nine-millimeter round through it. He blew imaginary smoke from the barrel of the pistol. "Nice shot," he said. J.R. couldn't keep from joining in our raucous laughter even though he didn't have a clue about the Bookends and our private joke.

I flipped my ashes into Dean Stanley's good ear. Ben asked what we were going to do with Stanley and the other two. "Good question," I said. "Witless protection program, maybe?"

J.R. Tyson laughed. J.R.'s Marine pals were going to put the three into safekeeping for us.

I used my portable telephone to check my Message Center. With a few minutes of peace, I was beginning to worry off in Buffalo. Debbie didn't strike me as a person who would hit the Urgent button for no reason, so I returned the call. I could tell from the background noise that she was pushing her big rig.

"Rob, I don't know what to make of this, but I went to the State University neighborhood the other night and picked up some cigarettes. I found the goddamnednest message in the package," she said.

"What did it say?"

"It said. `They're going to kill me. Joe French. Texas Colony.' "

I thanked her and hit the disconnect button with a shaky finger. We had another quick smoke while we sketched a plan that might keep a few of us from dying for our next cigarette.

235

CHAPTER 32

It wasn't the place I would have suspected as the host city for a protest. But it came during the Tuesday meeting of the Combined Utah Air Police. At Tuesday noon the Utah Air Police would meet to commemorate the blessed arrests of Edgar L. Newhouse, L.R. Eccles, Noble McKay and John C. Lynch. The men had been arrested at the Vienna Cafe on Main Street in Salt Lake City after Newhouse lit a cigarette and McKay a cigar. The arrests at the Vienna Cafe came in violation of Utah State Code Section 4, Chapter 145, which dealt with smoking in an enclosed public place. In another time the men would have been taken to court for a brief appearance and then summarily dispatched to one of the three Smoker Colonies but the smoke at the Vienna Cafe had come in 1923. It was the first anti-smoking arrest in the history of the nation and the Utah Air Police chapters enjoyed commemorating it.

Troopers from the local Smoke Jumper outpost always joined in the Tuesday gathering. Mormon Utah was historically one of the most anti-tobacco states in the union and there was little else to occupy the small Jumper contingent.

This Tuesday was different. Heather Reisner and two of her friends showed up with picket signs. Heather's read simply, "Smokers Have Rights, Too." Her wobbly script was sincere in its message and inadequate to express her outrage. Her husband had been dispatched to the Nevada Smoker Colony only three months earlier. A stern-faced Human Relations representative from the Office of Tobacco Abatement had come to her home on Sunday to notify her that her ex-husband had been killed while trying to escape.

The Air Police demonstrators ignored the three women

and their pitiful signs until Heather Reisner dug deep into her purse and produced an ancient .32 caliber pistol and a package of cigarettes. She solemnly handed a cigarette to each of her friends and struck a match, lighting all three illegal weeds.

A Smoke Jumper Lieutenant moved toward the trio and Heather Reisner stopped him by pointing the little .32. A female Jumper recruit screamed: "Drop the cigarette. You're killing your baby!"

Heather Reisner responded by dragging deep on the cigarette and the Jumper opened up with her automatic rifle. Heather Reisner and one of her companions went down. The third woman was hit in the leg and fell slowly, still puffing defiantly on the cigarette.

The shooter compounded her mistakes by clubbing a cameraman from the Mormon Church-owned television station and trying to seize his camera. Bystanders subdued the Jumper and the cameraman zeroed in on the protester's face, contorted by pain but framed in a halo of smoke. The last footage he took was of the Smoke Jumper lieutenant, who tossed his gun and badge to the ground. He picked up Heather Reisner's cigarette and put it between his lips.

"My God, what have we done?" he said. "She was right. She was right." He picked up the bloody protest sign and walked away.

CHAPTER 33

Worst week Winston DeWeerd can remember. Bozos in Office of Tobacco Abatement Surveillance Division should have had goddamned little half-brother dead to rights. Illegally watching OTA Colonies video. They didn't need anything else. Could have booted in and untangled the two. Should have had the cuffs on them before the cunt got on little Rob's lap. Before she freed his little peter for the whole world to see. They don't go in. They sit. They watch the tape. Little Rob bangs the Veronica French broad. Big deal.

OTA surveillance clown sells the damned tape to biggest porn dude in town. Little brother all over the world by now. Satellites took him. Little Rob's banging the hot-natured cunt in twenty-eight languages. How many languages are there, anyway? Cecilia, she'll know.

Goddamn Brits would love it. Hate to see headlines if the Brits get the story. "Anti-Tobacco Senator's Kin Seduces Smoker's Ex On Illegal Surveillance Tape." Some shit like that. Brits always a pain in the ass. Especially Brit newspapers. Winston Churchill crap. Never forgave Winston Churchill stuff. Winston smoked like hell.

Goddamned OTA. Could have grabbed little Rob. Conspiring with the bitch to try to bust her ex out of the Texas Colony. Plenty of ways to shut her up. Just need to get the bitch to a nice, clean OTA cell. Little Rob...different case. Little prick has to go. Goodykoontz, too. And the Polack. Milano Nagurski. What kind of Polack has a Dago first name, anyway.

Polack who could blow the whistle on the drugs he brewed. Heavy shit. Kept the Colony clowns under control.

238

Goddamned clowns at OTA agree on everything. Get little Rob. Get the Polack. Get Goodykoontz. Clowns tell their hired goons, Shitz and Fritz or whatever their names were: waste Goodykoontz. Waste little Rob. Right there on goddamned golf course. Backup. They got backup. A goddamned cannibal who can't eat straight. An agent who can't shoot straight. Some backup for Gritz and Schlitz. Can't be much. Little Rob wastes Mitz and Blitz. Bunch of rich broads shoot our cannibal in the ass. Backup backs off. Some goddamned backup.

Office of Tobacco Abatement, my ass. Sonsofbitches couldn't abate tabasco. Fire every one of the sonsofbitches.

Little Rob's on television. Like he's some kind of goddamned hero. He thinks he's so damned cute. He knows too damned much. Frigging Goodykoontz knows everything. Every frigging everything. Hospital was a disaster. Send in twenty clowns to grab Ben Goodykoontz. Wind up with three dead Smoke Jumpers. Four more on OTA medical leave. Clowns probably couldn't find their damned health-insurance cards. How could you if you can't find a fifty-year-old dork with a bad wing. The District Chief of Police is a shithead. Having trouble buying story a bunch of Jumpers went nuts at the same time.

The damned Jumpers still can't find the Polack, the Nagurski clown. Ten-thousand dollar tracking watch. Not a goddamned peep. Watch dies five minutes before Jumpers supposed to grab the Polack. Supposed to hit Ben and little asshole Rob at the country club. Gotta be a leak. Somebody tipped the Polack. Simple. The damned Jumpers supposed to grab the Polack the same minute Knitz and Britz were taking down Goodykoontz and sweet little Rob. Jumpers get caught in traffic. Hundred million dollars worth of helicopters in the budget. They get caught in traffic. Idiots can't find a bugged white-faced Polack in a bunch of darkie dorks. Fire 'em all. Start over.

All Air Monitor links cut, one by one. Even got to the one that keeps the money. Cecilia calls to tell the idiots to grab the money before Goodykoontz moves it. Sit on their butts. Goodykoontz shifts millions to foreign account. Goodykoontz knows all the tricks. Little prick ought to. He put them in.

District cops outside the building. Damned news media crawling all over the Air Monitor. Stupid when media covers media. Kinda like incest with your ugly sister. Jumpers won't even think about going in. Could have gone in when they got the nicotine buzz from Goodykoontz's office. Then the damned bug deader than a smoker's lungs. Can't even threaten the bastards any more. Trying to act like they're goddamned real cops, for crissakes.

Real cops wouldn't have shot up everything in goddamned sight in Austin. Ten puny puffers bite the dust just a little ahead of schedule. Dying anyway. Damned cigarettes. Everybody's making a federal case out of it. Just bad luck. One creep had to be the damned quarterback of the damned football team. Hadn't have been for the damned quarterback it wouldn't have been all that big a deal. President getting cold feet. Worried about his image. Image, my ass. Wimpy sonofabitch worried about the orders he signed about the jails and the damned Colonies. He wanted the Clean Lung Dividend worse than anybody. We got it going now. Wimp bastard wants to appoint a commission. See if maybe the Smoke Jumpers have gotten too powerful. Ground floor. Got video of the President. On the ground floor. Got tapes of the President. On the ground floor. Got video of the President. Smoking. Smoking in the White House bedroom Lincoln liked. Smoking like John Wilkes Booth's gun. Maybe his goddamned commission ought to get a look at those. Hypocrite sonofabitch.

Goodykoontz on television every fifteen minutes, like he's something except a goddamned two-pack-a-day shithead from the Texas Colony. Says there are "major developments" in the attempted assassination yet to report. He'll tell the world at the same time. Tomorrow, maybe. Or maybe later. Or maybe before.

What the hell is he doing? Why wait? Where the hell is the prick half-brother? Where the hell is the J.R. Tyson clown?

Got to get them. Especially sweet little Rob. Need to tell him the Jumpers might have missed his local squeeze. Sweet little Barbara Savage. Looks like another goddamned leak. Goddamned Jumpers leak like a Catholic rubber.

She's talking on the telephone to little Rob. Twenty minutes later, bitch is gone. Goddamned Smoke Jumper clowns got her sweet daddy, Old Ed Jones, though. Hard to miss an old fool in a mansion in Center, Frigging, Montana. Couple thousand bucks worth of weeds in his little basement. Dumb sonofabitch. Probably really did screw sheep. Old Ed's already on his way to the Texas Colony. Be all over the goddamned news in a couple of minutes. Ought to smoke out his pretty little daughter. Pretty funny. Smoke out his little daughter. Smoke out the bitch and maybe the goddamned Jumpers can put a kink in little Rob's little dick.

***

It took several stabs of his index finger before Winston DeWeerd hit the intercom button that connected him to Cecilia Word's private office. Her wonderful voice calmed him, but only slightly. Cecilia was the only woman he had ever known whose voice could have been exciting, yet placid, in the middle of a nuclear attack.

"Bring two," he said.

"Are you certain? You've already had two. We have the Western States reception tonight. Two more might be a bit much."

"I said bring two," DeWeerd said, his voice an assertive hiss. "And do it frigging now!"

Cecilia left them on the coffee table. She moved gracefully away from DeWeerd's clutching hand. "Not now," she said.

"Do it for me," he said.

"Do it yourself."

DeWeerd glowered at her back as she walked away, shaking in frustration and anger. He had to use both hands to get the flame to touch the marijuana cigarette.

CHAPTER 34

My celebrity from the Healthcrest Country Club shootout was serving us well. A week ago I couldn't have gathered up my cohorts of the Washington's media without hiring one of the District's heavily armed Jamaican gangs. Today we were together on one of those tilt-rotor transport airships that flies like an airplane and lands like a helicopter. J.R.'s six Marine buddies were wearing their old uniforms and carrying their new automatic weapons.

We flew low over Amarillo, Texas, and headed south toward a certain landing and an uncertain reception in the Texas Smoker Colony. A correspondent from Reuters News Service looked down at the bleak countryside and nudged the AP's Nick Coughran. "Bleakest country I've seen since Saudi Arabia," he said, "what do people do out here."

"Hunt and screw," Coughran said, concentrating on editing his computer notes from the morning briefing Ben and I had conducted, with some help from Ben's friends.

The Reuters guy was quiet for a moment, then mused that he hadn't seen a living creature on the ground. "What do they hunt?" he asked.

"Something to screw," Coughran said earnestly. Then he dissolved into waves of laughter.

*****

Jerry Ray Tyson had gone without sleep for three days during the last Middle East war, but that was a few years ago and he was stifling yawns as he worked at the computer in Benson Goodykoontz's office.

Goodykoontz had left him alone, interrupting J.R. only

occasionally to ask if he needed a cup of coffee or any other assistance.

Goodykoontz knew Tyson's work as at an end when he saw the right hand rise toward the ceiling, then descend in a graceful arc that ended with a gentle tap on the Enter key.

"That's all of them?" Ben asked.

"Yep. Every suspected smoker and smoker sympathizer from the Office of Tobacco Abatement's very own computer files, plus the names of the people Rob and I have been keeping."

"They're all notified, then," Ben said.

"They've got the whole story," J.R. said. "I hope they read it and look at the video footage we that goes with it."

"I just hope they believe it," Goodykoontz said.

"Good point," J.R. said. He stood and put on his shoulder holster.

"I think I know where to find Barbara Savage," he said. He ran to the helipad on the roof.

Benson Goodykoontz reached for the buzzing telephone with his left hand and reflexively tapped a cigarette out of the pack with his right. He looked longingly at it for a second, then put it back into the pack.

***

You never know what is going to turn out as the mob-journalism "angle" of any story. I thought the OTA undercover hit squad and the fact that convicted cannibalism killer Dean Stanley was the streets on an OTA expense account would be the grabber for the group. They homed in on it, all right, but there was extensive examination of the story behind about the Barranca Lopez tape.

"You mean the little bitch locked her mother out to die in a blizzard because she didn't want cigarette smoke in her damned hair?" Coughran asked.

The woman from the Foundation for Hearing Impaired Citizens jumped in and said that apparently was the case. She replayed the tape of Alicia Lopez and patiently pointed out that Alicia's lips clearly formed the word "hair" while the OTA-released tape clearly carried the word "air."

"Mrs. Lopez plainly told her daughter `screw your hair' and the Office of Tobacco Abatement clearly altered that to `screw your air'," she said. A video expert Ben flew in from Georgia pointed out that OTA had altered the tape in other subtle ways to make it more dramatic. He explained how the OTA's videophiles had enhanced the snowstorm that piled in on little Barranca but had failed to remember to phony up a dusting of snow on the kitchen floor. I didn't understand a word of his technical lingo and figured most reporters wouldn't do much better. So I had Ben send a jet for Hormel Schlegel so Hormel could be with us. I figured I owed him some celebrity time. He was the one who tipped me off. And Hormel was an internationally renowned anti-smoking activist who would have credibility with Winston's national power base.

Hormel backed up everything the woman from Foundation for Hearing Impaired Citizens said. He added: "I think the OTA was wrong in what it did but I will always believe that little Barranca Lopez was right, even if she was right for the wrong reasons. Her mother was killing her with secondhand smoke."

That brought catcalls and other expressions of disdain from the crowd. Hormel couldn't hear then but his keen eyes recorded the hostility. The tide was turning.

***

I was in what passes for deep in thought for me. I was trying to think of some telling quotations about freedom. I guess being a celebrity, even for a couple of days, tends to bend a person toward pretension.

Coughran broke my concentration, which wasn't all that deep on the freedom quest but had gained intensity because I was worrying about Barbara Savage.

"How long before we get to the Texas Colony?"

"About twenty minutes," I said.

"Great," he said, "we've got time for some entertainment."

He paddled to the video player and inserted an unlabelled tape.

"What's this?" I asked.

"Picked it up at a shop in Alexandria," he said. "I think

they call it The Second Coming. And the Third. And the Fourth..."

He hit the play button and I recognized the tape immediately. I hadn't had a chance to review it closely until now and was again awed by the silky strength in the heaving of Veronica French's wonderful little body.

Coughran adopted his best imitation of a television sports announcer. "The big guy needs to work on his couch technique, but I believe the judges will give his floor routine about a nine-point-nine."

One of the only non-journalists on the tour was Pierre Latouf. Pierre had given a brief presentation about his part in alerting me to the strange messages found in cigarette packages. The normally serious Latouf looked at the videotape with the eyes of a Frenchman, not as a functionary of Amnesty International.

"In France, the man would be honored," he said. "The woman! Ah, the woman! She would be declared a national treasure." There was applause.

I thought about some of my fellow celebrities of the past to see if I could come up with guidance. The FBI had made audio tapes of the Rev. Martin Luther King, frolicking in the hay with various women. But audio wouldn't count for a celebrity of the video age. I settled on the 20th Century actor Sylvester Stallone. Stallone avoided military service and was making whoopie for the porno flicks while the Vietnam War was going on, then made war movies as "Rambo" after peace broke out.

***

The pilot said we had received the warning that we were violating an Office of Tobacco Abatement restricted air zone.

Coughran yelled: "Damn the torpedoes! Full speed ahead!"

A young woman from a Philadelphia newspaper piped up from the back. "What's a torpedo?"

Coughran looked at me over his bifocals. "Guess I'm getting old," he said.

The pilot put the aircraft down flawlessly in a soccer field amid what the OTA Public Affairs people have always told us were the "comfortable, middle-class dwellings of those sentenced to the Smoker Colony." They were uniformly empty.

J.R.'s Marine pals fanned out and trained their rifles on the Smoke Jumper platoon that had burst out of the main gate. The protective helmets and breathing gear made them appear to be an invading force from outer space. It was great television. We were live, all over the country. There was the problem of staying that way. Live, I mean.

I had the microphone for the airplane's Public Address system. "That's far enough. You know who we are. You know we're coming in and you're not going to stop us."

I noticed that about twenty automatic weapons were aimed my way. There were so many red dots from laser sights steady on my white shirt that I must have looked like a chunky barber's pole.

"Don't let them bluff you," Coughran said. I glanced at his shirt and didn't see a red dot of any kind. It reminded me that a politician in North Carolina once described journalists as "the people who hide during the battle and come down after it's over so they can waste the wounded."

I had gone through my General Custer repertoire when Veronica French and I discovered the secret OTA surveillance device, so I rejected the idea of yelling "Take no prisoners." I was trying to dredge up what Stallone's Rambo character would say. It was no help. Stallone probably would have discarded the warrior role, raised a white flag, dropped his pants and said: "Bring on the broads." Dirty Harry was the best I could do. Dirty Harry was the tough cop figure who was played by a rugged guy named Clint Eastwood.

I knew Harry Callahan wouldn't have said anything. He would have walked toward the Jumpers, daring them to do something stupid. I was trying to justify an honorable death with millions of people watching. I was trying not to notice that the dots on my shirt were beginning to come together on the pocket over my heart.

I had taken a couple of steps on legs that felt more like Eastpulp than Eastwood when we heard the helicopters the mobile armored vehicles. I looked up only after I noticed that my shirt was white again. Soaked with sweat, but white. I thought it probably blended well with the yellow streak that was once was my spine.

The slow-talking voice boomed from the lead helicopter. "You Smoke Jumpers put 'em on the ground and flop your yellow-bellied asses on your face beside 'em and jest maybe we won't have to do anything you backshootin' sonofabitches are gonna regret."

Little Miss Philadelphia Newspaper moved to my elbow. She obviously thought I looked more approachable without the red dots.

"What does that mean?" she whispered.

"I believe he said we've got the Texas National Guard on our side." I made a mental note to read up on Colonel William Travis in case I ever do this again. He was the commander at the Texas freedom shrine they call the Alamo. That Dirty Harry stuff can't work more than once.

CHAPTER 35

J.R. Tyson saw the van bump to a stop in front of the bar. He threatened the helicopter pilot into landing on the street as the four Smoke Jumpers piled out. He shot one and was puzzled to see the second Jumper fall from a shot from inside the bar. The remaining two men dropped their weapons and slowly drooped to the sidewalk.

"Barbara!" he yelled.

The voice was strong. "Rob? Is that you?"

"It's J.R. You can come out."

J.R.'s face collapsed in shock when he saw the three people who walked from the bar that called itself The End. Barbara Savage had a small pistol in her right hand. Milano Nagurski was to her left. J.R. Tyson looked with approval at the lead shielding over the OTA tracking watch. His jaw drooped anew at the woman at Barbara's right.

It was Winston DeWeerd's Press Secretary. The beautiful and abominable Cecilia Word.

"What the hell is that bitch doing here?"

Barbara smiled. "I understand what you're thinking, J.R., but you really shouldn't call my baby sister a bitch."

"Hadn't been for Cecilia I'd be a dead man," Nagurski growled.

J.R. had a few hundred questions he wanted answered but was worried by the crowd that was gathering. There were several Gay Air Police volunteers in the group. They appeared to be transfixed by the screen of a teenager's portable television.

"Look at that," one slender GAP volunteer breathed. "Cigarettes. Making cigarettes in the goddamned Texas Colony."

One GAP volunteer sprinted toward them. J.R. leveled the gun at his chest but the young man made his way directly to the prone Smoke Jumpers and began kicking them. "Lying fascist bastards!" he screamed.

The rest of the crowd moved and joined the attack on the Smoke Jumpers. J.R. motioned to Barbara and they sprinted to the helicopter.

***

On a good day Winston DeWeerd was a tower of abuse to his staff people. Today he was a skyscraper. He screamed for Cecilia Word. She was nowhere to be found. He screamed at Ronnie Peebles, his Chief of Staff. Peebles said Cecilia had called and said to tell the boss to read the note in his electronic mail.

Winston DeWeerd had overseen the appropriating of billions of dollars worth of technology for the Office of Tobacco Abatement and its Smoke Jumpers.

He had never managed to learn how to get into his computer files. That was one of the reasons there were people like Cecilia Word on the payroll.

DeWeerd felt relieved when Peebles told him Cecilia had told him the password to the electronic mail.

"She thought you might need some help," Peebles said.

"Shut the hell up and let me see what's in there," DeWeerd growled.

The password worked and the note from Cecilia flashed onto the screen in larger-than-normal type. Winston's eyes narrowed to slits as he read it.

"Senator:

If you're reading this, that means it's over. Light up another joint. I left them in your credenza.

Cecilia

P.S. Tell Ronnie to call up the Cecilia Jones file from the National People Information Base. Have him bring up the Cecilia Jones from Center, Montana. I wrote you a resignation speech. You can read it at the party convention this morning. It's pretty good. Have a short life."

DeWeerd wanted to smash Ronnie Peebles in his smirk-
ing face. "You've already looked, haven't you?"

"Yes sir," Peebles said. "It seems that our Cecilia Word
is really Cecilia Jones. Her dad is..."

DeWeerd's backhand slap kept Peebles from ending the
sentence.

CHAPTER 36

I recognized the eyes at fifty yards. The man didn't look the same, but the eyes told me I had found Joe French. He was puffing on a cigarette and talking with the young newspaper-woman from Philadelphia.

They had stopped talking and their eyes were glued to her portable television set. I stopped and listened.

"That's the one we called Two Shoes. What the hell is a two-pack guy doing on television?"

"That's Benson Goodykoontz," she said. "He's the publisher of the Air Monitor."

I strained my eyes to hear what Ben was saying. He was telling a packed news conference how his computer knowledge and financial skills had resulted in his being plucked from the Texas Colony and installed as the OTA's front man at the Air Monitor. The financial analysts finally would understand how Ben managed to take the Air Monitor from an obscure sheet to one of the nation's most pervasive publications. Government money, managed by a financial wizard from the private sector. I wondered fleetingly if the formula might work in, say, the Department of Education. Then I said: "Joe."

"You're...You're Bob Reynolds."

"Close. Rob."

"How'd you recognize me? I don't look anything like the guy whose ass you kicked in Syracuse that night."

"Veronica is a friend of mine. She knew there was something wrong from your tapes. She kept after me until I said I'd try to do something. Probably none of this would have gotten out if it hadn't been for her."

Joe French smiled. "Well, guess that makes two things she's good at."

I tried to look puzzled. I'm pretty sure I didn't pull it off.

French looked at his cigarette as if he were seeing it for the first time. "I'm putting these goddamned things down," he said. "They're nothing but trouble for me."

***

Winston DeWeerd could feel the glacial chill of the crowd when he walked into the gathering of the party faithful. He had smoked two joints while he read, then shredded Cecilia's resignation speech. He had made some notes. He didn't need the bitch, anyway.

The party executive tried to block his path to the microphone. Someone had once said that the most dangerous spot to be in a dangerous District of Columbia was between Winston DeWeerd and a microphone or television camera. Winston pushed his way to the podium and raised his arms in the victory sign that had become his emblem.

"To Clean Air," he roared, waiting for the responding thunder he knew would come. It always came. The air-conditioning unit was the only sound in the darkened auditorium. His marijuana-dimmed eyes weren't focusing well, but he could see movement everywhere. There were hundreds of clicks and hundreds of scratching sounds.

The strident sound of the tobacco alarms filled the room. Someone brought up the house lights. Almost everyone in the audience was smoking a cigarette. Most appeared to dislike the experience immensely. Everyone kept their cigarettes burning.

DeWeerd's glassy eyes tried to find the Smoke Jumper unit that always accompanied him on public appearances.

"You're all under arrest! Smoke Jumpers, front and center. Block the exits!" he screamed.

He yanked his arm from the person tugging on it. The burly District of Columbia cop moved back in and secured DeWeerd in a choke hold. All but a few people in the audience extinguished their cigarettes when the babbling DeWeerd was handcuffed and led from the room.

CHAPTER 37

Maybe my grandchildren will get to know how the Winston DeWeerd era came to a close, assuming I have any grandchildren. You've pretty well got to have children before you have grandchildren and Barbara hasn't said for sure she's going to marry me. I think she will.

I didn't mean to imply that Winston was anything more than a filter-tipped Hitler. But I hope my half-brother taught us some lessons about freedom and tolerance. Negative, lessons, for sure, but lessons. Maybe we'll remember what Winston and his followers taught us, when we have a real crisis. Something with more meaning than a man or woman making a decision to drag on a bit of leaf wrapped in white paper.

Only a few months have passed since the week that began with my trip to Buffalo, but life has changed for a lot of people. The Smoker Colonies are closed.

The Smoke Jumpers in the Nevada Colony were the last to give up. The federal government called in the 82nd Airborne Division from Fort Bragg, North Carolina, to convince the Jumpers it was over. The 82nd only lost five people. Twenty Jumpers went down before it was over.

There were no troops involved in the North Carolina Colony. The public just mobbed the place. We've never gotten a good count on the Smoke Jumper death toll from there, because they retreated with their dead and wounded and tried to get to safe haven on the Jumper island just off the Carolina coast. A couple of the helicopters went into the Atlantic and several more provided target practice for Marine pilots from Cherry Point.

Most of the Reformed Felon Smoke Jumpers on the island killed one another. A few of the survivors got away.

The government says it will take a couple of years before its people can completely entomb the experimental nuclear fission units that furnished electricity to power Winston's illegal cigarettes- and-power empire. The experts say the generators could have been a major advance in making electricity if they had been shielded properly and built with the idea that people, not smokers, had to work around them.

Ed Jones, Barbara's dad, died of a heart attack just after we got inside the Texas Colony. I never got to meet him. Katricia Coyne is among the missing. The Justice Department says she probably ran to Canada.

I hear from Veronica French occasionally. She has turned down quite a few million-dollar offers to be a porno movie star. That irritates me, but only a little. I haven't had a single call from Hollywood, or Sleazeball, Oregon, or wherever it is they make porno movies. They probably know I would turn them down. That's probably why they don't call.

I got Benson Goodykoontz to pay a half-million of the Air Monitor's ill-gotten gains to Bentley Benning, the former tight end who thinks he played close catcher for Buffalo. Bentley has his own sports bar in Miami Beach. Barbara and I flew down for the grand opening. I had assumed Bentley would show tapes of his pro football exploits with the Buffalo Bays. He did, but the one that was the crowd pleaser was his three-table tackle of the guy who was going to kill me in the Holiday Inn. The quality was pretty good, for a security camera in a dimly lighted bar.

Milano Nagurski is on his way to becoming a millionaire. His cure for smoking looks promising and has to go through a few more months of testing by the Food and Drug Administration before it goes on the market. He will ever worship Cecilia Jones. Cecilia telephoned him once a week to keep him up to date on Senator DeWeerd's latest craziness and had made the telephone call warning Milano that DeWeerd's psychoses were about to boil into murder. The Smoke Jumpers had Nagurski under constant surveillance. Nagurski had been a primary target. He knew too much.

Barranca Lopez was charged with killing her mother in New Mexico. She skipped bail in the company of a Colombian drug dealer and hasn't been heard from since.

Collier Smythe was fired as president of the University of Texas at Austin. Ben Goodykoontz said Smythe called him from a pay telephone in Washington one afternoon, asking Ben if he could possibly use his influence to get him a federal job of some sort. Ben hung up on him.

J.R. Tyson is no more. No less, either. He is now J.R. Clemons-Tyson, having moved to Tigard, Oregon, to marry Marcia Clemons. I didn't realize that Marcia had two-name tendencies when I saved her from being gang-geeked by the accountants in the bar.

I hate two-name families. I can only think of one case in which I would willingly accept a hyphenated family. There's a football coach at East Carolina State University whose name is Bill Wacker and a writer at the New York Times named Sharon Talley. I always wanted to get them together so they would be Mr. and Mrs. Talley-Wacker.

I've told Barbara I'll change my name to Jones or Savage if she'll marry me but that I won't go through life as Robert J. Reynolds-Savage-Jones. I want to try to write some fiction and a name like that would bleed off the dust jacket.

Benson Goodykoontz is wearing short-sleeved shirts and is making millions as a lecturer on freedom. He says he'll never wear a watch again. He can afford to hire a brain surgeon to wear one and tell him the time. Ben figures he still owns the old Air Monitor, which is now simply The Monitor. A few dorks in Congress tried to get the Justice Department to seize it but Ben came into possession of some videotapes featuring our Beloved President and some of the most powerful people in Congress.

I don't want to imply that Ben blackmailed our Beloved President and the others, but Cecilia Jones is now the general manager of the Monitor Corporation. Ben made the President sign an Executive Order giving him clear title to the Monitor. Then he got the President and Winston's cohorts in Congress to sign letters of resignation. It was amazing. That many non-smokers stepping aside for "reasons of health." Ben and I still play golf once a month. We had a great round last week at Freedomcrest Country Club. That's the new name for the old Healthcrest Country Club. The nicotine monitors and the jerk golf professional are gone and one of the video memorabilia displays has black and white film of Arnold Palmer, striding up the Eighteenth fairway, smoking like a barn fire.

I tried to put the shootout on Number Sixteen out of my mind when we got to its tee. I hit my drive within a couple of feet from where it landed the last time Ben and I played Sixteen. Ben looked at the little plaque to the left of my ball and said, "I guess I should say nice shot."

The plaque marks the spot on Number Sixteen where the shootout with the OTA goons started. Ben ordered it be put up. The plaque simply says: "A fight for your freedom began at this spot." I keep hoping I'll run into the four women who saved our lives, but Ben says they have joined a club nearer their homes. Worst of all, they've taken up tennis.

Cecilia Jones is still the most beautiful woman in Washington. Her inner beauty almost matches her sister's.

Joe French is in a hospital, getting treatment with some of Milano Nagurski's drugs to try to reverse some of the side effects of the junk they filled him full of in the Texas Colony. Joe will be a rich man once the new Supreme Court rules on the lawsuits that flooded forth from Joe and the thousands like him. I visit him occasionally and he says he wants to try to get back together with Veronica if Nagurski can find the counter drug for the one that killed his sex drive. Life with Veronica might kill him, but at least he'll die an unbelievably blissful death. Joe is still off the weeds. He didn't need to ask Nagurski for a new shot of the Colony drug that cured him once before.

Winston DeWeerd is still in a federal funny farm. I get an occasional letter from him. He says he's going to kill me if he ever gets out. Barbara says I could get a court order to keep the creep from threatening me but I refuse. It doesn't bother me to allow Winston an abuse the freedom to be irresponsible. Besides, I wouldn't mind if they let him out. I've always wanted to beat him to a bloody pulp and I'll never get to do that with Winston guarded around the clock and locked in a padded cell.

That probably strikes some people as insensitive. But fewer all the time. The various Total Sensitivity movements began withering under the light of the Smoke Jumper scandal. I'll know they're gone for good when Bentley Benning reminisces about his glory days as a tight end.

The little red-roofed fast-food places are back to being Dairy Queens. I hope they sold the name Sensitive Stop to a national chain of hemorrhoid clinics.

The Police Chief who investigated the shootout at Healthcrest called me the other day. He said two guns registered to Benson Goodykoontz's guards had been found at the scene of a shootout involving rival drug gangs. "They sent me ballistics reports on the guns," he said, "but I'll be damned if I didn't lose them. What do you think of that?" I told him we should have dinner some evening and talk about old times. He said he would be happy to join me. He added: "I remember when I lost them. I'm certain I was watching the Texas thing on television. I think I lost them about the time I saw you, walking toward those twenty Smoke Jumpers with all those aiming dots on your chest."

I appreciated the Chief's losing the incriminating ballistics reports, but I know I could beat the rap. I could show the videotape he was talking about and any jury in the world would acquit me on grounds of temporary insanity or permanent stupidity.

I got an urge to go to the National Park Service ceremony down on the North Carolina-Tennessee border. Barbara and I got to watch as the head of the Department of the Interior put up the old sign that proclaimed the beautiful place to be Great Smoky Mountains National Park. I got that little gulping feeling and probably would have cried if a young woman hadn't elbowed her seatmate in the ribs and hissed, "It's him! I tell you, it's him!"

I assumed they would ask for the autograph of the idiot who faced down the Smoke Jumpers on the West Texas Plains, but it seemed they had been on a long Asian vacation. They had missed the television coverage of the Smoke Jumper cataclysm but had seen the Veronica French-Rob Reynolds video at a joint in Hong Kong. One of them asked Barbara for her autograph. I thought that moderately flattering.

Several people were smoking during the Great Smoky Mountains ceremony. One of them was a reporter from the newspaper in Johnson City, Tennessee. He approached us after the ceremony. He flipped two cigarettes up in the package and insisted that Barbara and I take one.

"First legal pack I've ever bought," he said. "I figure I owe it to you." He took our picture, clapped me on the back, then hugged me before he walked away. I got that little gulping sensation.

Barbara turned the cigarette in her elegant fingers. "What do you think?" she said.

"Same as you," I said. "Now that no one says I can't, I don't think I want to."

We dropped them into a trash canister. That's freedom.